VIENNA AT NIGHTFALL

RICHARD WAKE

MANOR AND STATE, LLC

This is a work of fiction. All incidents and dialogue, and all characters with the exception of some well-known historical figures, are products of the author's imagination and are not to be construed as real. Where real-life historical figures appear, the situations, incidents, and dialogues concerning those persons are entirely fictional and are not intended to depict actual events or to change the entirely fictional nature of the work. In all other respects, any resemblance to actual persons, living or dead, events, or locales is entirely coincidental.

To Mary,

My true love, my best friend, you are the person who gave me my life.

NOVEMBER 1936

d like one. Leon was a Jew, and even though we were
dred yards away, I could see where this was headed.
, let this one go. There's five of them," I said.
no."
police station is two blocks down—let's just go get

k that—the cop will probably help beat him up."
n was running now, Henry right with him, me a step
. We got there, and there was a lot of yelling. Thankfully,
e was armed—especially after Henry de-bottled the one
nd smashed the schnapps against the wall. Leon was soon
ging with both fists, and Henry was whaling on this one fat
. I managed to identify the guy on the other side—in bar
s, or any kind of group fight, there is inevitably at least one
ho had no interest in fighting, either. It goes unspoken, but
both know that neither of you is going to throw a punch.
at tends to happen is that you each grab the other guy by the
els, and shout a few indignant *fuck yous* at each other, and if
u play it just right, your jacket is minus a button, or maybe has
n easily mended tear along one of the seams. So no real
amage is done, but you have a small sartorial badge of honor.

Which was how this one was going to end, that is, until one of the Nazis pried a loose paving stone up out of the street and brained Leon. It staggered him, and it cut him above the eye, and blood ran down his face and dripped into the gutter as he tried to steady himself on one knee. Henry found a stone of his own, and, as he picked it up, a police wagon careened around the corner. Four cops piled out.

The Nazis ran. The cops did not pursue them. Instead, they stood there—shiny helmets, green capes, superior attitudes—and questioned us. Particularly this one scowling giant who smelled of beer, among other things.

"Let's see some identification, gentlemen."

1

The American Bar on Kärntner Durchgang was where we often began the night. It was all sharp angles and geometric patterns and dark wood and a green-and-white marble checkerboard on the floor. Masculine. It was a tiny place, a bar and three tables and not much else, including women. But it was where we drank Manhattans and got fortified for our pursuit of the aforementioned women, albeit somewhere else.

"The starting blocks," was what Leon called the place.

We hadn't gotten together, the three of us, in nearly two months, mostly because I had been traveling so much but partly because Henry had been occupied with a certain Gretchen, a porcelain doll, and a clingy one—until, that is, she got a better idea of how Henry's family made its money. It wasn't the first time this had happened, and he shrugged it off in what had become for him the time-honored fashion: a bottle, a 48-hour monastic sulk, and then, all better. Anyway, there we all were, two Manhattans deep.

"So where was this trip?" Leon always asked, mostly because he said he found my life in Vienna so dull by comparison.

"Dresden, Koblenz, and Stuttgart," I said, trying to suppress a smile. Trying and not succeeding.

"Koblenz? Isn't that . . .?"

"Yeah, the Gnome." I couldn't help but grin.

I was a magnesite salesman, which was about as exciting as it sounds. My family owned a mine in Czechoslovakia. My father ran the business, and my shit of a younger brother sat at his elbow. I lived in Vienna and serviced 24 of our clients in Germany and Austria, visiting twice a year, about 120 days on the road altogether. My Uncle Otto, who taught me the business, kept a half-dozen clients in his semi-retirement.

Most of our clients were steel mills, because of their blast furnaces—they used magnesite in the lining—and in those days, in Germany, the furnaces were working overtime. The Little Corporal had been very good for business. Most of the trips followed a familiar rhythm. I got to the place early in the afternoon, and most of the owners liked me to tour the plant while they chatted and joked with their workers. As if I cared whether they hated him to his face or only behind his back. Then we would go back to the office, where I listened to the owner complain about deliveries and such. Then I tried to get him to up his order by 5 or 10 percent. Ten percent had become my standard ask of our German clients—10 percent every six months—and I was getting it; *Heil*, etc. And then, when the work part was over, I took the owner out to dinner, followed by whatever, all on my expense account. Some were more interested in the whatever than others.

In Koblenz, Ewald J. Gruber owned the local steel mill. He was five-foot-nothing and stooped over besides, 70 years old, impressively unattractive, and truly believable as something you would put in your garden to ward off evil spirits and for nervy squirrels to piss upon. The Gnome.

But here was the thing about Ewald: He liked them young,

and blond, and tall—really tall. I ha
in exchange, I got my 10 percent
funniest thing I would see on the who
six-foot Brunhilda, hand in hand as the

"This time was a little different," I sa
two of them—12 feet of blonds, five
stepladder to help. I managed to make t
the girls, and when they left the café, I told
something for me. He was walking between
of them by the hand, and just at the door, the
swung him through the air, both feet off the gr

At which point, I reached into my breast p
out the photograph that the bartender had snap
the Gnome, both feet off the ground. Leon spit
his Manhattan.

"Alex Kovacs, I can't believe you do this for a livi

"Somebody has to."

We grabbed our coats and got ready to head to t
where there would be a band and some women and s
ing. It was a 10-minute walk, give or take, which wa
pleasant in November in Vienna if you were adequate
fied. Very quickly, though, we saw what looked like
ahead. In the late autumn of 1936, trouble in Vienna ten
be accompanied by a swastika, and it was this time. Well, a
swastika; the government had banned the party a coupl
years earlier, which drove the Nazis underground, but they w
still scampering in the dark. They didn't wear the full brow
shirts with the red armbands anymore, just little buttons wit
the hooked cross.

Henry and Leon walked a little more quickly in the direction of the scrum on Lisztstrasse. Four or five knuckleheads, one holding a bottle, surrounded a single man, pushing him, yelling at him, taunting him. He was probably a Jew, or at least he prob-

"You've got to be kidding me," I said.

"Does he look like he's kidding?" said his sidekick, who was more normal-sized except for his smirk, which was as enormous as it was well practiced.

"They were beating up this kid, and we were rescuing him," Leon said, "and my head is bleeding, and you're—"

"You're a Jew, yes?" It was the smirker.

"Listen," Henry said, taking a step.

"Identification, now," the giant said, taking a bigger step. It was not a request.

So, identification it was, followed by our names getting copied into one of those little leather-covered cop notebooks, followed by a lecture about brawling in the streets, followed by a warning that it had better not happen again. Within five minutes of talking, the smirker managed to use the phrase "the Jewish element" five different times. He looked at Leon the entire time, never even once acknowledging the kid who was still on the ground, head between his knees, cowering against a building. The cop probably couldn't tell that I had grabbed Leon from behind by the waist of his pants and his belt, to reinforce the importance of not taking a swing at these guys. Leon knew this drill well—every Jew in Vienna did—but a little reminder never hurt.

Then it was over, the cops piling into their wagon and speeding off, their fun for the night now complete. As we got him to his feet, the Jew we'd rescued finally had a chance to thank us. He was just a kid, not 20 years old. He could barely get the words out, he was so shaken. He had pissed himself but seemed fine physically. He said he was okay to get home.

Leon, though, was going to need stitches.

2

Leon wasn't really cut severely, as it turned out. It was messy but not that deep. A nurse had taken a quick look and said a doctor would be with us soon. The conversation quickly turned to fights in the past.

"The first fight you ever dragged us into?" Henry asked.

"Moi?" Leon said.

"It was Caporetto," I said.

"You guys fought together in Caporetto?" the doctor said as he walked into the room.

Henry said, "We won, call it by the right name: Karfreit."

"Nah, Caporetto sounds nicer," I said, turning to the doc. "We fought in the battle, but the fight I'm talking about happened in a café near Caporetto."

This was in September of 1917, about a month before the Italians graciously ran like babies down the mountain as we chased them. Our army was resting and resupplying, and we'd had a night free in Klagenfurt. We'd learned over the years that Leon would fight about anything, for good reasons and bad reasons. Most of the time, though, the fights were for female reasons, which could be good or bad, depending.

We had only known each other for about a month. Leon talked a good game, but, seeing as how we literally went days without even glimpsing a woman, it was all talk as far as we were concerned. Until that night in the Falling Leaf. It was a pretty prosaic name for a standard-issue shithole, but the place did have the two prerequisites for soldiers on a night off in town: a lot of beer and, at a nearby table, a supply of giggling girls.

We flirted with all of the skill and energy that three 18-year-olds could muster, which is to say, with more energy than skill. Henry and I devolved into what we believed was charming goofiness, and we got our share of laughs. But Leon played on a different level, a first-division game. He zeroed in on the prettiest, and the blondest, and the least Jewish of the three—although to be entirely accurate, the closest any of these girls had come to a Jew was in the pages of Leviticus. He locked eyes with her and wouldn't let go, even when talking to somebody else. It was masterful.

When the blond got up to use the facilities, Leon immediately followed, and Henry and I were left at the table with our two new friends. It was clear that we were going nowhere with them, and would settle for a peck on the cheek at the end of the night and a pleasant nocturnal memory later on, but that was fine. Because Leon would have a story to tell, and it would be the kind of story that we could get him to tell and retell, adding new details with each recitation, a new moan here, an extra fondle there. It is true that traveling armies are fueled mostly by manpower and horsepower, but the under-appreciated accelerant is sexual bragging. Just the week before, we had marched all the way from Wolfsberg to Völkermarkt—maybe 10 miles—without even realizing it, so enraptured were we by Corporal Friedhoffer's tales of the summer he spent working in a bakery with two twins from Steyr.

So it was all delightful until a man burst through the front door, glanced around, zeroed in on the two girls sitting with us, and bellowed, "Where is she?"

In subsequent years, we would encounter this type of situation multiple times on our nights out with Leon. Dozens of times, once or twice a year, easily. It would become a game for Henry and me. The guy came into the café, started looking around, got increasingly agitated when he couldn't find the female he was seeking, and Henry and I would make eye contact and give each other a sign: one finger meant boyfriend, two meant husband, three meant father.

Three fingers were the worst. And although we hadn't yet developed the code, that first night would have been three fingers. He wasn't sober, and was starting to pat the knife on his hip—yes, the knife. The girls said the lovely Heidi was in the bathroom and that they would go get her. We grabbed an empty glass from a nearby waiter—who typically would have been affronted by our impudence, but who this time was very happy that someone else was taking care of the matter—and our new friend sat down, the beer calming him almost instantly. The three girls were back in a minute, the blond so sufficiently put together that only in your imagination could you see where Leon's hands had been. The subsequent conversation was as awkward as you might expect, and Henry and I drank up and waved for the bill and started for our coats. It was going to be a clean escape, until we prepared for our final swallow and everyone raised their glass for a farewell toast. It was then that the old man got this quizzical look on his face, and then the anger built in the boiler, and then came the accusatory shout as he pointed at the table: "Whose glass is that?" Followed quickly by, "Where is he?"

It was all instinct at that point: I grabbed the knife and Henry took a single swing at the old man, which dropped him back in his chair. I literally threw our money at the waiter, and we ran. We ran all the way back to our camp, probably more than a mile, where we found Leon waiting for us. In the end, our story was better than his.

The emergency room doctor was laughing and shaking as he stitched up Leon. Leon said, "Hey, Doc, calm down. You sure you're okay to do this?"

"It's six stitches along your eyebrow—my father was a butcher, and he could have done it. No one will ever see."

"Where was your father's shop?" I asked.

"Jokl's, on Fruchtgasse," he said. And then it all clicked in.

"Are you Karl Jokl?"

"Yes," he said, tying the final knot and snipping the suture with a tiny pair of scissors.

Karl Jokl had been an assistant professor of surgery at the university. His name had been in the newspapers multiple times over the years, commenting on new techniques and such. He had even been a government minister for a time, advocating for prenatal care for mothers. They'd built a lot of clinics when the Social Democrats were in charge. They were all closed now, though. And now Jokl was stitching up a brawler on a Friday night, the only doctor in the place, with more brawlers undoubtedly to come.

He saw the question before it was asked.

"It's all they'll let me do now. I never had a private practice, you see—I was always in academic medicine, and then I worked in the government. But when it came time for me to be a full professor, well, they call you into the office, offer you coffee and cake, and tell you that the professorship just isn't possible. You know, 'Because of the current situation,' and they suggest that it's time to leave the university, except it isn't a suggestion. This is all I can do, the only job I can get, repairing street fighters on a night when no other doctor wants to work. I'm ashamed to admit that I was hoping you were more seriously hurt so I could have a chance to operate on you. So this is me, stitches on the Sabbath; my mother would cry. She was so proud. She cut out the first newspaper story that mentioned me and framed it."

Leon was seething, and Jokl patted him on the arm. "Stop," he said. "I have other options. I could go to Paris tomorrow and live with my cousin if only I didn't hate him so much. But he did make the offer, and I am thinking about it. But what about you, my friend? You will continue beating up Nazis in the street until you run into one with a knife?"

"I am a journalist," Leon said. "*Die Neue Freie Presse*."

"So you will try to tell the truth until they take the printing presses? It is hopeless, I fear, but it is our only hope. Truth."

Jokl hugged Leon, and then he was off to his next patient. Leon put his shirt back on and, miracle of miracles, there was no blood on it; there was only one small drop on his jacket sleeve. He looked in the mirror, combed his hair with his fingers, and smiled. He looked as if he had been in a fight, but he didn't look as if he had lost.

He turned from the mirror and said, "I don't feel like dancing anymore. But maybe one more at the Louvre?"

3

Café Louvre was a newspaper hangout at the corner of Wipplingerstrasse and Renngasse, really a foreign correspondents' hangout. Leon first went there to make contacts, and later started bringing Henry and me. Newspapermen are a little smarter than average, and a little more cynical than average, and a little more disreputable than average. In other words, our kind of people.

The American correspondents were at their regular table in the far corner. A group of visiting American students had kind of joined them, getting sloppy, yelling about Hitler. Even if they weren't speaking English, that's how you knew they were Americans: the yelling. On the subject of Hitler, the rest of us mostly tended to mutter and whisper.

It was nicely crowded, comfortably warm. The adrenaline from the fight had gone, leaving a quiet glow. We hadn't seen the sun in a week, which wasn't all that unusual for Vienna in November, but depressing nonetheless. You fought the black feeling in places like this, with a glass in your hand, in a crowd where you didn't tend to look at anybody in particular but still felt as if you were seeing everything.

Which, I imagine, was how I noticed this guy walking toward my table from about 50 feet away. I was sitting alone, as Henry had just left for the bathroom, and Leon had invited himself to sit with three blonds a few tables over. He said it was one of the rules of Shiksa Roulette—a game of his own invention—that there needed to be an odd number of shiksas for the single Jew to have a chance. He was fingering his stitched-up eyebrow, and they all seemed suitably impressed.

The guy reached the table and introduced himself as Robert Something-or-other, and he was the Vienna correspondent for *Prager Tagblatt*.

"Do you know the paper?"

"Of course," I said. He already seemed to know that I was from Czechoslovakia, or he wouldn't have come over, but I told him anyway and offered a seat. The social dance.

We began chatting. I asked him about the latest with Schuschnigg, which is really a question about the latest with Germany, which is where every conversation seemed to end up, and he told me a bunch of stuff that I had already read in the papers. He asked me about my work, and I filled him in on the fascinating life of a sales representative for a magnesite mine. As I was droning on about blast furnace linings and maximum temperatures, I caught him staring at a nearby brunette's nearby ass, and he caught me catching him, and he shrugged and said, "Maybe in a little while."

After a quick laugh and an uncomfortable pause, he leaned in and said, "Look, I have something to tell you."

"I kind of sensed that."

"A representative of the government in Prague would like to speak with you."

"About what? My company has an office in Brno. I really just take care of the accounts in Austria and Germany. I can give you the number—"

"It's not about the mine. It's more delicate than that."

There was nothing delicate about what I did. It was just sales. Which I tried to explain to a newspaper reporter who clearly wasn't listening, who was digging into the meat of his hand with his thumbnail with enough force that he was near to drawing blood.

"Look," he said. "The guy they want you to meet," and here he leaned in uncomfortably close and whispered, "is from the intelligence services."

"What are you talking about?"

"I'm telling you what I know. They want to talk to you about something. They want you to meet a guy on Sunday at 1:30 in Stephansdom."

"What?"

"You go in the main door, head up the right aisle," he said, and now he was reciting quickly from memory, the words tumbling out, faster and faster as if he was afraid he would forget if he slowed down.

"Just in front of the third pillar, a man will be kneeling and praying. There will be a copy of *Die Neue Freie Presse* in the pew in front of him. If the paper is there, you sit in that row and don't turn around and look at him. If the paper isn't there, you keep walking."

"You've got to be fucking kidding me."

He assured me that he wasn't fucking kidding me. He said that if there was a problem, the guy would be there at the same time the following Sunday. If I didn't show up then, they wouldn't bother me again. And then the guy walked away, this time not looking as he passed the nearby brunette with the nearby ass, and grabbing his coat and hat from a rack and heading for the door, not saying goodbye to anybody.

The whole thing didn't take five minutes. Henry was back from his piss as it was ending. "Who was that guy?" he said.

"Newspaper guy from Prague. Wanted to know if we had a common friend. We didn't."

We ordered another drink and talked about nothing. Actually, Henry talked, and I nodded over my sudden preoccupation. Why the hell would the Czech intelligence service want to speak with me? I could tell them where to get drunk in Graz, or where to get laid in Düsseldorf, but those weren't exactly state secrets. And as for magnesite: Yes, it had military uses, but I knew as much about the stuff as anybody who could read an encyclopedia. This just didn't make any sense.

Meanwhile, Henry was talking about Leon and the three blonds. "Has he given the signal yet?"

"I haven't seen it, but I haven't been paying attention."

The signal was just a tug on his right earlobe. When he did it, Leon needed help. That is, he was doing well but needed companions for his girl's friends before they would let her leave. It was a pretty standard strategy. Sometimes it even worked.

"There it is," Henry said, as Leon tugged his earlobe.

"Do we have to?"

"What's wrong with you?"

"I don't know. I just don't feel like it tonight."

"You have to come. Just me doesn't work."

So we went over. Mine was cute, as it turned out, and all three of them looked like they came from money. We ordered another round, and it was all charmingly inane. It became pretty evident that this wasn't happening for Leon after all when the girls went to the bathroom together and then sat in different seats when they returned, but then an odd thing happened. Mine, Johanna, sat in the same seat, leaned in, and asked me if I would be her date on Saturday night at the opera in her family's box.

"Saturday like tomorrow?"

"You're probably not busy," she said.

"What's on the program?"

"Why do you ask?"

"It's an appropriate question, I think."

"It's an appropriate question for someone who cares. You don't impress me as someone who cares. When was the last time you attended the opera?"

I laughed. The last time was on a school field trip, when they took us backstage and showed us the big costume wardrobe, and I got a big laugh from my mates by grabbing one of those blond Brunhilda wigs and putting it on when the professor had his back turned.

"'Attended' is such an imprecise word. I can tell you that I walk by the opera every day and admire it. It's a very handsome building."

She smiled for a millisecond. "That's what I thought. Be outside the main entrance at seven. I'll meet you there."

It suddenly occurred to me that I had never actually agreed to go, but now it was certain that I was going, regardless. During the walk home, I played the conversation over in my head and still hadn't come to any conclusion when I saw Hannah, our secretary, bundled up and sitting on the steps of my building, a handkerchief balled in her left hand. She was crying.

"Hannah . . ."

"Oh, Alex. . . . It's Otto. He's dead."

4

We hugged each other for I don't know how long, out there on the steps in the cold. We cried together. I believed I was closer to Otto than anyone on the planet, to the man who made me what I was as an adult, for better or for worse. Hannah believed she was closer to Otto than anyone, her lover for years, though unacknowledged publicly.

She didn't know much. A telegram had arrived at the office from the Cologne police, a detective, Adalbert Muller. It said that Otto's body had been found two days earlier "within the jurisdiction," and that he would appreciate being contacted "at your earliest convenience" to arrange for identification of the body and its release from the city morgue. When we got inside my apartment, I tried the contact phone number, but there was no answer, hardly a surprise at 11:30 p.m.

And then we sat, with a bottle from the cupboard, two glasses and our shared grief, still raw and unformed. We could only guess at what had happened. A heart attack was the most likely. Otto had suffered what he passed off as "a flutter" a few years earlier. The doctor had no real explanation and prescribed some rest. Otto stayed off his feet for precisely 24 hours and then never mentioned the whole thing again.

"I'll call in the morning and then get on a train," I said.

"I should come with you."

"I don't know."

"You shouldn't have to do this alone."

"You're not going to help me with the identification—there's no way I'm going to allow you to do that. And the rest is just a long train ride."

"He loved that train ride," she said, and then went silent. I loved that train ride, too, when it was on one of the days of the week when the Orient Express connected Vienna to Cologne. It was one of the things Otto had taught me, to love luxury. Or, rather, as he said, "To love the finer things but also to appreciate them. To live humbly but to splurge extravagantly. That is a perfect life—especially when the splurge is on your expense account."

Otto had taken me in when I was in high school. I was 16 and came to visit for the summer with my favorite uncle and thought I knew everything. I found out I knew only one thing: that I had no desire to go back to Brno and sit in an office with my father, learning the mine's account books. To this day, I can't believe he let me stay. Just before graduation, the army called. That's where I met Leon and Henry. Our outfit was transported back to Vienna after the Armistice, and I was determined to stay with Otto and learn his end of the business: the sales and the clients. He agreed immediately when I asked, and so did my father, who likely knew that my brother, Ernst, was a much better fit for the other side of his partner's desk. Ernst's nose had always been a better fit up Papa's ass than mine ever was.

And that's how it began. For the first six months after the war, in between a bit of schooling—finishing at Akademisches Gymnasium at one point, a semester of university later—I traveled with Otto everywhere, learning the paperwork requirements and the caring and feeding of the clients, from the office meeting to the evening debauchery to contact between visits, just to make sure everything was okay. I learned about a French cognac named Hennessy and a Leipzig madam named Clarissa and the fine art of padding an expense account. Or, as Otto used to say when he was filling out his monthly form, "When you hit your knees before bed, always remember to thank the Almighty for the man who invented the taxi cab."

Soon, Otto was giving me a few of my own clients, mostly the smaller ones where the head of the firm was younger. Within a couple of years, we were splitting things pretty evenly. A couple of years after that, Otto was in his mid-fifties and starting to give me more and more work. I would have taken it all if he'd let me, and not for the money, because while I did enjoy the commissions, I craved the freedom of being out on the road even more.

Somewhere along the way—I think it was about 1925—Otto hired Hannah to handle the office. I don't know when they started sleeping together, but I became aware of it about five years ago. It coincided with Otto giving me another bunch of his clients, and I understood. He kept a handful of the mine's oldest and most significant clients, but that was it. He was 63 when he died.

"I have to call my father," I said.

"It can wait till morning."

"I think you should stay. There's plenty for you to do here. There's a funeral to plan. There are clients to inform. Maybe you can get a little lost in the details. Maybe it will help."

Otto hated my father, who was his brother. It was the first thing we shared. He understood entirely in 1917, when I explained why I couldn't go home. Otto was the older brother by a year, but he never got along with his father, either, and mocked his father's conservatism at every turn. The way Otto told it, this one time Otto ordered a steak in a restaurant, his father made a face and shook his head, and Otto yelled loud enough for the whole place to hear, "Austerity should be a temporary condition, not a way of life!"

So, when Grandfather Jakob died, he left the mine to my father, 100 percent, against all tradition. Otto was furious, but my father refused to give him even a small percentage. Otto worked for a salary and his commissions and nothing more—except, that is, for the expense account. And just as his father had cut Otto out of the will, I had no doubt that my father had cut me out of his own. So I did as Otto taught me. I lived the same life. I held the same grudges. I embraced the same pursuit of life's finer experiences while simultaneously keeping my distance from almost all of life's people, never coming close to marriage, not really interested in taking the leap between acquaintance and friend anymore.

That was me. That was Otto. Only the relationship with Hannah broke the pattern, but even then only partly. They didn't hide their love, but they didn't announce it, either. Marriage was never considered, at least not by Otto.

"Do you know, Otto never spent the night at my flat?" Hannah said.

"What? That seems . . . impossible."

"He never stayed. He never slept. He got dressed and left—1 a.m., 3 a.m., it didn't matter."

"So he was protecting your reputation?"

"He was protecting himself. Whatever he was doing, everything in his life, he always had one eye on the exit."

I found a small photo album in a desk drawer—the three of us on a day out in Grinzing. For some reason, the owner of the Pine Bough had a camera and sent Otto the photographs. There we were, clowning with the band, posing with pyramid-shaped glasses filled with spring wine that went down like lemonade but kicked the next morning like a mule. In the shot I liked the most, Otto and Hannah were dancing, her eyes closed and her head resting on his shoulder. It was the last picture in the book, and as Hannah stared at it and cried, I read the little note that Otto had penned on the flyleaf: *Grinzing, 1934. A grand life.* In his formal correspondence, he signed with a great flourish, "Otto A. Kovacs." But on personal notes like this, it was always a capital O with three parallel lines beneath it. When I saw that, I started crying.

"I see that signature, and I think of this note he once left on my desk. I was still just a kid, just back from a trip, and—remember Richard Gruber? From Saarbrücken? The old prick gave me a bad time about something, but he was still a pretty big client back then, and I was worried, and I told you about it, and you must have told Otto. And he left me this note that said, *Fuck Old Gruber. And make sure to put an extra bottle of wine on the expenses for your aggravation.*"

We talked and laughed and cried until four. I left Hannah asleep on the couch, warmed by a comforter. I went to bed and awoke to a knock on my door at ten. Hannah was gone. At the door was a messenger delivering the train tickets to Cologne that she must have ordered.

5

The police headquarters in Cologne where I was to meet Detective Muller and view Uncle Otto's body was at Schildergasse 122. It was a scary-looking building with a tower on one end that looked like a gun turret, with vertical slits just wide enough for a sniper and his weapon, and which offered subtle vantage points in every direction. In all, it was a perfect architectural manifestation of the Nazi relationship to the German people, a relationship built not on trust but on the simple calculus that you never know who's watching. If the tower hadn't already been there, the Nazis probably would have built one.

Muller's office was on the fourth floor. My heart was already pounding as if I was having a panic attack, and the four flights of stairs just amplified what was going on in my chest. Muller greeted me when I walked in, offered me a chair and a cigarette along with condolences that were somewhere north of rote but decidedly south of compassionate. I didn't smoke, but I took it.

He opened a file folder on his desk, then began talking. "Here's what I know. On the morning of Wednesday, November

18, 1936, the body of Otto Albert Kovacs, identified by the contents of his wallet, was found floating in the Rhine River, hung up in the reeds along the western bank at Mullergasse, near an athletic field, not far from the South Bridge. Given the currents, we believe that Mr. Kovacs jumped off the bridge and took his own life between the hours of midnight and 2 a.m. on the 18th."

I was stunned. I had spent the previous 36 hours convincing myself that it was a heart attack, that there was nothing more nefarious going on than Otto's criminal neglect of his own health. Or just bad luck. Or just life and death, and that it was his turn, his time.

Suicide seemed impossible. "Was an autopsy done?"

Muller arranged the papers in the file. "The coroner examined the body but did not do a full autopsy. This is standard for deaths where the circumstances appear somewhat clear and where the deceased is not a German citizen. He did say that there was no evidence of stabbing or shooting or any other obviously fatal wound. And we did find the body in the water, after all."

"But this would be so out of character—"

Muller interrupted, and in a tone that was suddenly even further south of compassionate. "Mr. Kovacs, in my business, you come to learn quickly that many people have troubles that are buried deep below the surface. Mental problems. Relationship issues. Financial concerns . . ."

"My uncle Otto had no financial problems. He was in a loving relationship. Mentally, there were no signs whatsoever. He was witty, charming, generous—"

"Mr. Kovacs, you do not impress me as being naïve or unworldly. You know people have problems they keep bottled up. You undoubtedly stew about issues that none of your close friends are aware of—not issues that would lead to suicide, but issues. We all have them. When does an issue become something bigger? None of us knows. And besides, I deal in evidence."

"That you spent exactly how long accumulating? An hour? Two?"

"The facts are what they are, sir. I find them to be compelling. Think about it—he was dead in the river, the examination of the body was unremarkable, and he was found down-current from the bridge where we see a suicide a month, maybe more than that. And you know what? The bodies all drift to approximately the same spot on the riverbank, all within about a city block of each other."

"But—"

Muller closed the file and stood. "It is the opinion of this department that the case will be closed once you identify the body and arrange for its transport back to Vienna. Are you prepared to do that now?"

He began walking, not waiting for an answer. The morgue was in the basement. It was very much like in the movies: cold, white tiles, doors in the wall containing bodies on stretchers. I waited at some distance, and watched as two attendants opened the eighth door in the long wall and retrieved a stretcher, the body covered in a white sheet. They hoisted it up and carried it to what was clearly the viewing area—a metal table in one corner. In what was already a blindingly well-lit room, the light in the viewing area seemed even brighter. Muller and I approached tentatively. One of the attendants did the honors and pulled back the sheet. It was Otto.

The whole thing was over in a few seconds. The attendants gave me the name of a local mortuary, and the arrangements were made to have Otto's body transported on the same train with me. I didn't cry, probably for a lot of reasons having to do with male vanity. But the reason I was half-smiling when I walked out of the police headquarters was the sudden realization that it was Wednesday, which meant that Otto's final ride home would be on the Orient Express.

6

Hannah decided that Otto would not have wanted a big funeral, mostly because he always said he didn't want a big funeral, and so there wasn't one. She did not put a notice in the newspapers. There was no wake. The priest agreed to do his business in a small side chapel—Hannah and I, my father and brother in from Brno, Leon and Henry, the three other guys in Otto's bridge foursome, and some random old man who wandered in off of the street and out of the cold. His name was Max. He smelled. The only part of the day that Otto would have liked was Max.

We split into two cars for the drive to the cemetery. My father and brother got the bridge partners, and the rest of us took the other car. Max begged off.

Silence would have been too painful, so Hannah began the round of inanities.

"Your father looks good," she said.

"Too bad he doesn't look sad."

"That's not fair. You don't know—"

"I know. Trust me, I know. The only thing he's worried about is Otto's clients. He started asking about them, and when I would visit them, but I shut him off."

"When?"

"Just now. In the fucking chapel."

I started laughing. So did everyone else.

"You know what your brother asked me?" Leon said. "If you had found Otto's will yet. And how much I thought his apartment would sell for."

Henry joined in. "I talked to him for about 5 minutes outside. It's probably been five years, but your brother is the same asshole as ever. I've got to admit, though, that he's a prosperous-looking asshole. He looks like he's gained 50 pounds."

It was probably 20 pounds, but I appreciated the sentiment. Inane had given way to cruel snark. It was my friends' little gift on a stressful day. Plenty of people have family issues, and the blame for most of them can be spread around pretty liberally, but not here. It was one of the aspects of my life of which I was most confident. Otto was not to blame, and I was not to blame. We were the victims in this family struggle, and we were the survivors, and we had the better lives, and we were happier. Except Otto was dead, and we had become me, and I was alone.

After the cemetery, there was a big, somber lunch at Griechenbeisl, big family-style trays of sauerbraten and dumplings the menu advertised as "light as clouds." Mine tasted like clouds filled with wet cement, but maybe it was just my mood. I couldn't wait to put my father and brother on the train, after which we commenced the serious drinking. Hannah stayed with us for one, and then was hit by the inevitable wave of exhaustion. Which left me, Henry, Leon, and the issue that none of us could shake.

Or, as Leon abruptly said amid a conversation about the SK Rapid center back with two left feet, "You know, the suicide explanation is utter bullshit."

Henry smiled. "Not just everyday, run-of-the-mill bullshit? All the way to utter bullshit? Is that the highest form? No, that's not it. The highest form in Leonese is 'complete and utter bullshit'—isn't that right?"

"Fuck you. You know it's bullshit, too. There's no way Otto jumped off that bridge."

"I know," Henry said. I could barely hear him. And then everything got very quiet. I was suddenly hit by the same wave of exhaustion that had hit Hannah, and Henry and Leon appeared to be getting swept under as well.

I had felt the way they felt about the suicide: that it wasn't possible, not Otto. I had sat in the magnificent bar car of the Orient Express for most of the trip home—the bartenders tending to me in shifts—staring out the window at the passing night, and then the dawn, cocooned amid the wood paneling and warm lighting, coddled by the white-jacketed deliveries of double Hennessys. Suicide? There was just no way. But if not that, what?

My mind started to change when I talked to Hannah. I didn't know how to tell her what the Cologne police jackass had said, and I'd been working on a little softening preamble, but I was still kind of drunk when we sat down, and I just blurted it out.

I had expected Hannah to melt, but she didn't. She just got quiet for a minute, clearly thinking, and then said, "He had a doctor's appointment last week."

"His heart?"

"I don't know, but I don't think so. At least, I asked him and he said no."

"So it wasn't just a routine checkup?"

"Otto? You know better than that, Alex. He never had a routine checkup. All he would tell me was, 'Doc wants to run a few tests. No big deal.' So I said, 'You mean you had another appointment and didn't tell me?' He said, 'We're not married, you know,' and then he put on his coat and left."

Hannah was crying. "It was the last thing he said to me. He got on the train to Cologne the next day."

Maybe he had gotten terrible news from the doctor. It was at least possible. So there was that, and then there was the phone call I'd received the next day from the man at Oberbank. He identified himself as the executor of Otto's estate, and asked me to come to his office for a reading of the will, the sooner, the better. So I went that afternoon.

Werner Schmidt was about as old as Otto. It turned out he was president of the bank.

"I've known Otto since we were both in our twenties and unmarried. I used to tell him that the only reason I got married was that he had exhausted me, but he never stopped."

"He stopped a little, in the last few years, finally. There was a serious woman in his life. Which makes me ask: Why isn't she here?"

Schmidt opened the file on his desk. "Because you are the only beneficiary."

Nothing for Hannah? It didn't seem possible. Otto still did a bit too much of his thinking with his little head, even at 63, but he truly loved Hannah. I was sure of that. How he had not provided for her seemed incomprehensible.

But as Schmidt read the whereas-es and therefore-s, it was clear that it was all mine—all being his three significant assets: his bank account, the deed to his apartment, and the contents of his safe-deposit box. Schmidt shoved a piece of paper across the desk at me. It contained the balance of his bank account, which was more than I expected by a factor of about three. God bless the taxicab, indeed. Between that and the proceeds from the apartment, I had just crossed from upper middle class to lower upper class, which is the bridge between striving and worrying to striving and, well, not worrying. Even after giving a good piece to Hannah, I would still be able to live a more comfortable life than I had ever expected.

"The instructions were for me to empty the safe-deposit box and give you the contents," Schmidt said, pushing an oversized mailing envelope in my direction. Then there were two pieces of paper to sign, one acknowledging the reading of the will and my acceptance of the proceeds from the estate, and another allowing them to combine Otto's bank account with mine. With that, Schmidt stuffed my copy of the will into the big envelope and sent me on my way with a solemn handshake and a dirty laugh about a story from a time long ago, involving him, Otto, and a sophomore named Gretchen. But I was barely listening, suddenly preoccupied with excitement about the money I had just inherited from a loved one whose body wasn't yet in the ground. When I realized what I was thinking, I felt shittier about myself than I had in a long time. But I kept returning to the money all the same.

When I got home, I opened the envelope from the safe-deposit box. It contained the copy of the will and another envelope with my name on the outside. Inside was a letter to me and a bank book from Brust & Co., a bank in Zürich. I opened the cover and saw that it was a joint account, in Otto's name and in Hannah's. Thank God. He had taken care of her after all.

I read the letter.

Dear Alex,

Well, kiddo, this is it. You have always made me proud, the son I never had—a sappy cliché, yes, but true nonetheless. I sometimes worry that I gave you too many of my bad qualities, especially my rootless tendencies, but your loyalty to

Leon and Henry always heartened me greatly. You are a good friend and a good person, and you also know a proper champagne for celebrating the signing of a new contract with a client. You are a man in full.

Take care of Hannah for me. Do not give her the bank book yet. Do your best to make it contingent on her leaving the country. The money will do her no good once the jackbooted vacationers arrive. She wants to stay, but you have to convince her. That is your task now, the only thing you can do for me anymore.

Except this: There is a bottle of Hennessy prepaid in your name at Café Louvre. Drink it with Leon and Henry, every drop.

He signed it with the capital O and three lines underneath.

As we drained the bottle, I told Henry and Leon about the mysterious doctor's appointments. I kept the rest of it pretty much to myself, except to tell them the date on the letter in the envelope: November 11, a week before he died.

Henry tried to knock down the implication. "Come on. Even if he was sick, the Otto we know would have set up a second room in the hospital where he could give all of his women a goodbye shot."

We all laughed, but just for a second. The waves of exhaustion just kept coming. As we drank the last of the Hennessy, I finally said, "It might not be utter bullshit."

FEBRUARY 1937

7

The tuxedo, thankfully, was not in a ball at the bottom of my closet—the odds were even-money that it was—which made this a lucky day. I had last worn the tuxedo about six months earlier at a wedding, and pulling it from the closet and looking at it on the hanger, well, it was a summer wedding, and I had barely worn the jacket at the party, and even though it hadn't been pressed, it looked okay. I sniffed it and barely caught the scent of the perfume worn by a bridesmaid named Trudy, whose hugs that night were desperate but not amorous; she was so drunk she could barely walk. I still felt privileged that she'd waited to throw up until after she got out of the taxi.

Being in my late thirties and perpetually single made me a valued commodity on most invitation lists. There was always a spinster, or a homely cousin, or a girl on the rebound who needed sitting next to. Truth be told, Henry and Leon were the same age and of the same marital status, but I was the safer invite: because Henry was continually in and out of love—plus the fact that his father was a small-time mobster; because Leon was renowned as a hound who couldn't be counted on to make conversation with Cousin Hilda for very long, plus the whole Jewish thing. Hitler and the Nazis might have raised it to a governmental art form, but the Viennese didn't need lessons from anyone in the craft and practice of anti-Semitism. Certain people would never—never!—consider inviting Leon to a family wedding, no matter how much he had charmed them at a café.

As I walked from my flat to the opera, I wondered if Johanna was one of those people. She certainly fit the bill. I didn't know her last name, but given how she was put together, plus the family box at the opera, I guessed there was probably a "von" in there somewhere. They wouldn't say it out loud—the whole "von" thing wasn't really done anymore, not since they whacked the nobility after the war—but you just knew that the whole lot of them were still clicking their heels and calling each other Count von Whatnot when among friends. You know, like when they were at the opera.

Our original first date never happened because of Otto's death. This was a rescheduling after another meetup at Café Louvre. I made sure to be early, partly because Johanna was so intriguing, and partly because she was legitimately frightening. It's a good thing, too. Right at seven, the big car pulled up to the curb. The chauffeur hopped out and hurried around to open the door and out came Johanna first, her hair done up, her fur down to just above her splendid calves; her mother next, an older version of Johanna but with a tiara; and then the old man. As I walked over to greet them, I noticed: Christ, he was wearing a cape—black on the outside, red underneath.

Johanna put out her gloved hand and said, "Mr. Kovacs, so nice to see you again. May I present my parents, Karl and Cecelia Westermann. This is Alex Kovacs."

Greetings all around, and then we were part of the flow of

people headed inside. We got to the door, and there were no tickets; a nod from the old man to the ancient usher seemed all that was required. And then we were inside, where even the lobby areas looked expensive—no scuff marks on the marble floors, red damask everywhere. Johanna took my arm and led us up the staircase and then to the left.

"I'm glad you were on time. Mother and Father don't wait for anybody."

"Somehow, I'm not surprised."

"Meaning?"

"Nothing. But I do have to apologize that my cape is at the dry cleaner's."

"It's a pity your trousers haven't been there recently."

"I think they look fine."

"I imagine you would."

Arriving at the box, an attendant opened the door and greeted Johanna and her parents by name. Sitting down, the magnificence of the sight really did hit me: the ornate stage, the circular seating area, lots of deep reds and gold leaf and a massive chandelier. The Westermanns' box wasn't in the best position, but it was close—on the second level, near the side of the stage. This stuff didn't impress me, but I was impressed. Johanna could tell.

"Close your mouth," she said. "Act like you've been here before."

Soon, the lights went down, and the performance began. It was *Carmen*, which the program informed me would last approximately three hours, including the intermission. The woman who played Carmen had a beautiful, powerful voice in my first-time-at-the-opera opinion, but her body was her most impressive feature in the same way a battleship is impressive. This was one big woman. I felt a small concern for the opera company, and how the extra yards of fabric in all of her costumes must eat into the nightly take.

I was starting to doze when Johanna woke me by gently resting her hand on mine. This was okay with me. I was enjoying her company. The more she belittled me, the more she intrigued me.

As we walked to the bar for a drink during intermission, I asked her, "So it's really von Westermann, right?"

She smiled. "But not anymore."

"I bet your father still uses it."

"Only when he's been drinking. So, only every day. Starting at lunch."

"Beats working. So what is he, a count?"

"No, only a baron," she said, smiling again. "But enough with the inquisition. Champagne for me, please."

I returned with two champagne glasses to find the old man holding two of his own, and Johanna and her mother making their way to the powder room. Which left us stuck in a situation that is never not awkward. Good thing I made small talk for a living.

"Baron, the view from your box is magnificent. How long have you been a subscriber?"

The old man smiled at the honorific and stood just a little straighter. "Call me Karl," he said. "I don't even know how long we've had it—it's been in the family since before I was born. Families kept them forever, until recently. It is one of the pities of our age."

After the war, the nobility was put out of business. The Habsburgs' property was confiscated by the state; that's how this became the Vienna State Opera instead of the Vienna Court Opera. The minor nobility, without a court to whom it could pay obedience in exchange for its lifestyle, was left to wither. Most of them were financially sinking, throwing a country home over the side this year, a couple of gardeners the next. Some of them were said to have taken the drastic step of actually going to work for a living, although most of that work was said to involve long lunches and enthusiastic glad-handing on behalf of one bank or another. But I was in no position to judge, seeing as how that's pretty much how I made my living.

Which is what the baron asked me about. I emphasized the part about being the scion of a Slovakian mining family and glossed over the part about personally knowing the proprietor of at least one shady café in 20 different cities between here and the Rhine. We were interrupted at one point by a Herr Doktor Klein, who offered some platitudes admiring the onstage scenery and then made his excuses.

Johanna's father caught my eye, and then shot a glance at the retreating Herr Doktor, and then quickly brushed the side of his nose with his index finger, just a quick flick, the universal, unspoken shorthand for Jew. Okay, then.

Just as I began to pontificate on the many industrial uses of magnesite, Johanna and her mother returned, and the lights flickered, and we went back to the box.

"That seemed to go well," she said.

"What did you expect?"

"He can be pretty intimidating."

"I'm more afraid of you."

After the allotted time, the performance finally ended, and everyone cheered as if it had been a great success. As the attendant helped Karl on with his cape, though, he said out of the side of his mouth, "I think that cow has put on 50 pounds since we saw her in *Don Giovanni*."

As we got outside, I asked Johanna if she'd like to get something to eat, and she did. I asked her parents if they would like to join us, and they did not. Within seconds, the car appeared, and the Westermanns were gone.

"Is there anyplace you'd like to go in particular?" I asked.

"You must have something to eat in your flat. Let's go there."

I had half of a stale loaf of bread, a few slices of liverwurst, and four bottles of beer. Which we did consume, eventually.

8

Six or seven streets fed into Stephansplatz. I counted them once in my head, then remembered another one, then resolved to make the circuit around the cathedral and count them accurately, then realized I didn't actually care. So, six or seven, not precisely like spokes in a wheel but close enough—with the enormous Stephansdom at the center.

If I had paid more attention during physics class, I might have understood the reasons for the phenomenon of the wind tunnel. But all I knew for sure was that, when you were walking there on what you considered to be a sort of breezy day, once you exited a feeder street and entered the main square, "sort of breezy" became one of those newsreels from Kansas. It was a powerful, comical phenomenon—comical because it left pretty much every man who entered the vortex stooped forward, with a hand clamping his hat to his head.

That Sunday was even funnier, or maybe I was still in a good mood from my night with Johanna. Because there was an open truck parked on Goldschmiedgasse, with a half-dozen 20-year-olds wearing swastika armbands (completely illegal) and waving a Nazi flag (also completely illegal) and hectoring passersby to give the Nazi salute (also completely illegal). I know, a laugh riot. But I stood and watched for a minute; this wasn't a common sight in Vienna, but it wasn't an uncommon one, either. I watched from about 150 feet or so, and saw an old, head-shaking woman ignore the young Brownshirts, and I smiled. But the thing that made me laugh out loud was when a scrawny 40-year-old man tried to ignore them, got stopped by one of the kids, who leaped from the back of the truck into his path, and then relented with a Nazi salute—at which point, the hat flew off of his head into the wind and swept down Goldschmiedgasse. As he chased after it, my guffaws were taken away in the same wind, camouflaged by nature, unheard by any of the Brownshirts.

You took your laughs where you could get them in February of 1937 in the country that shared a border with Germany and that was featured on the first page of *Mein Kampf*. First page, second paragraph, to be precise:

"German-Austria must return to the great German mother country, and not because of any economic considerations. No, and again no: even if such a union were unimportant from an economic point of view; yes, even if it were harmful, it must nevertheless take place. One blood demands one Reich."

I had lived in Vienna for all of my adult life. It was an odd thing: I considered myself a Slovak, and my loyalty was to Czechoslovakia first, but I had never actually lived in Czechoslovakia. It was just part of Austria-Hungary when I lived there as a kid. At the same time, I talked about Austria and got involved in loud arguments about Austria—always in private places—and always used the word "we" to describe Austrians. I did it reflexively, primarily when I was arguing against Anschluss, extra-especially when I was drinking and arguing. The Czech loyalty was an intellectual thing and a fiber-of-my-being thing, but I never got the ancient anti-Austrian bias that generally came with it. I loved Austria. It could be confusing, except it wasn't, seeing as how my two loves shared the same predicament—that is, a border with the Corporal.

All of this had been running through my head in the hours since the invitation to meet the spy had been re-delivered last week—same bar, same messenger, same everything. There was never any doubt that I was going to meet the man. Part of me wanted to do something meaningful—not to say arranging a threesome every six months for the bald, walks-with-a-cane president of the biggest steel manufacturer in Stuttgart wasn't meaningful. He was our biggest client, after all, and the size of his magnesite order seemed to correlate pretty closely with the attractiveness of the women I managed to wrangle for the occasion. But there was meaningful, and then there was truly meaningful, something I had been thinking about a lot since Otto's death, and doing something for the people of my homeland trumped my work as a procurer, however skillful. Exactly what that truly meaningful task might be was what had me baffled as I pulled open the big, heavy door of the cathedral.

On a Sunday afternoon, well after the last Mass, there seemed to be two kinds of people inside: well-dressed families, undoubtedly from the country, doing a bit of religious sightseeing; and old ladies. So there were two of the latter, heads covered, swaddled in scarves, kneeling at the Wiener Neustädter side altar and staring up at the carved figures or the Virgin Mary after lighting candles. And there was this tableau of the former: a mother shushing her giggling daughters while the father grabbed a three-year-old boy by the collar before he could sprint up the center aisle, after which husband and wife made eye contact that said clearly, but without words, "Let's get the hell out of here." Holy, holy, holy.

Meanwhile, I was standing in the back and looking up the right aisle and counting the pillars and seeing no one. But the pillars—they were enormous—did block the view of some areas, which I imagined was the whole point of the exercise. Even though my right hand, which held my hat, was shaking noticeably, and even though my bladder was suddenly speaking to me, I began walking up the right aisle, as instructed. I went slowly, making a show of stopping and admiring the stained glass and the statues, really selling it to who knows who. And when I got to the third pillar, there was indeed a man in the pew, kneeling and praying. And in the row in front of him, there was indeed a copy of the newspaper. And, well, what the hell? I kneeled down, careful to look forward at all times. There wasn't anybody within a hundred feet of us.

Quickly, the man spoke in a loud whisper.

"Were you followed?"

"How the hell should I know?"

"Christ. Do you think you were followed?"

"Look. I'm not a—"

"I know what you are. And I know what you're not. Just listen. Your government needs your help—"

"But—"

"Just shut up and listen before you turn me down."

So, I listened. The request was simple enough. What it amounted to was, he wanted me to be a courier. He said that my job got me into Germany on a regular basis, and that it got me there without suspicion, and that, because magnesite had both industrial uses and military uses, it got me into contact with influential business people, who, in turn, were in contact with prominent military people. And some of those people had information that could be helpful to the Czech government, and that he wanted me to be available to carry that information back to Vienna.

I finally spoke. "But isn't that dangerous?"

"Don't you carry lots of documents on your trips—contracts, order forms, schematics?"

"Yeah. Sometimes two briefcases full, depending on the trip."

"And has anyone at the border ever looked in one of your briefcases?"

"One time. The Nazis opened one."

"And?"

"They looked, saw a bunch of papers and folders, and closed it."

"You see what I'm saying. The danger is minimal to nonexistent for somebody like you. Your company provides an essential material for German industry. They can't build a steel mill without your shit, and they don't have any of their own, which means you are essential to the German military buildup. Nobody is going to bother you."

Truth be told, I had often thought the same thing. Once, I even put it to the test. It was only a couple of months earlier, for Leon's father, right before he left Vienna. They wouldn't let you leave Austria with much currency—almost none, truthfully. So after he sold the family home, Leon's father took the proceeds and bought diamonds, and then he gave me the diamonds, and I traveled with them on one of my trips to Saarbrücken. After meeting with my client, I went over the border to Metz, changed the diamonds for francs with a prearranged broker, and then deposited the francs into a prearranged bank account. The whole time, the diamonds were either in a money belt or in a half-assed false bottom in my briefcase. No one at any border crossing looked at me for more than a second before stamping my passport and waving me along.

Still, though, this was different. If I had been caught with the diamonds, I would have just said they were mine and played dumb. I might have had to bribe somebody to get out of trouble, but there wasn't really any risk. There was no way to play dumb, though, about a couple of pages of German military information hidden in the middle of the August magnesite delivery schedules. There was no way to bribe your way out of something like that.

"I don't know . . ." I said, finally.

"Christ. Do you know how important this is?"

"I think I do, which is why I'm not sure. Can you give me some time to think about it?"

"Look, we need to know before you leave for Cologne on the fourteenth."

"How the hell do you know when I leave for Cologne?"

"What do you think, that we're amateurs? This is serious. We are serious people. Think hard, Herr Kovacs. Two weeks. We'll contact you. Now you stay here for five minutes. Say a prayer."

I heard him get up as I continued to stare straight ahead, fixing on the massive altar in the distance.

9

The Vienna office of Kovacs Mining Company was one room on the second floor of a building filled with one-room offices—an accountant to the left, an architect to the right, an unnamed tenant at the end of the hall whose clientele tended toward the quiet and the desperate. I was pretty sure it was a place where Jews worked out their financial arrangements before they left town. That is, how they hid their assets.

Ours was a nice-sized room, just the one room. Other offices had divided their space, with a receptionist and a small seating area in front and a private office through a door. But seeing as how Otto and I went to the clients instead of the clients coming to us, we went with a more open concept: one room, two desks, one shared by Otto and me, one for Hannah. That way, she could look out the window onto Falkestrasse.

I didn't go to the office, other than to file my expenses, make travel arrangements, pick up money for an upcoming trip, or deal with my father. Once a month, it was a phone call. The rest of the time, it was correspondence by mail. Hannah took care of all of the paperwork details in between.

This day was for expenses. Or, as Otto used to say, "You always eat three meals a day on the road, even if you don't."

That's when he wasn't saying, "Add 20 percent to every expense—it's the only compensation you get for being away from home."

And when he wasn't saying, "If you're not smart enough to steal a good living from your father, you're no good to him as a salesman, anyway."

It had been a couple of months, and my emotions still seesawed when I thought about Otto. Hannah seemed to be doing fine, except she often found the subject of Otto awkward. Sometimes she talked about him endlessly. Other times, she avoided mentioning him altogether, even when telling a story where his name should have come up naturally.

I walked into our office with the standard office greeting, begun by Otto, continued by me.

"Hey, baby, how's business?"

Hannah lit up. "I was wondering if you remembered."

"How could I forget?" It was Otto's birthday. We always went to lunch together, and had a few drinks, and told all of the old stories, which generally meant making fun of my father and brother.

"We going to Café Central?"

"Reservation is made," she said. "But first we have to get a couple of things done."

She looked down at the expenses, focusing in for a second, shaking her head. "You know, the day is coming when your brother is going to refuse to pay one of these. You should have heard him last month—"

"Which is what you have told me every month for the past 11 years. And he has paid every time, and he will continue to pay, and the reason is simple: If he fires me, he'll either have to start making the sales calls himself, or he'll have to hire someone else to do it. And if you have learned anything about our family over the last few years, it is this: that the only people we trust less than each other are everyone else. To this day, I can't believe they let you handle their money."

She snorted. "Enough. Let's get through this."

She opened a file full of letters from various clients I hadn't seen in a while. We set the dates for my next visit, and Hannah would write them to confirm. Next was a file with letters from clients asking questions about their orders, or with specific delivery issues, or whatnot. I dictated replies as Hannah took shorthand.

"Okay, Linz next week," she said. "You've been putting this off, but we need to make the arrangements today."

The trip to Linz was going to be maybe the worst of the year. It was going to be one night in a hotel, two stops, both unpleasant. At the first stop, we were going to get fired by Ulrich Bain & Co. There was no way around it; we had messed up an order, and they were unhappy with the price accommodation we made as a result. But it wasn't just that. The guy I dealt with, Herr Ulrich Bain himself, was just about the most odious of the Nazis I was forced to deal with, and I just couldn't kiss his ass anymore, and he resented this fact. Then, after he fired us, I would have to visit a quarry for sale on the edge of town—not because we were going to buy it, but because the owner was somehow an old acquaintance of my father's, and we were just showing the old guy some respect.

Hannah looked down at the paperwork. "Why is this guy firing us again? We could give him more of a discount. Isn't it worth a try?"

"You want the real reason or the one we're telling my loving father?"

"The real reason."

I told her about the Nazi flag in his office, and the picture of

Hitler on the sideboard next to the tray of schnapps, and the map on the wall with the red pushpin stuck in at Braunau am Inn. The anger in her eyes was apparent by the time I was finished.

"So what do we tell your father?"

"Blame the bad shipment from the mine that started it all. Make it his fault."

She reached into her desk drawer for the train timetable. It wasn't necessary. Before she got it open, I just started dictating: three o'clock train to Linz on Thursday, six o'clock return on Friday night. One night in the Hotel Wolfinger. No need for a lunch reservation on Friday; the Nazi is firing us, so the Nazi is picking up the tab.

That was enough. We went to lunch, got drunk, told all of the old stories and cried a little.

10

"A schnitzel for two marks. Two! And it's good!" Leon dug in.

"A two-mark schnitzel and a room full of reporter assholes. Who could beat it?"

Leon looked at me with faux disapproval. "Now, now. You like reporter assholes. You like all kinds of assholes. You like me, after all. And do you own a mirror, by the way?"

It was like this most nights at Café Louvre. The big fat American from United Press had his own table in the far corner, his stammtisch. Michael Stern. In the unofficial foreign correspondents' clubhouse, Stern was their unofficial ringleader. He had a typewriter at the table and used the café as his office many days. The others either worked from home or in their cubbyholes in the telegraph office across the street, from which their copy was sent. Well, not all of it. The really urgent breaking news could be dictated over the phone to London and passed on from there. Routine breaking news, with a short shelf life, went by cable. The stories without any urgency were typed up and dropped in the mail because it was so much cheaper. Or, as one of the correspondents told me, "As long as this whining, broke former Habsburg count doesn't die between now and publication, what's the difference? His whining will be just as whiny two weeks from now."

Besides Stern, at the table tonight were Rand from Chicago, Hillary from Philadelphia, and Watson from the *Manchester Guardian*. I never asked for the first names. Watson was the guy they seemed to respect the most. You could tell because they all listened to him when he talked, rather than just showing off with some worthless nugget they said they heard from Schuschnigg's cook's husband in a café in Floridsdorf. As if any of them would set foot in Floridsdorf.

Heading to and from the lavatory, they would pass our table and offer Leon a nod or a wave. When it was her turn to parade by, the woman from Chicago leaned in and whispered something in his ear, and he seemed on the verge of blushing. This was borderline historic, because Leon didn't blush.

"Was that as dirty as it looked?"

Then Leon did blush, a little. "She said, and I quote, 'What wouldn't I give right now for a brief encounter with a man of the circumcised persuasion. If you can think of anybody, let me know.'"

"Jesus, she's pushing 50."

"Jesus has nothing to do with it."

"You mean you're thinking about it?"

"A source is a source. And the night is young."

Behind Leon, Vivian Montreaux and her husband, the French ambassador to Rome, walked in and were escorted to a booth on the other side of the café. She was unmistakable, even with her back to us, even from 50 feet away, because of her long red hair. She never saw Leon, and neither did her husband. This was all probably for the best.

"What are they doing back in town?"

Leon, his mouth full, answered anyway. "Not sure. But the

French chef de mission dropped dead the other day. He's been here forever, and the funeral's tomorrow."

"You seen her since?"

"First time."

Until about two years ago, Leon worked for *Der Abend*. In a city with 22 newspapers, from serious to scandal sheet, *Der Abend* leaned heavily toward the latter. They had an editor there named Jurgen R. Jager, and Leon used to tell stories about him that had me pissing myself. Like this: Jager had a rule that every photo that accompanied every story about a car accident had one requirement—a young woman with big breasts standing there and solemnly surveying the wreckage. One photographer, Dieter, had a sister who qualified and was always on call, in case he couldn't round up somebody appropriate from the immediate neighborhood. When he used his sister for the third time in three months, Jager caught him. "Dieter, from now on, fresh tits," he bellowed, but then he giggled. "Although I have to admit that I will miss what has been on offer."

Then there was the time Jager insisted on calling a murder victim an "Innere Stadt matron" even though she didn't live anywhere near the tony mansions of Innere Stadt. One of the reporters even pulled out a map and showed him. "It isn't close, boss."

Jager thundered, "It's close enough." And then he walked away, giggling. And, yes, he got his "Innere Stadt matron" headline.

This is the stuff Leon did, and he did it well. But he always wanted more: politics instead of society fluff, a serious paper, a nod from the *Manchester Guardian* at Café Louvre. And Mme. Montreaux was how he got it.

It was simple enough, really. Working the society beat one night—*Der Abend* was equal parts breasts, sports, and boldfaced names of the wealthy and privileged—Leon was leaning against one of the bars at a charity function of some sort in the Palais Auersperg. He ended up chatting with a young guy who was also hugging the bar, as bored as Leon was. It turned out his name was Herman Lutz, and he was the nephew of the German ambassador. He was 24, learning the diplomatic business—shuffling meaningless paper during the day, drinking free drinks after work at the stultifying reception du jour, the usual stuff. It was nothing—one drink, 10 or 15 minutes, a couple of stories, trading experiences about favored dance clubs, with Leon currently preferring Koenigen and Herr Lutz enjoying Mariposa. That was it. Leon wrote 400 words, including 28 names, and his work was done.

Until two weeks later, on a lazy Thursday afternoon, when the entire diplomatic corps was in the parliament listening to Schuschnigg prattle on about something or other and then cabling their advice to their governments. Leon just happened to be about 300 feet from the French ambassador's residence, when the door opened, and none other than Herr Lutz walked out, stopped, leaned back in, and embraced a woman whose face Leon could not see but who had a head of splendidly long red hair.

With that, the rest of it worked pretty simply. First Leon confronted Lutz at Mariposa. He thought the kid, who was a little bit drunk and who had a tiny brunette waiting for him at a small table, was going to cry. The next morning, he confronted the good mademoiselle at Demel, her regular café. She did cry. The deal was pretty plain. Leon didn't want state secrets, but he wanted political gossip from both of them, or else. Herr Lutz's services lasted three months until he abandoned the idea of a career in the diplomatic service and left town, returning to Heidelberg to obtain an advanced degree in biology. Mme. Montreaux lasted six months before she managed to get her husband transferred to Rome. But in that time, Leon broke a ton of political news and developed a variety of new sources—because that's how it works: When you start to know stuff, all kinds of people become attracted to you and begin to whisper into your ear. That success enabled him to get a job writing politics at *Die Neue Freie Presse*, which was probably No. 1 in seriousness.

Leon was good, and the other journalists all knew it, and these nights at Café Louvre were now ventures into a world that Leon used to covet, but in which he now clearly belonged.

He surveyed the place as we got another drink after dinner. And then he hit me.

"So, are you going to do it?"

"Do what? I'm not circumcised."

"Are you going to spy or not?"

I had not told anyone. Not Johanna, not Henry, no one. I could barely admit it to myself. I generally did about 75 percent of my yearly drinking in the 33 percent of the year I spent on the road, but I had been drinking every night since the meeting in Stephansdom. I was honestly frightened and just didn't know what to do.

When I asked him how he knew, Leon said, "I'm insulted you'd ask. I mean, I do this for a living. And they should never have used that chinless weasel from Prague to approach you—and to do it twice. He was embarrassingly easy to crack. As soon as I saw him approach you the second time, I knew it would be a cinch. So you are going to do it?"

"First off, fuck you. You didn't tell anybody, did you?"

"Our secret."

"Then I'll tell you the truth: I don't know what to do."

"You know what the right thing to do is, though. And that's all that matters."

"I don't know what's right."

"Yes, you do."

"It's more complicated than you think."

"Why, is Daddy going to be mad?"

"I repeat: fuck you."

"So what do they want you to do?"

I explained what the guy in Stephansdom said. We talked a little about the risk. He pushed. I pushed back.

"If they asked me, I would do it without thinking," he said.

"I have a lot more to lose than you do."

He got quiet. I got quiet. We drank some more. I left. The woman from Chicago was still at the correspondents' table in the corner.

11

I had been to the restaurant in the Hotel Weinzinger in Linz a half-dozen times. The food was okay but only okay. The decor dark and formal. The waiters old and decrepit. Nothing about the place was memorable, but I did enjoy the walk down to the Danube, which the hotel overlooked. Of course, this would be my last visit. I wasn't going back to a place where I got fired.

I was playing it out in my head during the train ride, how it was going to happen. I was about 98 percent sure, partly because of the botched order, partly because I could no longer hide my disgust from Herr Ulrich Bain.

Don't get me wrong—I kissed plenty of Nazi ass in the course of doing business. I would do the salute when I was in Germany and got cornered into it, mainly when there were military people in the room. Of course, I always made it quick and weak, convincing myself that it wasn't the same as the heel-clicking, stiff-armed assholes. I drew the line at laughing at Jewish jokes; I'd perfected a kind of eye roll/change the subject combination that got me out of those situations every time. I also would go out of my way to avoid the public displays of Nazi affection that seemed to pop up all the time; you couldn't take a walk after lunch in Munich without running into a parade where, if you didn't salute, you got slugged by a Brownshirt, or worse. I always managed to duck into a shop or an alley to avoid those things. But business was, well, business.

Except for Herr Ulrich Bain. He was worse than the Germans. A lot of people in Linz were. Hitler was born in Braunau am Inn, but he spent some of his youth in Linz, and the citizens seemed to be quite proud of their favorite son. I was actually in a bar once with a client where one guy said Hitler once slept in his house, another guy said Hitler once kissed his aunt when they were kids, and the owner of the bar said that Hitler used his bathroom. So proud, they were.

Anyway, the last time I was in Herr Bain's office, he was complaining about the messed-up delivery, and accepting a discount on the next delivery, but refusing to be placated, refusing to let it go. He was over at the sideboard, fixing us a drink and preparing to complain some more. I was fine enough with that. It was the job, after all. But then he did what he always did. He picked up the photo he had on the sideboard—which was in a much more expensive frame than the picture of his wife —and sat down with it in his lap. Then he looked down at it, and then he looked at me, and then he pointed at the photo and said, "The day will come, and it will come soon, when Austria knows the greatness of his leadership—"

I had heard the speech about six times before. It never varied. So this time I interrupted, picking up the speech mid-sentence, even adopting Bain's pinched accent. "—And the genius of his vision, and the purity of the Aryan race."

Bain was stunned; his mouth opened, then closed, then his whole face twisted in fury. You could disagree with a Nazi—

sometimes they even kind of enjoyed the argument—but you could never mock them. Suffice it to say, I drank up. I'm not sure either of us said anything after I shrugged and said, "Well, it is a memorable sentiment."

So now he was going to fire us. Lunch was set for noon. There was a particular protocol to this sort of thing. You ordered a drink and talked about the weather. You ordered the meal and talked about your families. You spent the better part of an hour avoiding the obvious subject until the waiter brought the coffee. It was an agonizing dance, especially when you knew all along that you were going to be on the receiving end of the bad news, but it's what you did. He wanted to make this as civil as possible in case he ever needed us again. We wanted the same thing. Business is business, after all, and that was the ritual.

Walking the several blocks to the Weinzinger, I was determined to just shut my mouth and endure the lunch. Then I got about a block away and witnessed Bain, across the street and with his back to me, screaming at an older man in a white apron standing outside of Goldberg's Delicatessen. Goldberg, probably. Another man was yelling, too. A policeman watched from about 50 feet away.

All I could hear was garbled anger, except for the, "Fucking kike!" that shot clearly out of Bain's mouth as he turned halfway toward me. More yelling followed. Goldberg raised the broom he was holding and menaced it in Bain's direction. The policeman bellowed, "Goldberg!" and that was enough for the old man to holster his weapon. He turned and went back into the deli. Bain and the other man laughed, shook hands, gave each other the Hitler salute and walked away in different directions, another job well done by the master race.

It is difficult to describe what I felt as I watched: anger, sorrow, helplessness, inevitability. It is hard to love such a shitty country, but I did, even if it was my adopted home. And I couldn't stand the idea of Hitler officially sanctioning every lousy impulse in the Austrian character, and making life impossible for people like Leon and Hannah.

At that moment, the only thing keeping the Germans on the other side of the border was Mussolini, who would likely object to Hitler swallowing us whole when he was still hoping to take a nibble out of us himself. But who knew how long that would last? Il Duce could get distracted, or bought off by Hitler—at which point, Austria would become a delicious lunch. Our army wouldn't last 24 hours against Germany's, if for no other reason than the fact that they wouldn't have the nerve to shoot all of their cheering brothers and cousins waving the Nazi flag.

So what were you supposed to do? I could ask a hundred people not to tell me any Jewish jokes, and it wouldn't matter. Leon could get in a street fight every night of the week if he wanted and it wouldn't matter. Hitler was too big for any of us to stop—and he was coming, and everybody knew it. We just didn't know when. A country might have been able to stop him. An individual, though? Leon talked all the time about "the human imperative to resist." But all it got you was brained by a paving stone and a half-dozen stitches, and that's if you were lucky.

Anyway, Bain went into the hotel. I waited two or three minutes and then followed him. He checked his coat and hat. I decided not to check mine at the last second, brushing past the man at the reservation stand and approaching his table.

"Herr Kovacs."

"Herr Bain. You're here to fire my company, am I right?"

He was taken aback. This wasn't how it was supposed to work. "Well, yes I am."

"Thank you. And go fuck yourself."

I turned and walked out, not waiting to see or hear his reaction. I was elated as I reached the sidewalk—it always feels good to tell somebody to go fuck themselves, especially when the retort isn't in the form of a balled fist.

My next appointment wasn't for two and a half hours, and I realized I had just missed lunch. I got a sandwich at Goldberg's.

12

The little local train from the Linz station got me to Mauthausen in about 20 minutes. Rather than taking a taxi to the quarry, I decided to walk. It was about two miles, but it was a nice day. The path wended through clusters of small homes built into the hillsides and on ridges that overlooked great valleys. The quarry was pretty far away; up in the distance, ruggedly imposing.

How my father knew Edgar Grundman, the owner of the quarry, was a mystery to me. The old man never traveled anywhere. Maybe Grundman had been to Brno at some point, I didn't know. All I knew for sure was that the Kovacs family had no intention of getting into the granite business.

"Who would we get to run it—you?" the old man said on the phone, laughing. It might have been the only time I had heard him laugh in a year.

"So why do I have to listen to him?"

"Just be polite when you turn him down."

"But this is a waste of time."

"You have plenty of time. Just do it."

I was slightly winded as I reached the quarry. Herr

Grundman was waiting for me at the door.

"I was watching you. That's a good walk in city shoes."

I looked down at my brogues, shined every week, now covered in gray dust. "City shoes? Country shoes? What's the difference?"

"The blisters on your feet when you take them off tonight will be explanation enough. You know, there is a world outside the Vienna city limits. You probably think a big nature adventure is a trip to get drunk in Grinzing."

He was right, but so what? Outside of Vienna was a world full of Hitler-loving anti-Semites.

"This is a pretty area," I said. "The quarry has a rough beauty that is hard to imagine if you haven't seen it."

The office was a working foreman's office, not an owner's office. Work schedules and delivery notices were posted on the wall, along with an Ottakringer beer calendar that featured two attractive swimsuits. A broken piece of some bit of machinery was disassembled on a side table awaiting a reworking of the mechanical jigsaw puzzle.

"You still get your hands dirty every day?"

"Not really. I supervise, mostly. But I like the work. I like being in the middle of it."

This isn't how my father ran the mine. He only showed his face outside the office to yell at people. My father wore city shoes always.

"So if you still enjoy it, why are you selling? And how do you know my father?"

"That's two different questions. I'll start with the second one. I have never met your father in person. I did know your mother."

Mama got the Spanish flu and died in 1918. It was God's last, worst joke. The war that was supposed to last six months lasted more than four years. And near the end, just when everybody thought it was going to be safe again, the flu epidemic wiped out millions more. They buried her before I was discharged. I didn't even get a photo of her.

"We met at a Fasching ball in Vienna in 1894. I was 19. She was 17. If I close my eyes, I can still see the dress she was wearing: pink, very light pink, with a ruffle at the hem. To say I was smitten doesn't begin to explain it. Well, maybe it does. She was in town for two weeks, and we saw each other every day—balls, the opera, coffees. I know it was quick, but we were both very much in love."

You never think of your parents that way, not when you are a kid, not even when you are grown. I knew her family was some kind of minor Czech nobility, and that they didn't entirely approve when she married the grubby mine owner's son, but they didn't cut her off completely. I knew my grandparents in the big house in Dukovany, on the banks of the Jihlava, with the fields and forest surrounding it. I learned to shoot a rifle there. I got my first kiss there, from the housekeeper's daughter.

"So why didn't you get together? Was it my father?"

"No, he wasn't in the picture then. The problem was that your mother was Catholic and I am Lutheran. It was impossible."

"That's it? Really?"

"A mixed marriage is still hard today for people of a certain station. It was impossible then, for her. I understood."

Every year in January, the anniversary of when they met, my mother sent a letter, updating Grundman on her life. He would reply and do the same. But the letter in 1919 was written in a different hand, a man's.

"Your mother saved the letters, and your father found them after she died. He wrote to tell me, and we have kept up the correspondence. It's mostly about business, but he does mention your brother and his grandchildren, and you, of course."

"All very complimentary, I'm sure."

Grundman smiled. "He loves you, you know. Your father just doesn't always understand you. He always says that he can't believe how much you are like his brother, Otto. I'm so sorry about his passing."

I thanked him. "I can't believe he writes you every year."

"Every year. I think it keeps your mother alive, for both of us, even though we never mention her name."

I didn't know what to say. My mother had another love. My father had a heart. This was a lot to process, and I was having some trouble with it all. The silence grew uncomfortable. Grundman jumped in.

"The other question—why am I selling if I still enjoy it? This is something I would never tell your father, and you don't tell him, either. But I would like to tell you in confidence. Really, you can't tell anyone."

He began with a quick survey of Nazi sentiment in Linz. I told him what had happened in front of Goldberg's, and about my very abbreviated lunch with Ulrich Bain. I still didn't know where this was going.

"It's terrible, probably worse than you think. There are thousands of Herr Bains. I grew up with these people and Hitler is one of them. Hell, his parents are buried right outside Linz in Leonding cemetery. We'll line up and put flowers in their rifles when the Germans march in. It's only a matter of when."

I mentioned Mussolini, our great Italian protector. Grundman said, "That fool? You could buy him off with a five-mark whore. He's no protection. Hitler will offer him a tiny sliver of the Tyrol, and he'll go away. Hitler will take the rest. We can't stop him."

"So what does that have to do with selling?"

"Part of it is strictly business. When the Nazis come in, I guarantee they take the quarry away from me within six months. 'Resources in the national interest of the Fatherland,' or some such. They might give me 20 percent of what it's worth if they're feeling generous. Most people here are so in love with him that they can't see the next move, though. So I'm selling now, and I'm going to get a decent price."

"Not from us. You know that, right?"

"Oh, yes. I just consider this visit an extra letter from your father, a bonus."

Now it was my turn to smile. "So will you take the money and leave Austria? Where will you go?"

"No, I'm staying. I have my little house in the village—you walked past it—and I plan to stay busy."

"Doing what?"

Grundman leaned in. "This is the part you really can't tell anyone. I'm only telling you because I think you'll understand. I just can't live with the idea that this thug is going to destroy my country. There are at least some people who agree with me and are willing to act. I want to organize them. I want to finance them."

"You'll be in Dachau in a week. These people aren't kidding."

"I can't think that way. I'm 62, but I still have my health. I can outwork a 35-year-old in the pit when I feel like it. So I have that, and I will have plenty of money when I sell. I have to do something. Most of the people who think like me are younger—younger than you. They have energy, but also stupidity. I can guide them, help protect them."

"It's suicide."

"Maybe. Maybe you're right. But what's the alternative? There is no hiding from this. Read *Mein Kampf*. He's not stopping until somebody stops him."

"But you?"

Grundman shrugged. The look on his face was part defiance, part helplessness. It's the picture I couldn't shake, all the way back on the train to Vienna.

13

It was Henry's place by then, but I would always call it Henry's dad's place. And place is the word—not restaurant, not café, not bar, not dance hall, not gambling emporium, not brothel. Because it was all of those things. Nowhere else in Vienna could you get a crisp schnitzel for three marks and an hour of individualized entertainment in one of the back rooms for 10 marks more. As his dad used to say: "I am in the business of quenching all thirsts." The sign outside said, simply, *Fessler's*.

The back rooms were, not surprisingly, in the back. Working forward, there was a decent-sized dance hall in the middle third of the building, with a five-piece combo in one corner and lighting that made the room not quite dark but not quite adequately lit, and of various faint colors that had been accomplished by dipping the light bulbs in food coloring. I'd once had a summer job with Henry's dad, and keeping up with the light bulbs was part of the task.

"Mood lighting, Alex," is what he told me. "So you can see but also so you can pretend you can't see, if you are in the mood to pretend."

The front third of the building was divided in half, a dozen tables for the café on the left, a long, handsome wood bar on the right. When I walked in, Henry was sitting at the end of the bar, as always. Come in at 2 p.m., and he was sitting there, inevitably with an open ledger book, going over figures. At 6, he was likely in conversation with a bartender or waiter about something or another. At 10, which was when I walked in, he was having his only drink of the night, a martini, before going home and leaving Max, his oldest bartender, in charge for the rest of the evening.

"A Monday night? What's the occasion?"

"Quiet week," I said.

It was anything but, of course. Half the time, I was walking around and thinking about Johanna. The other half of the time, I was repeatedly recounting the conversation in Stephansdom. Never before in my life had the wondrous daydreams about a new woman been crowded out by something else. But that's what was happening.

There were so many reasons not to get involved. There were business reasons, specifically that the Kovacs Mining Company was profiting somewhere between handsomely and obscenely off of the Nazis, and, well, who cuts off their financial lifeline for some kind of romantic fantasy? Because that's what this was. I hated him, and I might have hated his followers even more, but who was going to stop Hitler? Me? It was absurd, and the risk was genuine, despite what the guy in church said. I could end up in Dachau, the family business could be blackballed in Germany, and for what? So that the Czech government would know ahead of time the exact caliber of the artillery that would be firing upon St. Vitus Cathedral in Prague?

Thinking practically, thinking risk-reward—Papa would have been so proud, the man whose favorite retort to pretty much any idealistic notion was, "Don Quixote didn't live on the Danube"—there was just no real upside to getting involved.

"You seem like you're someplace else," Henry said, and then he smiled a dirty smile. "Is it that . . . what is her name?"

"Johanna."

"Come on, details."

"Aren't we a little old for details?"

"Okay, but there are details, right?"

I smiled. That would be my answer.

Headlights suddenly lit the bar, coming through the front window. A big-ass Daimler was parking on the sidewalk, right against the building. The driver's door slammed and in walked a police officer in a captain's uniform. Henry eyed him, and then looked at me. The smile wasn't dirty anymore.

I looked at him, quizzically. "Friend or foe?"

"Both. Just business."

I knew what the business was. Before he left, Henry's dad had his hand in a bunch of areas, some more legitimate than others. He employed dozens of what he called "my guys." Some of them offered "protection" for neighborhood business. Others collected debts. Still others worked in the family's discount alcohol and cigarette business. Then there was this place, from the front of the house to the back of the house.

By the standards of the day, Henry's dad was a benevolent mobster. He would not allow his guys to be involved with illegal drugs. The protection charges were not onerous and did actually offer an element of protection in a city where burglary rose in lockstep with the unemployment rate. The gambling and loan-sharking were real, and people who did not pay did occasionally get beaten up, but it was never worse than that. Henry's dad always told his guys, "Know your clients. Don't let them get in so deep that they are left without alternatives." He actually fired a guy once, a very good earner, and told him, "What good are these customers to me tomorrow if you have to beat the life out of them today?"

But that was all over now. The family had sold off just about all of their businesses, except for Fessler's. But given the goings-on in the back room, the police still had to be accounted for. That was why Henry and I watched the host, Max, reach beneath the reservation book at his stand up front, pull out an envelope, and hand it to the good captain, who pocketed it in one motion. It was just the cost of doing business. I had seen Henry's father hand the envelope to old Schindler in the back alley on Saturday mornings a few times.

But instead of leaving with his extracurricular salary, the cop walked into the bar and approached us. Introductions were made. Captain Hans Fuchs seemed to be the prototypical Nazi: late 30s, blond, athletic, confident, oozing smarm. The Vienna police department was full of his type. There were probably more devout Nazis working the second shift in Vienna police precincts than there were in most Munich beer halls. So this was nothing new.

The truth was, Henry and I made our livings in the same way—that is, by talking to assholes. Whether you're in the bar business or the sales business, mindless conversation with despicable people is part of the job. Yet Henry was having trouble here, while I talked with Fuchs about the cold weather and the misfortunes of FK Austria this year. "Even Sindelar is so messed up, he couldn't hit the Danube from the embankment," I said. Fuchs made some crack about the goalie being "like a sieve for spätzle," and I kept looking over for Henry to join in but he just kept withdrawing into himself, silence wrapped in obvious concern. Fuchs noticed, too.

"Quiet tonight, Herr Fessler."

"Problems here—staff problems. I'm sorry."

"There must be a lot of staff issues here. So many different jobs under one roof." His wink was about as unsubtle as a wink could be, cartoonish almost. No, cartoonish actually. Without the good manners to accept his bribe and be done with it.

"It's the kitchen staff. I must check something—excuse me, Captain." And Henry was gone, leaving me and my new best friend. We had done weather, and we had done soccer, which left Schuschnigg, but I wasn't going there, not with this junior Himmler in training. Thank God he was as uncomfortable with the silence as I was. He got to his feet and said a quick goodnight and was gone—door slam, headlights again flooding the bar, and then roaring off into the February night.

I waited a minute for Henry, but he never came back.

14

Whenever I didn't feel like making my own breakfast, which was most days, I ate at Café Hawelka. If Café Central was all marble and multiple domes on the ceiling and the faint odor of perfume wafting from the next table and waiters who seemed to have studied choreography, Café Hawelka was dark wood and beer cases stacked in the vestibule, and a clock permanently stopped at 12:31. There were four booths, and this was the kind of place where people scratched their initials into the wood. Or, because it was 1937, you sometimes got more than that, like two lovers' initials encircled by a heart and joined in the middle by a swastika. But the breakfast—eggs scrambled and served in a small cast-iron skillet with some bacon and cheese and the proper amount of grease on top to douse a hangover—made it just about perfect. And, because this was Vienna, the skillet would be placed upon a china plate, and the whole thing would be delivered on a metal tray.

I grabbed *Der Abend* from the rack and sat with it and my coffee as the food cooked. The wooden dowel holding the paper together was worn by decades of warm hands, cold hands, sweating hands, worn by thousands of people reading about Jutland and Versailles and Hitler and Daladier and Lenin and Freud and Marx and Lloyd George and Hitler and Hitler and Hitler. The shellac was gone from the knob at the bottom, and most of the cherry stain, too.

The headlines were a variation on a common theme this winter: Hitler this, Mussolini that. The only comic relief, as the paper chronicled for the third straight day, was the investigation into who hired the skywriting plane that drew a hammer-and-sickle in the bright blue Vienna sky the other morning, only to be chased unsuccessfully by six military aircraft.

Craving my eggs, absorbed by the paper, I was startled by a man in a dark suit and a darker expression who sat down at my table. I looked at him. He said nothing.

"Do I know you?"

The look on his face morphed into pure, aggressive disdain. He practically spat the word: "Stephansdom."

"I never got a good look at you. You told me not to look."

The look on his face grew even more disdainful, if that was possible. Only the waiter's arrival to take his coffee order softened it.

I had obviously been thinking about it pretty much nonstop. It really upset me—and I had the toilet paper receipts to prove it. I worried about Hitler, and about the future, like everyone in Vienna—but my worries were also wrapped around a comfortable life where money wasn't a problem, and my responsibilities were easily managed, and where Johanna was now in the picture. She was challenging but also . . . comfortably challenging.

I just wasn't really that worried. I'd survive if the Germans came. If I couldn't hack it, my family would take me back in Brno, God help us all. I also had some money stashed in a couple of bank accounts, in Zurich and Paris, enough to make a fresh start, even if I couldn't get Otto's money out. There were options.

But now, if I accepted this offer, this summons, everything would be at risk—including my freedom, and maybe my life. It was a small risk, granted, if all I was doing was bringing back a few sheets of paper hiding in my briefcase amid hundreds of pieces of paper. Small risk, maximum penalty.

The man sipped his coffee and said, "So when do you leave for Cologne?"

"Sunday. It's three cities. Nuremberg for two days, Monday and Tuesday. Frankfurt for a day and a half, then Cologne for two more, Thursday night and all day Friday and Saturday. Overnight train back on Saturday night. The Orient Express."

"I know that."

"So why did you ask?"

"Making conversation so you can take your mind off of the fact that you're about to piss your pants."

"I knew you were a charmer. So, your plan is to sweet-talk me into doing this?"

"My plan is to finish my coffee and send a message to my boss in Prague telling him that you're either in or that you're a chickenshit. So which is it?"

My new friend, a complete asshole whose name I did not know, was right. I had spun this a million different ways in my head but that's what it came down to: Was I in or was I a coward? I was torturing myself, all the while wishing that I just possessed even a slice of that thoughtless decisiveness that Leon lived. Whether it was a woman way out of his league or four thugs jumping a Jew on a street corner, it didn't matter—Leon was all in while I was always a step behind, calculating the odds and the consequences.

"I'll die younger, but I'll have more fun," is what he always told me, usually when we were drinking afterward, and he was nursing some sort of wound, physical or otherwise.

So this was my chance. I'd had others—I'd fought in a war, for fuck's sake. I always came out looking okay, but I was never really a hero. I wasn't a total coward, but I was always slow, always calculating. Don Quixote never got near the Danube. My father's son.

I looked across the table at my sullen, burned-out friend. "Explain to me again why this is so important. I mean, we all know Hitler's coming. What's the point?"

"The point is that our army is better than you think. And the point is that the German army is worse than you think. And the point is that these are facts that need to be continually updated and verified so that the politicians, if they ever decide to grow a pair, can understand our chances of holding him off, the Corporal, and maybe embarrass him, and maybe convince the French pussies to honor their treaty because the big bad Nazi wolf maybe isn't so scary after all."

"But if Hitler takes Austria, Czechoslovakia will be surrounded. It won't matter. And he's taking Austria if he shows up with three old men on horseback armed with broomsticks and a bugle."

"Exactly. Which is why now is so important. Maybe we can make a late mutual defense deal with the Austrians. Maybe we can organize military maneuvers near the Austrian border that will scare Hitler a little. Maybe we make a show of strength that makes him reconsider for a little while. We're playing for time here, and to embarrass the French pussies into living up to their obligations. But I'm telling you more than I should, although it's all just common sense if you can read the newspapers and a map. So, are you in?"

I sat there and stared at him, but not really focusing on him. I saw my father, and I saw Otto. I saw Leon and the doctor stitching him up in the emergency room. I saw Ulrich Bain in front of Goldberg's Delicatessen and, mostly, I saw Herr Grundman in the quarry. His was the face, more than any, that I couldn't shake.

"I'm in," I said.

"Good. Someone will contact you, or not. Just go about your business. You'll never know until it happens."

15

I had time for a quick walk over to the museum to say goodbye to Johanna before the trip. It was hard to know what to say. Because I was putting whatever we had begun to build together in jeopardy, too, and I didn't feel like I could tell her about it.

It was bad enough that Leon knew, although I was pretty confident he wouldn't tell anybody, not even Henry. On the one hand, I very much wanted to tell Johanna because it would burnish my reputation as a brave doer of good. But I very much didn't want to tell her because she might blab. And also—and this was the real reason—I wasn't sure she would approve. I wasn't sure she was all that interested in doers of good.

It wasn't that she was an outright anti-Semite. It was nothing like that. But when I told her about our fight to rescue the Jewish kid, there was no disgust for the injustice, or concern for the kid, or disrespect for the police or the Nazis. Instead, what she said was, "I guess boys will always be boys, even when they are men." And then she kissed me on the forehead, and then down lower than that, and we really didn't talk about it anymore.

I just didn't know. The title her family had, and didn't have.

The money her family had, and didn't have. Her father's flick of the nose. There was a little bit of an edge there. We saw one of the socialist newspapers that still got smuggled in now and then —somebody had left it on our chair in Demel—and Johanna said, "Who would honestly believe these lies?" But that's just politics. Henry hates the socialists, too, and I'd trust my children's lives with him if I ever had any. Before they were outlawed, even Leon wasn't a big fan: "They figure they have us Jews in their pocket because we have nowhere else to go, and they take advantage of it. Intellectual shitheads." So what did it mean that Johanna hated them, too? Anything?

The point was, I didn't know, and I kind of didn't want to know. Someday, but not that day.

"So is the magnesite king of Central Europe all packed?" I didn't even have to see her face to see the smirk. I loved it.

The museum had a small canteen next to the gift shop. The place was dead. The only other person there was grabbing a coffee to take back to her office, it appeared. She came over, Johanna introduced us, and I immediately forgot her name. She barely stopped walking, but did manage to say, "That was quite a proposal."

"Early days yet. Just an idea."

After she walked away, I said, "Proposal?"

"For a new exhibition. It's daring."

"I didn't think they did daring here."

"We'll see."

She offered no other details. We had a cup of coffee and didn't say much. We were getting more comfortable with the silences, which was good, because I was suddenly conversationally paralyzed, so preoccupied with what was about to happen on the trip, so conscious of not revealing anything to Johanna. It felt good just to say goodbye.

Walking back home along the Ringstrasse, I was thoroughly

preoccupied. My most persistent daydream was of a waiter handing me an envelope containing secret military assessments along with my bill after lunch one day in some clandestine hole in the wall in Frankfurt. The other recurring dream was of a Gestapo agent banging on my hotel room door later that same night. The dreams were like an entry at the racetrack, one following the other. I swear, I had lost 10 pounds since the whole thing started.

Soon I was walking past the Hotel Bristol. I usually remembered to cross the street, or detour around it, but with the daydreams, I just forgot. The reason for the detours was because the Bristol was home to the German tourist office in Vienna. The office had one of the hotel's big display windows, which for years had been full of beautiful Aryannesses, skiing in Garmisch-Partenkirchen, or demurely taking the waters in Bad Godesberg, or not so demurely busting out of dirndls as they hoisted massive steins of beer for Oktoberfest in Munich. Not anymore, though. The window had become an enormous shrine to Hitler. There was a big framed photo of him, and that was it, and people gathered around it at all times of the day and night, noses pressed against the glass: men and women, old and young, and not just the teenaged boys who used to gather for a closer inspection of the dirndls. It was worse at night, as the portrait was lit by a spotlight, the illumination of evil. People sometimes left small bouquets of flowers; it had become a shrine. A hotel employee came out to tidy up and clean the smudges off of the glass twice a day.

This day, it was quiet—an older couple, holding hands, just staring. The man actually took off his hat like he was in church and didn't put it back on until they walked away.

How do you defeat that? The question, along with the mental picture of that old couple, stuck with me for hours—

through the taxi ride to the station, and the porter setting me up in my compartment, and a solo dinner that was more about the wine than the food, and the dose of valerian and the Agatha Christie novel to help me sleep. Eventually, I did. The train arrived in Nuremberg at 8 a.m., right on time.

16

The place was dark. These places were always dark, wherever they were, in whatever country. There was a kind of international language spoken by the designers, understood by all, in the layout of these places: understated entrance off of the street, formally dressed man to greet you inside the door, booths around the perimeter with single candles on the tables, red the dominant color of the furnishings, a three-piece combo lit by a small spotlight, a small dance floor marked by dull floor lights around the perimeter, but dark everywhere else, dark in all of the spaces in between. It was part of the illicit ambiance, that and the single corridor off of the main room, the corridor that led to the rest, the entrance invariably marked by a red velvet curtain and guarded by a bricklayer in a monkey suit.

I was seated in one of the booths. My client, Thomas Scherer, was with me, along with Trudi and Gretl, no last names required. There wasn't a lot of heavy lifting involved on this night. Dinner, drinks, stumble past the man in the tuxedo. Trudi and Gretl appeared at the table within seconds, and Trudi and Gretl's hands found our laps beneath the table a few more seconds after the drinks arrived. This wasn't complicated. It never was, except when I heard Scherer start bragging to Trudi about the steel mill he owned, and about the important work he did in building up the defense industries of the Reich, as if she were the type who needed impressing.

I removed Gretl's hand and slid over in the booth, put my arm around Scherer's neck and yanked him close so that I could whisper something. I caught Trudi's eye and winked. I looked at Scherer with a conspiratorial smile, as if we were about to begin plotting the time when we would walk toward the red velvet curtain.

"I'm ready now," Scherer said, almost giggling.

"You didn't tell her your real name, did you?"

"No."

"Or the name of the company?"

Terror suddenly contorted his face. A couple of years before, he had done the same thing, the same bragging, and he told the girl that night the company's name—and the girl came looking for him at the office a while later, pestering and then threatening. I had to make a special, unscheduled visit to Cologne, to pay off the girl to keep her quiet, and to pay off the owner of the club to make sure he worked to keep her quiet. In my expense report, I called it an "emergency consultation regarding unexpected demand at Scherer Steel." And, yes, in thanks, my good friend Thomas did agree to increase his magnesite order by 20 percent on the spot.

"So, did you?"

"No," Scherer said, and the terror was replaced by the same drunken smile. "No, I didn't mention it. She doesn't know the name. I'm good."

"Try to keep it that way. Why don't you dance for a while?"

"Can't dance right now," he said, winking and pointing quickly at his lap.

"Okay, okay. But stick to safe conversation subjects. Compliment her looks. Tell her she has nice tits and see where that goes."

We both laughed out loud, big guffaws, two aging fraternity brothers drunkenly prowling. And as Gretl and I made our way to the dance floor, I tried to keep up the inane conversation while scanning the room, looking one by one into the dimly lit booths, trying to figure who it might be.

The Nazis closed down a lot of these places. Or, rather, they closed the most conspicuous of these places and then made a great show of it. But while Nazis might have been Nazis, they still liked sex as much as anyone. They merely demanded discretion—and, if you talked to enough of the doormen, payoffs to local police were also a requirement. Looking around, peering into the dark booths, I could make out at least a few military uniforms.

I hadn't been approached anywhere on the trip—not during the stay in Nuremberg or the time in Frankfurt, not in the train station or at the hotel in Cologne the previous day, not in the restaurant or the first café tonight. I was leaving for home the next day.

"You seem distracted. Perhaps I could better get your attention—" Gretl smiled, and her eyes darted quickly toward the red velvet curtain. On many nights, I had made the walk down a dark corridor like the one here, but not tonight. I would wait for Scherer and Trudi to shamble off and make my goodbyes while they were busy—and by goodbyes, I meant I would leave the money for Trudi and Gretl with the tuxedo at the front door.

"Maybe in a bit," I told her. As we got back to the booth, we saw that Scherer and Trudi had been joined by a man in a Luftwaffe uniform. He stood to introduce himself, but it was awkward in the booth, and I told him to stay seated. He said his name was Major Peiper, and then he and Scherer smiled and winked. Fake names all around, then.

Gretl, sensing fresher meat, slid in quickly next to the good major. I was suddenly the fifth wheel, but I was okay with that. I hated to admit how much these trips took out of me. I was only 37 and had been doing this for more than a decade, and while the travel seemed to be in my blood, it could sometimes be exhausting, especially the final day or two. I wouldn't mind getting to bed, alone, with the long train trip home to Vienna still ahead.

Before the major got himself too entranced in Gretl's handiwork, I managed to find out that he and Scherer knew each other through "business." I assumed that the Luftwaffe was a client of the steel mill.

After another drink, I began plotting my exit. Every client was different, but Scherer liked to have me stay until he made a decision about the red velvet curtain. But then there was the Gretl question. The money I left at the front door would be different if Gretl took the major down the corridor or if she didn't—and there was no question that I was now paying for both of them, whatever happened. It was all the cost of doing business. Maybe I would just pay the full rate for both of the girls and let the tuxedo pocket the difference if the major chose not to partake.

This was all going through my head when the major excused himself to use the restroom. Trudi was fully engaged with Scherer, and Gretl slid over and joined her, two sets of hands now exploring. This had not been Scherer's thing in the past, but he appeared to be considering the notion. All I was thinking about was the four-block walk back to the hotel in the sleet and a nice warm bed. And when the major returned from his piss, he signaled to Scherer that it was time to head for the red velvet curtain, and what lay behind it.

They all got up. I shook hands with the men and promised Scherer that I would expedite the updated contracts once I returned to Vienna. Money for the evening was not mentioned, the arrangements understood by all. After they had left, I slugged my drink, put down the glass and began to grab my coat and hat from the nearby rack when the major returned to retrieve the pack of cigarettes he had left on the table.

He looked at me and said, "It's an envelope taped to the bottom of the sink in the bathroom."

17

Like most people who travel a lot, I had my routines and my preferences—favorite hotel, favorite restaurant, all of that. In Cologne, the restaurant was the Brauhaus Sion, where the two waitresses—mother and daughter—wore dirndls and the sauerbraten was the best I had ever tasted. The hotel was the Dom Hotel, a big place near the cathedral that catered to businessmen and their needs. In my case, that meant a large room with a view of the cathedral, and it also meant the delivery of a typewriter on the last day of my stay.

After years of experimenting, the last day of a three-city trip was a workday in the hotel for me. The paperwork was excessive and could bury me if I wasn't careful. There also were notes that I made during conversations with clients, documenting the information for new orders and timetables for delivery and such. The typewriter was my method for making those notes legible so they could be acted upon by Hannah when I got home. I taught himself to type after frustrating her for years with my indecipherable handwriting and haphazard shorthand. It just felt better to sleep in after a night out with the client, and then get the detail work done so I could relax on the night train.

I had slept in and had a room service breakfast that was actually lunch. I finished typing at five and packed everything back into the briefcases—in the middle of which was shoved a small envelope containing several strips of microfilm.

I wasn't anxious about it at sometimes and paralyzed by the thought of it at others, which I found a little bit odd. Then again, my contact had warned me, "Half of the time you're going to feel like the almighty sheriff in one of those American westerns, and the other half of the time, you're going to feel like one of the wounded outlaws hiding in the barn." I didn't get it when he said it, but I did when it was happening.

On the last night, I always ate in the Dom's dining room. The train wasn't until 1:30 in the morning, so it was a leisurely meal, good for a hotel. Then it was to the front desk to order a taxi for one o'clock, and then to a chair in the back corner of the lobby, where one or two drinks would get me so far, and then a shower and a change of clothes would get me the rest of the way, and then the taxi and the train would get me home.

I was into the second schnapps and had not thought about the microfilm in half an hour, I realized, when I saw a man in a black trench coat walk into the lobby. He removed his hat, spoke briefly with the bell captain, and then began walking in my direction, passing one table, two tables, three tables, and not stopping. It was soon quite clear that he was coming to speak to me.

18

Put it this way: If UFA was looking for someone to play a Gestapo captain in its next widescreen blockbuster —*The Knock at 3 a.m.*—then this was their man. No screen test necessary.

"Captain Werner Vogl. May I join you?"

As if I had a choice. Had anyone failed to answer any question in the affirmative since he first put on that uniform? It was a question I wished I had the guts to ask him out loud.

"And how was your dinner, Herr Kovacs? I've always been partial to the medallions of pork in a black cherry sauce."

So he knew my name. He smiled when that dawned on me. So much for my poker face. The waiter arrived.

"I was about to order a drink. Can I tempt you?"

"Sorry. Still on duty for a few more hours. I try to limit myself to once a week when I play chess at Bischoffshausen on Wednesdays. It's a nice place—do you know it? It's right around here, maybe a 30-second walk from the back of the hotel. In by 7:30, home by 10. Anyway, you go ahead. Your train isn't for, what, five hours?"

So he knew my name, and he knew when I was leaving. I felt my hand begin to shake. I ordered another large schnapps.

"Yes, the Orient Express. It's my favorite train, even if I spend most of the journey asleep. It arrives in Cologne at 1:28 a.m., departs at 1:38 a.m.—but you already seem to know that. There are always a few passengers having a last drink in the dining car before bed. So many interesting people."

I was regaining my conversational sea legs. I could talk travel all day, to anyone—hotels, restaurants, trains. I loved trains. I could compare the quality of berths and dining cars depending on point of origin—food was best on trains starting in France, but berths were cleaner and more comfortable in Germany and Austria, for instance. Most of all, I loved talking about the mysterious luxury of the Orient Express.

"I once met a professor from London who was headed to Bucharest to meet up with a former student who was involved in a plot to take a shot at King Carol. I read the newspapers for weeks afterward but never saw a word about it. I always wonder if he was kidding me."

Vogl listened, but not all that attentively. But that was okay. Bored was more than all right with me. Part of me thought I was going to be able to talk my way through this because that was my living, talking my way into and out of things: late deliveries, price increases, whatever. So why couldn't I handle a pleasant few minutes with this guy, just because he was wearing a black uniform? But then it dawned on me: Maybe the reason he wasn't really listening to me was that his job was just to keep me busy while his partner—they all have partners, don't they?—was searching my room.

I was downing my schnapps and thinking about catching the waiter's eye. Then Vogl suddenly leaned in conspiratorially and said, "Are there ever opportunities for female companionship on the Orient Express?"

I'd been taking that train twice a year for the last dozen years, and I had one story. Truth be told, it wasn't even on the Orient Express but an overnighter from Berlin. But it is a great story, one of my go-to stories with the right audience, a story about a mother, a daughter, separate visits to my compartment, all under the unsuspecting nose of their husband/father. Or, as I always ended the story, "Or maybe he knew and just didn't give a shit."

It always got a laugh. It got a laugh from the good captain. But then it was on to business.

"So what brings you to Cologne?"

I caught the waiter's eye and then dove into the great and glorious story of the Kovacs family magnesite mine. I actually had three different versions of the story that explained my professional existence. I used the 20-second version when I was talking to an attractive woman, always ending with, "But enough about mines. How about yours?" It was stupid, but most of them at least giggled. Then there was the two-minute version for men who seemed genuinely interested. Then there was the five-minute version, with explanations of mining depths and maximum temperatures and the latest research on proposed new uses, which I unfurled when I was trying to get rid of somebody in a social situation by boring them into submission. Vogl was getting the full five-minute recital. The problem was, after three minutes, he was still nodding along with every point I made.

I kept thinking about his hypothetical partner as I droned on from memory. The microfilm was in a small envelope. It was stuck amid about 200 pages of contracts and delivery schedules in the one briefcase. I'd started the trip with about 500 pages in each but was down to about 200 in each. Maybe I should put all 400 in one case and leave the other one empty. I always balanced them off for, well, balance when I walked with them, but maybe combining made sense. I didn't know.

I was about done with the five minutes. Almost everybody I had ever subjected to this long explanation had thought up an excuse to leave before I got to the part about the difference between light burnt and dead burnt, and which works best in a furnace, but Vogl was still hanging in. I didn't have much left. So I went where I always went—getting the other guy to talk about himself. But, really, how many people make conversation with a Gestapo agent by asking, "So, are you from here? Married? Children?" Well, I did.

Vogl was from Koblenz, as it turned out. He had a wife and a five-year-old daughter. He liked chess. As he talked, though, he suddenly became distracted again. I looked over his shoulder, toward the elevator, and saw the door closing and someone with a dark trench coat walking toward the hotel exit. The partner? Could be. But Vogl's back was to the elevator when the guy got off, so whatever was distracting him wasn't that. Then, for whatever reason, Vogl stood and made his excuses and left.

I was pretty sure I was physically slumping in my chair as I watched Vogl leave through the hotel's front door. I looked over my shoulder to see what might have distracted Vogl. There was nothing there, except for the enormous mirror that gave him a view of the entire lobby, including the elevator doors.

19

Up the elevator and down the hall, I kept telling myself that they would have grabbed me on the spot if somebody had searched my room and found the microfilm. I couldn't assume they had found anything. I couldn't assume they even searched the room. What did a black trench coat even mean? I mean, come on—I owned a black trench coat.

I opened the door and took a small step inside, almost on tiptoe. The light was on. Had I left the light on? I couldn't remember. I had turned on the desk lamp when I was typing, but the overhead light? I just didn't remember.

I closed the door and scanned the room, still hesitant to take a step. My typing was in a pile on top of the typewriter, where I left it. Looking into the bathroom—no light on in there—my shaving kit was packed up and on the sink as before. My suitcase was open on the rack at the foot of the bed, re-packed. The two briefcases were on the bed, both unlocked and unlatched, both open. Check.

The briefcases were all I was worried about, specifically the one with the small bit of green ribbon on the handle. That was for the last client on the trip, the other one for the first, or first and second clients. I riffled through the papers, looking for the small envelope containing the microfilm. I didn't see it. I took out the stack of paper, riffled again, and the envelope fell out on the bed. It was still sealed.

I put it all back into the briefcase and exhaled for the first time. My Czech contact, whose name I still didn't know, had warned me, "There's a fine line, just a filament, between awareness and paranoia—try not to cross it. Be aware. Don't be paranoid." It was good advice. Of course, it was easy for him to say. I was the one who just received a hearty hidey-ho from the Gestapo.

The fact that I couldn't find the envelope when I was specifically looking for it told me that I had nothing to worry about. At the same time, though, I had whined enough before I left that my contact gave me a way to hide it even better.

When I got to the station it was after midnight, but the place was far from sleepy—not bustling, not precisely, but the café was open, and the newsagent, and the wine store. That was my stop, after dropping my bags with the porter and hanging on to the one briefcase with the green ribbon. I had practiced the line, over and over, and could deliver it flawlessly, if I do say so myself. I walked into the empty shop, and the man behind the counter acknowledged me with a nod, and I said, "I'm looking for a nice German wine for my Slovak father."

I felt like winking, to make sure he got it. I settled for earnest eye contact. But there was not a hint of acknowledgment on his part, just a quick search of the shelves behind the counter, the grabbing of a bottle that he then presented to me.

"You must try this Riesling from Rüdesheim. It is one of our best."

That was the recognition code. Hot damn. I really was a spy.

The Orient Express arrived exactly on time, naturally. About a dozen people boarded with me. It always gave me a thrill, that train, and it did that night, too. The feeling was more of elegance than opulence, of old money and hushed conversations to which I would never be privy, but which I could pretend to be understanding as I caught small snippets in passing. There were plenty of people on the train like me—businessmen with healthy expense accounts—and the truth was, those were the people I tended to end up talking to. We all seemed to gravitate toward each other as if the practice of commerce provided us with a magnetic sheen that drew us together. But it was the rest of them—the old couple that had the look of faded royalty, silently eating a late snack; the two swarthy 30-year-olds in ill-fitting suits, maybe Italians, maybe Turks—that stuck in the imagination.

When I got to the compartment, I fished into the briefcase for the envelope and then, taking the wine bottle, fiddled with the cork until the secret compartment revealed itself. I took the tiny strips of film—two of them—out of the envelope, doing my best not to smudge them with fingerprints, and inserted them into the void, then replaced the loose bit of cork and jammed it back in with my thumb. Even if it fell out, there really wasn't anything to see. Then I burned the envelope in the little metal sink in the compartment, as instructed, put the bottle in the other briefcase, and went for a drink in the dining car to calm myself down.

I didn't feel like talking to anyone, and I didn't. Sleep came easier than I'd thought it would. Breakfast was breakfast, although even the coffee on the Orient Express tastes better. The border crossing into Austria was at Passau. We would get there around 11 a.m. For years, the train would stop and the German border agents—there were always two of them—would knock on the door of the compartment, check the passport, ask if there was luggage. I would point to it, they would nod, the passport would be stamped, and that would be it. They would finish, the train would run for about five minutes, and Austrian border agents would get on and repeat the process.

But for at least the last two years, everybody and their luggage had to get off at Passau, walk up to two German border guards sitting at a table, and go through the same process. The inspections were just as cursory, performed by inspectors who looked just as bored, and the stamps in the passports looked just the same. Other than taking three times as long and being a boon to the waiting porters on the platform, who worked for tips, it seemed like a complete waste of time. Of course, this would be the first time I ever came across the border armed with a wine bottle fortified with what I presumed were German military secrets, so there was that.

It was, as always: a line of passengers, and luggage, and porters, shuffling up to the table. Greetings, what was the purpose of your visit, anything to declare, glance at the bags, nod, stamp, next.

"Guten tag. What was the purpose of your visit?"

"Business appointments in Nuremberg, Frankfurt, and Cologne."

The truth was, this guy had not been listening to anyone in the line ahead of me, but he suddenly really wasn't listening to me. He was on his feet, walking away from the table, back over near the platform. He had my passport in his hand, open to my picture. He consulted with another guy who was holding a clipboard. The guy looked at the passport, then down at his list of names. He nodded.

My guy returned and handed me the passport. "Herr Kovacs, to my colleagues, please. It is just routine—and have the porter bring your luggage."

He pointed over to his right, about a hundred feet away. A doorway to a room, a man standing at attention, armed with a machine pistol. The black uniform was unmistakable. He did not look bored. I did my best to affect a shrug and a smile as I began to walk over. Glancing over my shoulder to make sure he was following, the porter suddenly looked worried, probably about his tip.

20

The Aryan specimen opened the door as I approached, standing at attention again just inside. "Come in, with the luggage," he said.

I was first, holding the briefcase with the wine bottle. The porter was next, with my suitcase and the other briefcase, the one with the papers and the green ribbon around the handle. The muscle signaled with a flick of his head that the porter could leave. He did not dawdle.

"Wait here." Then the door was closed, and I was alone.

It was a makeshift kind of space, with a bit of a cave quality to it—you didn't have to stoop over, but the ceiling was just a little bit low, and the back wall was cement. Maybe it had once been used for storage. The only light was from a single bulb overhead. A small wooden table and two chairs were the only furniture. I sat, waiting.

I had played this out in my head a hundred times over the last few weeks. I just kept telling myself to act the way I had acted the other time they had looked through my bag. It was last year, coming back from Leipzig. The same kind of setup, pretty much, except there wasn't a guy with a clipboard and the second table was also out on the platform, not in a separate room. That one seemed more random. I tried to remember how I acted with that Gestapo agent—I think he was a second lieutenant. I was just, well, normal, I guess—not angry at the delay, not guilty because there was nothing to be guilty about, kind of friendly, not overly friendly, just answer the questions.

The door opened. I stood up. "Herr Kovacs, I am Sturmhauptführer Rabel. Please be seated."

Sturmhauptführer. Another captain. Shit.

He held out his hand. I gave him the passport. He pulled a notebook from his pocket and began to write. "I understand you were here on business. Can you please explain in some detail where you were and who you met with?"

I began, explaining the magnesite sales business, and all of my clients, and taking him on the trip from Nuremberg to Frankfurt to Cologne. I left out the part about how I pretty much had to carry Herr Feldmann of the Nuremberg Steel Works and drop him into a taxi to take him home, and the club in Frankfurt where I had to pay off the maître d' to keep him from calling the cops on handsy Herr Lindemann. I also left out the part about collecting the small envelope taped to the underside of the porcelain sink in Cologne.

"This magnesite—it seems an important material for manufacturing, and perhaps national security. Do you have many contacts with the military?"

"I have some, yes. The steel mills who are our clients are all private business concerns, but many of them have military contracts. Probably most of them. As a result, when I meet with my clients, I sometimes come into contact with military personnel. They can sometimes explain better than the client what is needed in the manufacturing process."

I stopped talking. Rabel continued to write. Then he looked up. "And any military contacts on this trip?"

I thought I had danced around it, but no. Any military contacts on this trip? The only one was the guy who passed me the microfilm.

"Let me think back, just to be sure," I said, buying a few seconds.

In the half-assed training I was given by my Czech contact, one thing I remembered him saying was, "Don't lie if you don't have to." He had talked about how life is full of coincidences, and odd little events that defy rational explanation, and not to get caught up lying about meaningless things just because you think they look bad.

"The lies are the hardest thing to keep track of," he said. "Only lie when it matters."

So where did the major in the club fit in? I could tell the truth—that I was in the club with Herr Scherer, and that the major was a friend of Scherer's who we ran into, and that I left them soon after as they continued their evening. It was all true and as innocent as it sounded—except for, well, you know.

But the sturmhauptführer was sitting there, writing. He probably had dozens of those notebooks, stored in his office, organized by date, the information cataloged for easy retrieval. He probably went to his office every day and reviewed the latest entries in order to take the appropriate actions. To put Scherer's name in that notebook, however innocent the story, was to put him in the Gestapo's sights. Then again, maybe he was already in the Gestapo's sights—in which case, my bringing up his name would attach more suspicion to my name. Then again, lying about an innocent contact could also hurt me if they ever found out about it. For all I knew, they already had found out about it. I mean, why did Vogl come to the hotel? Why was my name on that clipboard?

In the end, I went with my gut, making a show of searching my memory.

"Nuremberg . . . no. Frankfurt . . . no. Cologne . . . no. No, no military this trip."

Rabel wrote some more. His face betrayed nothing. He might actually be the one guy on the planet who could successfully lie to his wife. I sat there, trying to keep my breathing even. He got up, pulled on a pair of black leather gloves, opened my suitcase, and began to paw my dirty underwear. His heart wasn't in the task—it was all pretty cursory. You would have thought he'd have an underling for such work.

Gloves off, briefcase next. He looked in at the stack of paper, a couple of hundred pages, and riffled through it without attempting to read even one of the pages. He now seemed as bored as the border guard outside.

"Two briefcases?" he said, his hands outstretched. I handed it over.

"On a trip to three clients, I start with more paperwork than can fit in one. I unload some at each stop and am left with this: contracts, orders, delivery schedules. The second briefcase is usually empty on my return. Except for this time . . ."

"I see," he said. He was actually smiling.

"It's for my father. He lives in Brno. He loves German Riesling."

Rabel held the bottle up to the light bulb. He read the label. He looked at the cork. He turned it again, squinting, studying.

"I wonder," he said. "You leave the important papers with the porter. Yet you carry the wine bottle yourself. That seems backward to me."

Easy, now. Steady. As evenly and matter-of-factly as I could, I started to speak, hoping my voice didn't crack like a 12-year-old's.

"You're right, it is kind of backward. I did it the other way in Cologne—I carried the paperwork. But the way the porter was tossing the bags around, I really thought the bottle might break.

I didn't want to ruin the bag, so I carried the wine when we got here."

Rabel continued to study the bottle.

"The bottle didn't break," he said, "but the cork did."

He picked at it, just a bit, and the pre-broken piece popped into his hand. He looked again at the bottle. The single light bulb left the secret hiding place in a bit of a shadow. Even then, the microfilm was further secreted into a sliver of space that had been cut into the cork, probably with a razor blade. He would be very fortunate, and I would be very unfortunate, if he found it.

He looked at the void in the cork one more time, intently. He probed into the hole with his pinky. Nothing. "Ah, look, I've made it worse," he said, and then took the broken piece and shoved it back into place, admiring his handiwork. "Good as new. I'm sure your father will enjoy it."

He handed me the bottle and the briefcase. "You may rejoin the train. Have a pleasant remainder of your journey."

I thanked him, because that's what you do. As I wrestled the three bags out the door, looking for the porter, Rabel was writing something else in the notebook.

21

Leon with Hildy, who can properly be described as one of the women in his regular rotation. Henry with Liesl, a new girl, a librarian, of all things. Me with Johanna. The bottle of Riesling back in my apartment, in the small wine rack.

Drinks at the Grand Bar. Then the movies, to see *The Hour of Temptation,* which was fine enough for a crap mystery, except for the *Strength Through Joy* newsreel that they were tending to show more and more, apparently to appease the German government, which was convinced there were too many Jews in the Austrian film industry. Then something to eat and a few more drinks at Café Imperial.

I had been home for several days, and nobody had contacted me about the microfilm. It was on my mind constantly the first day back, then hourly the next couple of days, then less. I made it through the whole movie without thinking about it once—well, not once after the newsreel, which featured about a hundred men, stripped to the waist, about to go for a swim in one of the Fatherland's massive new indoor natatoriums, giving the Hitler salute. Heil Backstroke!

The conversation at dinner was fun, light, perfect. Hildy had nothing much to say, which was typical. A couple of months ago, when Henry had brought up this fact, Leon had assured us, "I promise, her mouth works fine." Which apparently was why she remained in the rotation. Her entire contribution to the evening's conversation came after an impromptu riff that Henry made about the quality of Stalin's mustache, followed by a general admiration for the facial hair of many Russian politicians. At which point, Hildy offered, "I hate borscht."

Liesl was more interesting. She spoke four languages—German, French, Italian, and Russian—and was clearly smarter than most of the women Henry had dated. In fact, she was clearly the most intelligent person at the table, and it wasn't close. But the most interesting thing she said had nothing to do with the Austrian National Library, where she worked inside the Hofburg, or with the Turgenev, which she was currently reading in the original Russian for fun. It was when the conversation had somehow turned to the idiosyncrasies of our parents, and Leon was telling the story of how his father always went for the same walk, down the same streets, every night after dinner, never varying no matter how much Leon made fun of him. "One day, you will understand the comfort of routine," his father told him.

To which, Henry replied, "My father was like that, too. Like clockwork: reports from his guys on Monday, bookkeeping and the bank on Tuesday, inventory and orders on Wednesday, deliveries on Thursday, inspecting the new inventory on Friday . . ."

"Especially the new blond inventory," Liesl said, and everybody laughed, partly because it was funny but mostly because it sounded funnier coming from a librarian. But what it meant most of all was that she knew what Henry really did for a living, and what his father had done for a living, and she wasn't fleeing the scene. This was big and pretty much unprecedented, and it explained the look on Henry's face. He tended to be so perpetually anxious around his girlfriends, never quite relaxed, always seeming to anticipate the end when it was only the beginning. But not here, not with Liesl. Here he looked content.

Liesl asked Johanna about the museum, and she offered some details about the mysterious exhibition she was planning, the one that she had said would be "daring." As it turned out, it was going to be a show that featured the works of three modern artists. "Very arresting—there is a boldness to the lines and the subject matter that is captivating," she said, and I guess that was daring, seeing as how the Rudolf Museum was an old-money, aristocratic kind of place whose board was full of people like her father. But it wasn't that daring.

This was: "Max Ernst, Felix Nussbaum, and Max Beckmann," she said when Leon asked her the names of the artists. He fancied himself a connoisseur, even if his museum visits had been limited to openings where he cadged free drinks and compiled lists of boldfaced names for *Der Abend* before he moved up to the *Die Neue Freie Presse*. The truth was, he had not been to a museum or gallery since he had stopped being paid to go.

Ernst. Nussbaum. Beckmann. Jew. Jew. Jew. The only people at the table who got it were Leon and I. We made eye contact immediately. As the conversation shifted, I was able to turn to my left and offer Johanna an arched eyebrow. She half-shrugged, half-smiled. Then she leaned over, kissed me on the cheek, and whispered, "I told you it was daring."

That didn't begin to describe it. Vienna had always had an uncomfortable relationship with its Jewish population. Some tried to assimilate, like Leon's family, which had come from somewhere near Budapest in the 1870s. Leon was third generation and barely religious. He always said he had more Gentile friends than the average Jew in Vienna, and the ability to exist in both worlds was an attainable goal for people like him, even if there was never true equality. The way most people figured it, Jews could excel in the professions, Gentiles could control the civil service and the military, they would share the business landscape, and everybody could go on with their lives. If Jews would give up the practice of their religion, they could even intermarry. Their lives would be complicated that way, but not impossible.

But then there were the eastern Jews who came after the war, who packed into Leopoldstadt. They were peddlers, not professionals, and they didn't want to be professionals. They didn't want that for their kids, either. They didn't want to fit in—but it wasn't just a we-don't-care-about-fitting-in mindset. They actively did not want to fit in. They kept their beards long, and they kept to themselves, and the youngest among them who weren't Zionists were Communists. The truth was, Leon had much more in common with Gentiles than he did with the new Jews.

The one thing they did share was support for the current government under Schuschnigg, and the one before that under Dollfuss. Neither one was a liberal—hell, Dollfuss would have kissed Mussolini on the mouth, with tongue, if he were standing next to him, and he had a stepladder. You see, Dollfuss was about four foot eleven, which generated all manner of unkind humor. There was an especially funny one about how a Nazi plot to kill him had been foiled when investigators found a loaded mousetrap outside the door of his apartment. Of course, that one became a little less funny in 1934, after Dollfuss was assassinated during an attempted coup by the Nazis.

Since then, Schuschnigg kept up with the Nazi ban that got Dollfuss killed, and at least occasionally gave lip service to the rights of Jews. But it was lip service, and every Jew knew it. As Leon said, "The best thing Schuschnigg has going for him is that we're afraid of what might come next if he gets kicked out."

So if Jewish professors couldn't get tenure anymore at Vienna University, well, they would live with that and adapt, like the doctor who sewed up Leon that night in the emergency room. And if the two musicians from New York who came for a series of performances were forced by the Konzerthaus to anglicize their names in the publicity materials, well, the shows were still excellent. And if the Boy Scouts now insisted on separate troops for the Jewish boys, well, it was a way to reinforce Jewish values on impressionable young minds. In Vienna, in 1937, there was a rationalization for almost anything if you wanted there to be one.

Ernst. Nussbaum. Beckmann. Jew. Jew. Jew. This would not go over well in the world of the Vons, and this was their museum. Johanna's father really was on the board of directors. Her credentials for getting the job on the museum staff were unquestioned, but neither was her lineage. This exhibition, if it were to take place, would be viewed as a direct attack on that lineage.

I think I loved her. It was on this cloud that the rest of the evening floated.

Just before we were getting ready to leave, a man I did not recognize followed me into the bathroom. I started peeing as he waited behind me. We were the only two inside. I finished, buttoned up, headed for the sink, and saw him there, leaning against the door to force it shut, to make sure it was just us.

I nodded an acknowledgment as our eyes met, what polite strangers do. He looked at me, a little tiredly, and said, "Go for a ride on the Prater, Tuesday afternoon at one. Just bring the microfilm. And I was told to tell you to enjoy the wine, that it actually is very good."

22

I probably hadn't been on Tram 1 in 10 years, but the cars hadn't changed, not a bit, since the first time I had been on one after the war. The only things that had changed were the circumstances.

The ambiance was worn, dark, old, the windows scratched by kids with coins. The leather seats were shiny from decades of asses, shiny when they weren't worn through entirely and split, the horsehair spilling out. The floor was perpetually dirty, nicked and scraped and sticky in places. Somebody once told me they hosed down the cars every month and pushed the standing water out the doors. You knew they never used any soap—not that it would have helped.

On a Tuesday afternoon in February, seats were plentiful, and there was only a handful of people in the car when I got on. That was different, because the only time I had ever taken the tram out to the Prater was on a packed Friday or Saturday night, with some combination of Henry and Leon and whoever else, accompanied either by girls or by hopes of meeting girls. Those were terrific, entirely carefree times for a teenage soldier just home from the war, even if Vienna was overrun by the unemployed and struggling terribly with its new post-war status. It once had been the capital of a vast empire, with all of the size and grandeur befitting that title. Now, thanks to Versailles, the size and the grandeur remained, but the empire was nothing, just a bunch of farms linked by towns without industries and people without prospects.

That didn't matter to Leon, Henry, or me. We all had some combination of work and school—Leon and Henry with their parents, me with Uncle Otto—and we weren't getting shot at by Italians anymore, and we were successfully managing to pursue the kind of fun that teenagers pursued. Thinking back on it, I'm pretty sure I was never wholly sober on any of those Friday or Saturday nights—which was really the only thing about the tram ride that hadn't changed over the years. Because, on this day, I had drunk the entire bottle of Riesling after I had removed the cork, pried out the microfilm, and put it into an envelope that was now hidden in my shoe.

I got on at Schwedenplatz. There were seven stops to the park, which was the end of the line. Five of the stops were on this side of the canal, and there were normal people doing normal workaday things riding along with me. I eyed them all up and down—the smiling schoolboy who undoubtedly had a note from the school nurse in his pocket about some phantom stomach ailment; the woman with a package from someplace, wrapped nicely as a present; a handful of men dressed for business; and the people who got on with me: a pregnant woman with a baby in a carriage, and an old couple lugging a string bag of winter produce, a bag that now sat at their feet. I wondered which one might be following me, which was silly. But it's what you did when you had an envelope containing microfilm hidden in your shoe.

The car began to empty with each stop. I mean, nobody was going to the Prater on a Tuesday in February. I actually called before I left, to make sure it was open. It was a benign enough day, the sun in and out, the temperature in the high thirties, but it wasn't precisely Ferris wheel weather, even if the cars on the famous old ride were enclosed.

One by one, my fellow passengers got out. After the sixth stop, the only ones going to the end of the line were me and the people who got on with me at Schwedenplatz. At which point, the silent panic that had become my best friend settled in for another visit.

There were entire days when I couldn't shake the feeling in my stomach, the fear. It was during those times that I couldn't believe what I had gotten myself into. I was paralyzed, not physically but mentally. I couldn't think about anything else, couldn't concentrate on work or Johanna or whatever book I was reading. My mind would just wander, mostly to Captain Vogl and our chat in the lobby of the Dom Hotel. Thinking about it, the search at the train station was more dangerous, but I could shake that memory for some reason. Vogl, I couldn't shake. I guess it was the fear of the unknown that he represented.

At the end of the line, the tram lets everyone out, then drives empty a few feet where it lands on a wooden turntable and is, well, turned in the opposite direction, back toward the city. I got out first, helping the woman with the baby carriage out the door. The old couple followed. I eyed them up and down again, trying to get some sense. But, really: a pregnant woman with a baby carriage and an old couple? Neither would be able to keep up with me if it ever came to that. The whole thing was stupid. Still, I walked extra fast away from them, heading left into the park and toward the Prater. It was probably a half-mile away. I turned after walking for about three minutes. The old people looked as if they had barely moved from the tram, that's how far back they were. And the pregnant woman was nowhere to be seen. She had either headed in the other direction or taken one of the trails toward other attractions in the park.

With that, my blood pressure settled a bit. The envelope in my shoe was uncomfortable, but I left it there, an annoying reminder. There was almost nobody in the amusement park when I got there, and pretty much everything was closed. A small snack stand was open, and so was the Prater. I thought about a cup of coffee but decided against it—let's just get this over with. I didn't know who I was meeting, or where, but I figured the thing to do was go for a ride. I bought my ticket and walked through the cattle chute to the entrance. Two people were waiting for the next stop—a couple of 16-year-old boys who had pretty obviously ditched school. I was pretty sure I wouldn't be handing them the microfilm, but I didn't know what else to do but get on. It was only at the last second that a man in a brown overcoat handed the attendant his ticket and made us a foursome. It was the same guy, my regular contact.

The enclosed cabin probably had room for 30 people, so we weren't exactly crowded. The two boys headed to the front left and looked out the window. I walked to the back right. The brown overcoat followed me.

"So, do you have it?"

"Not even a hello?"

"Fine. Good day, Herr Doktor Kovacs. Now, do you have it?"

I sat down on the bench. "It's in my shoe."

He snorted, then shook his head. "You're right, they never look there."

Fuck this guy. That was all I could think as I took off my shoe, removed the envelope, and handed it over. I mean, really: fuck this guy.

"It went okay?"

I told him about the pickup in the club bathroom, and the Gestapo captain at the hotel, and the wine bottle, and the search at the train station. He seemed slightly bored. "So, it was pretty routine."

"Routine for you, not for me," I said, my voice rising, and he kind of shushed me with a hand gesture, just to make sure the boys wouldn't hear. But seeing as how one of them was in the middle of telling a joke involving two kittens and a brassiere, and telling it loudly, there wasn't a lot of risk.

"I don't know if I can do this anymore. This is eating me alive. It's killing me."

His face softened when I said that, just a little. His tone changed. "Look, it's always like that at the beginning. The first time is the hardest. You get used to it, I promise. You never want to lose your caution, that edge, that little bit of nervousness. But it stops being paralyzing. It becomes your routine, a routine of awareness. You stop having a stomachache all the time."

"But what if I want out?"

"If you want out, you get out. I know people who've done it. But if you think you're drinking a lot now to get through this, think again. Because there is no drinking like the drinking you do to live with the fact that you're a coward."

I glared at him. He said, "Look, you don't need to make any decisions now. A lot of times, these little delivery missions are a one-off, and they never contact you again. And if they do contact you again, and you can't handle it, just tell me, and that'll be that."

The ride on the Prater lasted maybe 10 minutes. We didn't say much for the last five, but I felt better just saying out loud what I was feeling, and hearing him say that I could walk away. When we got out, he headed one way, and I headed the other, back toward the tram. At the exit from the park, the old couple with the string back full of carrots and turnips was seated on a bench, taking in a sliver of February sun. I looked back and saw my contact headed toward a different exit, followed by the pregnant woman pushing the baby carriage.

23

Emil Fassbender came into town once a year from Salzburg to meet with the head of the bank that employed him as a branch manager. We'd all fought together in the war, and it gave us an excuse to get together and tell all of the old stories, which I hated. Especially the story where I was the big hero who saved 10 of us singlehandedly.

We decided to keep it simple and meet up at Fessler's. There was a small private dining room where we could be loud assholes without disturbing the regular customers, and the loud assholes part was pretty much a given whenever Emil was around. It was as if he had to bottle up his personality for 51 weeks a year and hide it behind the sober propriety required of a bank manager, and then he just let it all loose on the 52nd week, like somebody shook a bottle of beer and it exploded all over us.

Through drinks and dinner and more drinks, all of the old stories were retold. Leon and his various female conquests took up half of the night, as always—and he never disappointed, always adding a new detail with each yearly retelling, of a birthmark or a squeal or a sister in the next room. Then there was the one about the time Emil had to order a flanking maneuver at Udine because the captain was too drunk to function, and the time we raided the wine cellar in a mansion in Pordenone, and the time when the cook nearly killed us all with a version of sauerbraten that left us throwing up for days outside of Villach. It was getting late, and I thought I might escape this year, but then Emil banged on the table and nearly knocked over the seven empty wine bottles and said, "Alex! Hero!"

"Nah, I'm bored with that one."

"Then I'll tell it," Emil said, and thus began a slurring, semi-incoherent recitation of a story that had become an established truth for all of us, but which was much more fiction than I had ever been able to admit.

The setup was accurate enough. We were in Gorizia. There were 10 of us trying to hold on to our position at an abandoned farm. We had been led to believe that reinforcements were coming, but that we were on the extreme right flank of our army's position, and that it was vital we not be turned. I had no idea if this was true, but that's what they told us. And if the 10 of us were the army's right flank, the barn where I was positioned alone was the right flank of our right flank. We had all just scrambled for cover when the shooting started, and I was a hundred yards away from a large henhouse, where two others were stationed, and 300 yards from the main house, which occupied some higher ground and where the other seven were located, including Henry, Leon, and Emil.

So that was the setup. It was a hellish hour as we fought and waited. Two guys in the main house were shot, but not that bad, one in the arm, one in the thigh. One guy in the henhouse got it worse, in the shoulder. I can still hear him screaming. I had the sense that there were a lot more of them than there were of us, but I wasn't sure, because they had the advantage of cover from the woods that encircled the farm, and then the cloud of dust that was beginning to be kicked up.

So that's all true. And we did manage to hold the position. And when our reinforcements showed up, the shooting stopped. And when we began to advance, there were eight dead Italians at the tree line across from the barn, on my side.

"Eight!" Emil yelled, again banging the table, again nearly toppling the empty wine bottles. It was quickly established that the dead were in a position to the right of the barn and that the only person in our group of 10 with a clear shot at them was me.

"Eight! If they get through, we're all dead! Dead! Every one of us is dead—they would have got us from two sides!"

That is the way the story has always been told, and that is what it says on the commendation. And the truth was, I was a good shot, and they all knew it. But the truth also was, I didn't shoot any of those Italians, not one. The fact was that I fired randomly out the window of the barn a couple of times, but that I spent nearly the entire hour crawled up in a ball in the corner of the barn, sobbing, literally shaking. Only when the shooting stopped, and our reinforcements arrived did I manage to pull myself together.

Nobody scrutinized the bodies, other than to count them. If they had, they probably would have seen they had all been shot in the back, or maybe from the side, by friendly fire. I wasn't sure, but I just knew it wasn't me. And I remembered saying at the time, "Guys, I don't know. I mean, eight?" But everyone's adrenaline was up, and the bodies were there, and it was almost as if everyone needed this to be true. And so it was.

I had never retold the story, not once. It was about the only reason I could live with myself. But I never denied the story, either, and never admitted the truth, not to anyone. I came close once with Uncle Otto, but couldn't quite get it out. He knew something wasn't right, though, and he offered this blanket absolution: "The shit of war deserves to stay where you left it. Whatever it was, it has no place here."

I didn't know if that made any sense, but it was all I had. It was the only way I was able to deal with the notion that a fundamental lie was a part of the foundation of the friendship I had with Leon and Henry. A lot had happened since then, obviously, and we were friends for a hundred reasons that occurred after the war, but in the back of their minds, somewhere, their friend Alex was still the hero who killed those eight Italians and probably saved everyone that day at Gorizia.

It was why I hated when Emil came to town every year. And as I was walking home from Fessler's, for some reason, all I could hear in my head was the guy in the brown overcoat from the Prater:

"Because there is no drinking like the drinking you do to live with the fact that you're a coward."

AUGUST 1937

24

Nothing happened on the trip to Berlin, Leipzig, and Hannover in March. Or on the trip to Bremen, Hamburg, and Lübeck in April. Or on the trip to Bamberg and Mannheim in May. Or Munich, Linz, and Salzburg in June. Or Dresden, Koblenz, and Stuttgart in July—although it was noteworthy, in Koblenz, that the Gnome was back to preferring one six-footer at a time.

With each trip, the anxiety eased. Maybe it really had been a one-off, and Czech intelligence wouldn't need me anymore. It wasn't as if anything had changed. Whatever information I had carried back from Cologne in February must not have been very important.

My last trip of the summer, though, did include Cologne. It was the same as in February—Nuremberg, Frankfurt, and Cologne, which did have me a bit nervous. But I was actually hopeful. This trip was always the same time every year—in the first week of August, no later, because with temperatures rising and the lakes beckoning, no self-respecting titan of industry wanted to do any meaningful business for the rest of the month.

It was also essential to get the Nuremberg part of the trip out of the way before the first week of September, which was when they held the Nazi Party rally every year. Part of that was practical—the town was completely paralyzed for a full week, with no place to eat or stay—but most of it was just the sheer horror of hundreds of thousands of fawning Nazis assembled to pay homage to the great sociopath. I used to try to dismiss it all as a seven-day drunk for the Brownshirts, an excuse to get away from the missus, and nothing more meaningful than that, but it became impossible. The unavoidable newsreels, even if they were polished up by the Goebbels boys, told the most disturbing story—not because of the sheer size of the rallies, or the banners and the torches and the salutes, but because of the looks on the faces, the fervor, the devotion that bled into adoration. Those faces were what always made me feel the most helpless.

The client in Nuremberg was Herr Josef Steinbach of the Steinbach Works. We did what we always did, touring the plant, meeting with his engineering staff, then getting down to business in his office. With minimal prodding, he upped his order by 12 percent. In fact, I'd only suggested 11 percent when he insisted on 12—such was the level of rearmament going on in Germany. Iron ore became steel in a blast furnace, which became toys for the Wehrmacht and Deutschmarks for people like Herr Steinbach. And, well, me.

After the meeting, I took Steinbach to dinner. He wasn't a player, so it was always just dinner and one bottle of wine that we split. He sometimes brought along his wife or his oldest son. But we were alone this night, and it was all pleasant enough. The truth was, I liked Steinbach. He was a funny guy, he wasn't an obvious Nazi—we never did the Heil Hitler thing when we met at the plant—and he apparently was very content with himself and his life. That last part was what I admired most.

So we were sitting there, pushing the last bit of strudel around our plates, talking about nothing, winding down the night, when a man in uniform suddenly appeared at the table. "Josef!" he said. "It's been too long!"

Steinbach stood, and I expected a Heil. Instead, they hugged. Steinbach turned and said, "Alex, I'd like you to meet General Fritz Ritter, an old friend. Fritz, this is Alex Kovacs, a business associate. Sit, sit."

The coffee and dessert were cleared away, and a bottle of cognac was produced. Ritter and Steinbach had served together in Verdun for a short time but mostly in the east. As it turned out, they were at Tannenberg, Ritter a colonel and Steinbach a captain. They hadn't seen each other in about five years, and caught up on their lives and families. Ritter was in the Abwehr now, military intelligence. "Spies, spooks, whatever," he said. "When you get to my level, it's just pushing paper. This is just a different kind of paper."

Through the first drink, and into the second, Ritter kept looking at me to the point where it was becoming uncomfortable. The whole Abwehr thing went right up my colon, and I thought I hid it okay, but the paranoia that had ruled me for months, and that had finally started to recede, was now back. Had he seen my name on some list from the Gestapo? Did Captain Vogl send some kind of report in triplicate about our meeting, and whatever suspicions he might have held, and did one of the copies end up in some Abwehr file that Ritter had seen? Did the Gestapo even talk to the Abwehr? Should I just make my excuses as quickly as possible, check out of the hotel early, and get the night train to Frankfurt?

I didn't know how much of this worry was showing on my face. Steinbach was telling a story about a corporal on an overnight transport train who'd proposed a wager for the men in his car that he would be able to drink a pretty big bottle of Tabasco sauce in one gulp without throwing up. As it turned out, he drank it down and won 20 marks.

We were all laughing when Ritter suddenly appeared to be struck by a moment of clarity. He pointed at me and said, "Your name is Kovacs, right?"

This was it. Should I run?

"Did you know Otto Kovacs? Was he related?"

My panic turned to, well, I don't know what. "Otto was my uncle, almost a second father."

"Are you in that same business? Mining or something, wasn't it?"

"He trained me. I took over his clients when he died. You knew him?"

"My condolences. Let me tell you a story, another example of what a small world it is," Ritter said. And with that, he began a fantastic tale that started on a November night in Munich in 1923.

Otto was in town to see a client but had a free night. Ritter was on a temporary assignment to the Abwehr unit in Munich. They both were staying at the same hotel, the Torbräu. They ended up sitting on adjoining stools at the hotel bar. Both mid-forties, both unattached, both properly fortified, they decided to find out what a Thursday night in November might have to offer in terms of female companionship. With a few suggestions from the hotel bartender, they headed out. Passing the Bürger-bräukeller, they saw a big crowd for some kind of political meeting and decided to head in a different direction. They were jostled by several groups of men in brown uniforms who filled the sidewalks, and kept turning away from them until they came to one of the dance halls on the bartender's list, the Daisy. There, they met two moderately attractive sisters, the Freys. Once the sisters were adequately fortified—it's all about fortification in such circumstances—the four of them went back to the girls' flat, wending their way through an ever-growing number of Brownshirts who were gathering for some purpose. In a city and at a time when political parades were a daily occurrence, it didn't seem all that odd.

And it was in the flat, which happened to be on the same block as the Bürgerbräukeller, where an amorous evening that was about to turn into something more was interrupted by gunfire. And it was from their knees, half-unbuttoned, that Ritter, Otto, and the moderately attractive Frey sisters peeked out of the window and watched the start of what became known as the Beer Hall Putsch. Soon, Ritter and Otto sneaked out through a back door of the apartment building and made their way back to the safety of the hotel, avoiding the shooting that left 20 dead, and Hitler arrested. The subsequent trial would essentially be the start of his political career. *Mein Kampf* would be written during his short prison stay.

Ritter could tell a story, which I admired. So after recounting the hurried re-buttoning and race back to the hotel, there was his last line, obviously well-practiced: "So if anyone ever asks me what I have sacrificed for my Führer . . ."

Steinbach and I were roaring. I was also wide-eyed. I couldn't believe Otto had never told me this story.

25

Thomas Scherer had turned into my most exhausting client. Not the business part—that was easy. An 11 percent increase was agreed upon without anything beyond my initial ask. There were no delivery issues, no quality control issues, nothing. All Herr Scherer wanted was a night out away from his wife, and the nights were getting longer with each visit, and the drinks more plentiful. I swore I could press into my side and feel my liver growing.

He wanted to meet at the hotel bar, where two Manhattans began the process of lubrication. Then dinner, accompanied by two bottles of Spätburgunder and brandy after that. Then through the nondescript door on Bruckenstrasse, his favorite, all dim lighting and red furnishings and illicit possibilities, where the two who joined us in our booth were named Karin and Jana.

Manhattans for us, champagne cocktails for them. Inane conversation above the table, active hands below. Pretty quickly, Scherer began to eye the doorway guarded by the ape in the tuxedo. I was not above joining one of my clients in the journey down one of these hallways, but I hadn't done it in a while and had made a half of a pledge to myself that, given my growing feelings for Johanna, I would stay out of said hallways. The problem, of course, was the alcohol, which tended to render most of my promises moot. Which was how I ended up walking down the hallway with Karin (or was it Jana?) and then into one of the little rooms, where my pants were soon around my ankles.

The regrets, which generally came in the morning, hit me immediately this time. I said my goodbyes, financial and otherwise, to Karin, or Jana, and headed to the bathroom down the hall to get cleaned up and wallow in what a miserable human being I was. As I was re-buttoning myself, the door to the restroom opened.

"Be out in a minute, pal," I said, without turning away from the mirror over the sink.

The intruder was silent in reply, so I turned and looked. It was Major Peiper—at least that was the name I knew him by. He locked the door behind him. My miserable feelings about myself were transformed instantly to fear. I had been to about 10 cities over six months, and I really thought I might be out of the spy business. Now, with my shirt half tucked-in and my pants only half re-buttoned, it was starting again.

"Fuck me," is what I said, evidently out loud, because Peiper smiled and made a comment about a room down the hall where that request could be accommodated. But the smile just as quickly disappeared. This was a business meeting, after all, regardless of the absurdity of the location.

"Before you get started, I'm just not sure—" was how I began. Peiper interrupted me immediately.

"Look, you have no choice but to listen—I'm blocking the door, after all, and it won't take long. We don't have long."

He began by telling a story from the previous year, when the Germans marched in and remilitarized the Rhineland in violation of the Versailles Treaty. It was always German territory—that was never an issue—but the Frenchies had insisted that there be no military presence permitted along the Rhine, as one further defensive measure against the time when the Germans inevitably resumed playing their national sport. And, well, one fine day in March of 1936, Hitler decided to march the Wehrmacht into the Rhineland and see what happened.

"You have to realize how unprepared we were," Peiper said. "Our army was a joke. We didn't have significant numbers. We didn't have much equipment. Our training was laughable—we could barely march straight. There was no way we could shoot straight. The people at my level, the staff officers, knew this was crazy. If the French had come at us with a hundred Boy Scouts on bicycles, we would have had to turn and run. And I'm not kidding—and we told this to our generals, and our generals told Hitler, and Hitler told them they were weak, and defeatists, and that they all worried too much.

"We were shitting ourselves that morning as the operation began. I can't tell you how nervous we were. We knew the people would welcome us, and they did. But what if the French came at us? I literally didn't sleep for the three days after—none of us did. It became a kind of no-win for people like me. If the French retaliated, the army would have been humiliated and there is no telling how Hitler would have reacted—we all probably would have been sacked. But if the French didn't retaliate, Hitler would have been rewarded for his boldness, and the generals would have been mocked for their caution. Which is where we are now."

"So which is worse?"

"The first would have been worse for people like me. The second is worse for everybody. Fucking French cowards."

I remembered what my Czech handler had told me, that the German army wasn't as strong as we all thought it was, but I had no idea it was this bad. I wasn't not sure anybody knew. And it seemed that Peiper was really telling me two things: that not only was the German army nothing like advertised, but that the German general staff was continually advising Hitler to slow down and continually being ignored. That disconnect between Hitler and his high command might have been the most interesting part of the information, which was what I told Peiper.

"It is the key thing," he said. "The generals are the ones to watch. I don't know what might get them to act, but they're probably the only ones who can stop Hitler at this point. And they think we need years more to rearm—years, not months—before launching out on the Corporal's next adventures."

"To Austria? Czechoslovakia?"

"Both. And then beyond."

"Are you sure?"

"Can you read a map?"

"So it's just your military intuition?"

"No," the major said. "It's more than that."

He went on to tell a story that had been told to him by his immediate superior, of a meeting attended by a handful of the top military—Blomberg, Fritsch, Göring, some others—in which Hitler outlined the whole thing, using small wars as spurs to the economy, and for the creation of Lebensraum, living space. Peiper said the generals weren't sure if it was an actual plan, or just a general statement of principles, but whatever—all the dominoes were there, waiting to be toppled, Austria followed by Czechoslovakia followed by the rest.

I asked, "But Austria first?"

"Absolutely. Austria first. But if somebody would just confront Hitler, the whole thing might crumble. Mussolini, the French, the English, the Czechs, someone. It wouldn't take much to embarrass Hitler, and that might be all the generals need to get him out of the way. Because the thing is, it's only going to get worse. We might not be strong now, but the army gets stronger every day. Hell, you know that. You can't mine that shit you sell to the blast furnaces fast enough, am I right? And they're all running three shifts, 24 hours a day. Am I right?"

This was just the kind of information that could make a difference. I knew that. It was exciting just to know it. It was the other side of the fear, the exhilaration of possessing knowledge that few others possessed. The whole spying business, I liked to tell myself that I was involved for all of the right and noble reasons—but the excitement was at least a part of it, just a bit of a drug. And if it didn't completely balance out the fear of getting caught, it wasn't nothing. It was all I was feeling as I was standing there in the most ridiculous setting, leaning on a sink.

"So," I said, "you want me to go back and tell my handler what you have told me?"

"Yes," he said. "but there also is some more documentation, more about troop strengths and armaments. More microfilm. It is hidden and you will need to pick it up tomorrow before you get the train."

26

My hangover cure after a long night out in Cologne, be it the winter trip or the late summer trip, was the same. At about 10 a.m., no later, I got my sorry ass out of bed, pulled on some clothes, left the hotel, and headed toward the river. The Rhine.

It was about a half-mile walk from bed to riverbank. About halfway there, regardless of the weather, I ducked into a café that was always willing to sell me a bottle of Kölsch to take away. Admittedly, this worked better in the summer—I often needed to wear gloves to hold the beer in the winter—but it was more than okay either way. I'd take the bottle down to the riverbank, sit on one of the wooden benches, and consume the victor's breakfast in the presence of grandeur.

Grandeur? From someone who lived in a city hugged by the fabled Danube? Yes, grandeur.

Nobody would ever write a waltz about it, but I'd take the Rhine. It was a real river, not a dance. It was, at once, a great working river—you sometimes wondered who kept track of all of the coal barges, so that they didn't collide—and, at the same time, if you took one of the tourist boats, the view of the cathedral was nothing short of breathtaking. Even in February, bundled up against the inevitable cold wind, the Kölsch-and-Rhine cure never failed. And on a day like that August day, sunny and calm and warm and inviting, it was without a doubt better than any patent medicine on the shelves of any apothecary. And that was true, even while acknowledging the new reality: that the Rhine was where they'd found Otto's body.

I looked to my right. The bridge was out in the distance, maybe a mile, really not close to where I was. The place where the body washed up wasn't close, either, and it was on the other bank. I turned and looked to my left. The nerves soon crowded out the thought of Otto. The truth was, maybe I was just too nervous to be hungover, from the night before and from the knowledge that a small envelope containing some more microfilm to be ferried back to Vienna was supposed to be taped to the bottom of the wooden bench upon which I was now lounging.

I had arrived at the riverbank at the agreed-upon spot. I had sat on the proper bench, the first one after the small red brick building that housed an antique shop full of nautical-themed crap. Now it was just a matter of reaching beneath the bench on the right side as I faced the river and finding the small envelope that was supposed to be taped there. But as I leaned forward, elbows on my knees, beer in both hands, staring at the river, and then sat back slowly and nonchalantly reached beneath the bench seat with my right hand, there was a problem. No envelope. Which meant I was going to have to get down on my hands and knees and look under the bench to see if it was there, just out of reach.

The problem was that, on this beautiful morning, there were all manner of people on the river walk: old people, mothers with prams, messengers dawdling, office workers enticed into a few minutes of playing hooky by a spectacular day, maybe one of the last ones of the summer. And, for some reason, every 10 minutes or so, policemen—sometimes alone, sometimes in pairs, also drawn away from their routine work, from the beats they walked in the nearby Cologne neighborhoods, by the weather and the water.

It was easy enough to see when a policeman was coming. The problem was the civilians. In Germany in 1937, Hitler had been in power for four years, which meant the Gestapo had been in power for four years, which meant that it was getting harder and harder to trust anyone. Sometimes out of belief, sometimes out of fear, sometimes out of indoctrination, people who would have otherwise spent their lives minding their own business now reported friends and neighbors and strangers to the Gestapo for crimes, real and imagined. So, maybe out of spite because of his noisy dog, the man in the first floor flat was reported by the widow on the second floor for holding what seemed to her to be clandestine, late night meetings with strange men. Or, maybe because he was a true believer, a man would call the Gestapo and tell them about a coworker who told a Hitler joke in the lunchroom at the plant. Maybe it would lead to an arrest and Dachau. Or perhaps just a warning and another name written in meticulous penmanship in another small notebook with a leather cover. Either way, the effect on the population at large was the same. It was paralyzing and exhausting, always walking with your eyes down while simultaneously trying to look back over your shoulder.

So would the cute old couple, holding hands, saying nothing, looking so content, be the ones to call the Gestapo because they saw a stranger on the riverbank on his hands and knees, feeling around for something underneath one of the wooden benches? Or the young woman walking hand in hand with a four-year-old who was hugging a small white blanket? What about her?

You could drive yourself crazy with this stuff, I knew. So I finally settled on the old man who appeared to be mumbling to himself as he approached. I leaned forward again, elbows on knees again, this time jangling a handful of change in my hand, then clumsily dropping it, then getting down on my hands and knees and picking up the runaway pfennigs, reaching for the last one and getting my head all the way beneath the bench and looking up and seeing it: a small envelope, just like the previous time, taped to the slat. It came away quickly when I snatched it.

Gathering myself, the old man was now even with the bench, not five feet away from me as I sat down again. He was still mumbling.

The rest would be easy enough. Major Peiper told me to remove the three strips of microfilm from the envelope and place them beneath the thin piece of leather on the inside sole of my shoe. He said it was just glued down and would come up easily, and it did when I yanked on it back in the hotel. Peiper said, "It's not good enough for a professional search—you should do the thing with the wine bottle again, same code phrases, same everything—but it's good enough for a casual search, especially if you glue the leather back down when you're done. Ninety percent of the time, that's plenty."

And the other 10 percent? I did everything I could not to think about it as I untied my shoe, took it off, and shook it exaggeratedly for whoever might be watching, as if I were trying to dislodge a small stone that had been pestering me. It was easy enough to slip the microfilm beneath the leather without anyone possibly seeing or being suspicious about what I was doing. Which left me with the tiny envelope. On the train the last time, I'd burned it. This time, I balled it up and tossed it into the river.

I still had about two sips of beer left in the bottle as I got up and began walking back to the hotel. In the distance, I saw the mumbling old man talking to two policemen. I knew it almost certainly had nothing to do with me, but I immediately turned and walked the other way.

27

I was almost back to the hotel, right near the cathedral, when a big black Mercedes pulled up beside me. The window rolled down, and Captain Vogl leaned out and offered a hearty, "Herr Kovacs! So nice to run into you!"

Whatever good feelings I was carrying after successfully collecting the microfilm were gone before Vogl got the words out. Last time, back in March, in the hotel lobby. Now, here. This could be random, sure. But was it? At a certain point, coincidences nag, like when you are out for a walk, and there is something in your shoe that shouldn't be there.

Standing there at the curb, I chatted with him about the weather. He asked if business was good and I told him it was. I was going to ask him how his business was but thought better of it. The conversation was going nowhere, and part of me honestly felt as if it was about to wrap up, when Vogl said, "You must let me show you my office."

I attempted to beg off, citing work demands. He correctly pointed out that my train wasn't for 14 hours. I thought about inventing a phantom appointment but reconsidered; if he knew my train reservation, he likely knew my meeting schedule and my work habits, how I always spent the day before traveling typing up orders and other paperwork in the hotel. Hell, he probably knew about my hangover routine, which might explain our chance meeting, and made me feel even worse about how he might have been watching me on the bench along the river.

"It's a quick drive, not five minutes, and the building is so interesting. You must see it," he said, opening the door and sliding over in the back seat. There was no way to say no.

Vogl was right; the drive didn't take five minutes. We pulled up in front of a brownstone building with a plaque on the front. "EL-DE Haus? What's that stand for?" I asked.

"We rent the building from a jeweler. His name is Leopold Dahmen. Those are his initials—L. D."

Standing on the sidewalk outside, there were a series of grated windows that reached from the ground to about our knees. They were open, and we were hit by two waves that pummeled our senses: the stench of an open sewer, and the screaming of a man in severe distress.

"Yes, the smell can be difficult in the summer," Vogl said. He did not mention the screaming.

The building was unremarkable upon entrance: a foyer, a central staircase that wound up and up, with marble tile floors, and marble walls up to about hip level, framed in black. There was white-painted plaster above the marble, all the way to the ceiling. The banister was black iron.

Vogl's office was just an office, not big, not small, not well decorated, pretty standard—desk, two chairs, file cabinet. A picture of his family sat on the small table behind him. Hitler looked down from the wall to his right. There was nothing particularly ominous about it, or creepy—except, that is, for the person sitting behind the desk.

"Cologne is such an enjoyable city," Vogl said. "The cathedral. The river. It brings in so many visitors from all over the region.

But the mixture makes this a hub of problems, too. We are quite busy."

He pointed to the file cabinet. "They are bringing me another of those later today—this one is bursting. Quite busy."

I wondered about my file. There was no question in my mind that I had one, and that Vogl would remove it when I left and make a notation. Assuming I left, that is. As I recrossed my legs and my right foot hit the floor, I felt the microfilm hidden there, ever so slightly.

Vogl said, "I can see you are thinking. Most people have a misapprehension about our work. The files are mostly for the protection of our citizens. Many—no, most—identify individuals whose loyalty to the Führer is unquestioned. There are enemies sprinkled in, to be sure, and they do take up a significant part of my time, but the bulk of those files are a celebration of men and women who place the Führer and the Fatherland first in their hearts, and whose loyalty is demonstrated by action."

Ah, so the snitches get files, too. Of course.

"But you must be busy—so many reports to write, as with me. It is difficult to keep up sometimes, but I pride myself on knowing everything that happens on my watch, everything in this station. I must get back to it. But here, let me walk you out and show you the rest of the building."

There was nothing to see on the third and second floors, just more offices. As we reached the level where we came in, I made for the door and began saying my thank you-s for the tour when Vogl grabbed my arm. "No, the basement. You must see the basement. It won't take but a minute."

Down we went, through an iron door. The smell was overpowering again. There was no screaming.

I counted quickly as we walked. There were 10 cells, all with locked iron doors and peepholes. One of the doors was open, and I looked inside at an empty room, maybe 30 feet square but one about four feet wide. There was one window, up at the level of the ceiling, and it was barred. There was a bed, bolted to the floor. In the corner was an empty bucket. All manner of graffiti decorated the walls—crude calendars with x's in the squares, simple strokes as if counting off the days, and words. One read, *Everything will pass so keep your head up high.*

Vogl caught me reading, and I hesitated. "No, no, go ahead. We have left the writing there for a reason. It is just as easy to paint over the words, but we decided to leave them there for subsequent prisoners to see. Some of our guards believe it gives the prisoners too much hope, makes them less cooperative. I disagree. Besides, we are not savages. We are not in the business of taking away people's hope."

He guided me to the next cell and signaled for a guard to open the door. Inside, in a room that wasn't 10 feet wide, were five men, barefoot and in their underwear. Two sitting on the bed, two leaning against the walls with their arms folded, one finishing up a piss in the bucket in the corner.

They made no eye contact with Vogl, but all looked at me with a kind of tired, questioning look. What was I doing here? Was I to join them in the cell? I was wondering that myself.

Vogl snapped his fingers to get the attention of one of the men leaning against the wall. He motioned for the prisoner to move out of the way, which he quickly did. Then Vogl pointed at the wall and said, "Look at this one, Alex. It is my personal favorite."

These were the words, tortured graffiti, scrawled by a prisoner who was faceless now and unknown:

Perhaps the hour will arrive. Perhaps they'll let me go. Perhaps we will be able to say farewell to the Gestapo in my homeland, in my homeland, to a reunion we will strive.

Vogl said, "It is beautifully expressed, but so naïve. We need to better communicate the mission of the Gestapo to the population. It is our greatest failing, that communication. If people understood our goals, they would understand why saying farewell to the Gestapo would be Germany's biggest mistake."

As we left the cell and the door was shut, the enormous hinges screamed and then there was a heavy clang. We walked further. There was a common room where two Gestapo guards lounged and read the newspaper, secure behind an iron gate. Farther down the hall was clearly another room of some sort because it was from that direction that the silence was pierced by a scream that was equal parts terrifying and heartbreaking. It was also loud enough to actually make me jump just a little in place. Neither Vogl nor the two guards reading the paper reacted in any way.

Vogl began walking back to where we had come in. I followed without prompting. Soon we were up the stairs and opening the front door, standing on the threshold and saying our goodbyes.

Vogl said, "Do not let what you have seen leave you with a false impression. There are 23 men and two women in the cells today. In all likelihood, at least 20 of them will be home tonight with their families. We are here to gather information about potential enemies, to protect the Fatherland from those who would harm us. It is what every nation does. Self-defense is the first obligation of every government. Did you know that in the American citizenship oath, all new citizens swear to protect the country against, and I quote, 'all enemies, foreign and domestic.' That is all we are doing—but we do it with vigilance."

He paused, then pointed over my right shoulder. "I'm sorry I don't have time to drive you back to the hotel, but it is a beautiful day, I am sure you would agree. Right down that street."

I agreed. It was a beautiful day. When I got about a block away from EL-DE Haus, I threw up in the gutter.

28

By the time I got back to the hotel, I had pretty much decided that I was getting out of the spy business. There was no way they weren't on to me. Maybe they were being extra cautious because I was a foreigner, or perhaps it was because of the magnesite—the blast furnaces wouldn't work without the magnesite, and the steel couldn't be made without the blast furnaces, and the armaments factories couldn't be built without the steel, and the Führer couldn't dominate the world without the armaments. So maybe I was safe, and maybe Vogl was just fucking with my head, just in case. Or maybe he was just waiting for permission from a higher-up to strip me down to my underwear and throw me into one of his playpens in the cellar at EL-DE Haus.

Either way, Vogl had succeeded. I was getting out. I was going to lift up the little leather strip from the sole of my shoe, and take out the three tiny pieces of microfilm, and burn them in my hotel room's bathroom sink, and rinse the ashes down the drain, and then rinse them again, and then wait for my train with a determination never to have anything to do with this whole business again.

I mean, it was insane. I was just a fucking magnesite salesman. I was in so far over my head that it was beyond absurd—and for what? I didn't know what was on the microfilm, but from what Major Peiper had told me, the information wasn't all that different from what Czech intelligence already knew. It would reinforce the idea that the Wehrmacht wasn't all that the Goebbels propaganda machine said it was, and maybe it was even weaker than the Czechs expected, but we were talking about a matter of degree here. For that, for a matter of degree, I was supposed to risk electrodes from a car battery attached to my balls—this was my most common nightmare about those screams I had just heard at EL-DE Haus—followed by a taxi ride to Dachau? No. Hell no.

Besides, from a purely operational standpoint, even my controller in Vienna, if he knew about my second meeting with Vogl, and his tour of the home office, would probably conclude that I had been compromised and that the prudent thing to do was destroy any evidence and protect myself.

"First rule—don't do anything stupid and don't get yourself killed," was what he told me, right at the beginning. Well, ignoring what had just happened with Vogl would be stupid. Everyone would agree with that.

Nobody followed me on the walk back to the hotel—I was pretty sure of that. Besides, the Gestapo wasn't likely to be all that subtle if they were coming to get me. Returning to the room, I locked the door and put on the chain as well, as if that would hold up to a persistent black boot. I looked around again for any sign that anyone had been visiting. The problem was that the maid had been in, and the bed was made, and the bathroom had been cleaned, and everything had been tidied. The briefcases appeared to be where I had left them, and the desk and the rented typewriter were in place and ready for my afternoon of paperwork, if I could find the ability to concentrate.

I grabbed a glass of water from the bathroom and tried to wash the taste of vomit out of my mouth. Then I sat down in the desk chair and removed my shoes, determined to rid myself of the evidence. Sitting there on the third floor, with the window open on the warm September day, I suddenly heard tires screech and doors slam—two big black cars, four men getting out, two in black suits, two in black uniforms, standing on the sidewalk, looking around. One of the suits saw me, gawping out the window. He stared through me. I was frozen in place. I'm not sure I exhaled until I saw them turn toward the apartment building across the street and one of the uniforms began pounding on the door. There was no immediate answer, and he pounded some more.

After a minute, a woman opened the door. The uniform insisted that she come outside, gesturing, pointing. She hesitated, but only briefly, ultimately staying with one of the suits while the other three rushed inside. It wasn't two more minutes before they were back, half-carrying a man in an undershirt, no shoes or socks, and trousers with the belt still undone. The woman screamed but quieted when the man in the black suit menaced her with a raised arm and a balled fist. Her brother/husband/lover/whoever was shoved into one of the cars and handcuffed to a railing inside. The cars then drove off, tires again squealing. The woman remained on the steps, now alone, wailing. Looking around, a dozen windows up and down the street were filled with faces. The whole thing didn't take five minutes.

And then I looked down at my shoes on the floor. And then I thought again about that quote on the wall of the cell, the one that Vogl said was his favorite:

Perhaps the hour will arrive. Perhaps they'll let me go. Perhaps we will be able to say farewell to the Gestapo in my homeland, in my homeland, to a reunion we will strive.

This was not my homeland. Maybe Czechoslovakia was, maybe Austria, but not here. But I couldn't shake the thought that if somebody didn't do something, there would be cells just like those on the Ringstrasse in Vienna within the year, and on Na Prikope in Prague within a year after that, and everybody knew it—Chamberlain in England, Daladier in France, Mussolini in Italy, and Schuschnigg and Beneš, too. They all knew it in their hearts. But somebody needed to remind them that they had hearts.

What would any of them have thought, or done, if they had just witnessed the scene outside my window? What precautions would any of them have taken against Nazi aggression if they had toured EL-DE Haus, smelled the shit, heard the screams?

I was sitting on the end of the bed, physically shaking as it all played out in my head. I don't think I had ever been more afraid, not even in that barn in 1917—because that was a terror imposed upon me by great forces and this was a terror imposed upon me by my own decision.

I could walk away. I wanted desperately to walk away. But I kept coming back to the man who had just been piled into that Gestapo taxi. Was he now in one of the cells, pants gone, dignity gone, sitting either with a few others or maybe by himself, alone with his bucket and his terror?

I put the shoes back on and ordered room service and began with the pile of paperwork.

29

Routine was always the answer—order forms, delivery schedules, client complaints and suggestions, notes for Hannah about this and that, everything unfinished in a stack to the left of the typewriter, everything finished in a stack to the right, one stack shrinking, one stack growing, a mindless sense of accomplishment with each piece of paper pushed. I would go minutes at a time without revisiting the picture in my head of the Gestapo officer staring up at me from across the street.

I took my time and finished at about seven, which left me about six hours before the train. Eating and drinking were the only options as a way of filling the time, and not in that order. Typically, I would be a little bit careful, because getting too drunk that I missed the train would cost me a day. But careful wasn't going to be an option on this night, not after the afternoon I'd had. Besides, this was going to be one of those times where my adrenaline was such, and my nerves, that I probably wasn't going to be able to get drunk no matter how hard I tried.

After dinner, I tested the theory at a little bar down the street from the hotel, Herschel's. It was one of my go-to spots to kill a couple of hours before the Orient Express pulled in, a hole in the wall that seemed to be a favorite with off-duty police. It was there, sitting at the far end of the bar, almost entirely in the dark —Herschel was a little slow to replace burned-out light bulbs— when none other than Detective Muller grabbed the stool next to mine. Muller was the cop who'd investigated Otto's death.

He was pretty much incoherently drunk, based upon his difficulty in placing his shot-and-a-beer order with Herschel, who made him say it three times. I was pretty sure Herschel understood it the second time and insisted on the third merely for its comedic value. It was a long day tending bar in a place like that, and you took your laughs where you could get them.

Muller didn't look at me and likely would not have remembered me, given his condition. But after hitting the men's room —where the smell triggered a memory of the basement of EL-DE Haus, which really shook me and left me wondering if I would be reminded every time I went to the shitter—I sat back down and decided to start a conversation.

"Detective Muller?"

Muller turned and looked at me. There was no initial reaction, and then a glint of recognition, and then some verbal shambling as he searched for the connection, a staggering down several dead ends that I allowed to go on for far too long, again because of the entertainment value.

Finally, I told him. "I'm Alex Kovacs. You investigated the death of my uncle, Otto. Drowned in the Rhine."

He started to tell me that no, that wasn't it, but just as quickly agreed that it was. "The Austrian Czech!" he said, exclaiming as if it was a triumph. "A suicide! A jumper!"

He stopped, looked at my face and realized through his alcoholic fog what he sounded like. "I'm sorry. I'm sorry for your loss."

I could go a day or two at that point without even thinking

about Otto at all, which was how I coped. It was also as shitty as it sounds. Although in Cologne, I thought about him a lot. They were mostly good thoughts, funny thoughts. I thought about him in my hotel room when I was finishing up the reports, laughing at how he made fun of the neat pile I always handed to Hannah in five minutes while he spent the better part of his first day back from every trip trying to decipher little scraps of paper he had stuffed in his pockets and quickly scrawled notes in the margins of documents, dictating his translation of the hieroglyphics to Hannah for processing.

I didn't have a lot to say to Muller, but I gave it a shot, telling him about my sales trip and my reservation that night on the Orient Express. Muller said he once drew the assignment of delivering a Hungarian diplomat on some kind of trade mission to the great train. "Unpronounceable asshole," he said. He stumbled over the "unpronounceable," but the "asshole" rang out loud and clear. Then he laughed. "But the overtime was good. But why is that train always so late?"

I tried to explain that it wasn't late, that it left London Victoria at 3 p.m., and made its way to Brussels by about 10 p.m., and that Cologne got one-something in the morning because of geography, but he wasn't buying it, mumbling about how "a German train would never run late like that. It's the damn English."

This was going nowhere. If I left at that point, I could have one more at the hotel bar and then grab a shower before heading to the station. So I stood and began to reach for my coat, but Muller grabbed my arm and stopped me. "Sit," he said, and he suddenly seemed a little more sober.

"I have something to tell you. Just listen. I never lied to you—understand? I never lied. But the story of recovering your uncle's body is a little more complicated than I said.

"Shhh," he said. I wasn't about to speak. He was shushing

himself, it seemed like. And he leaned in a little closer and whispered:

"He definitely went into the water off of the bridge. He went in at about the time I said he did, and his body floated down the river to where they all float. That's all true. The coroner did look at him, and there were no fatal injuries like a shooting or stabbing."

"So he drowned?"

"That's what I asked the coroner. He said, 'Fuck if I know. His lungs were full of water, but they all get full of water after they've been in the river for a few hours.' Then he said, 'There's no reason to think it's anything but suicide.'"

Muller stopped, lost in the middle of his own story. I had actually become okay with the notion of Otto's suicide. Given the thing with the doctors, and the date on the letter he left for me, it made sense. If he really thought he was dying, I could see him making that decision. Cologne hadn't made much sense to me as the site, but he might have been drunk and talked himself into it. And the truth was, he really did not want to be a burden on anyone. He had so few people close to him, and sometimes I got the sense it was because he didn't want to feel obligated to anyone about anything. So I could see it. I could see him jumping off of that bridge rather than having Hannah and me tending to him in a hospital bed for his final months.

I tried to snap Muller out of his fog. "So—"

"So, this. Just listen." Muller was now speaking so low that my ear was just inches from his lips. "The coroner said your uncle had bruises in several places on his body. They weren't fresh, but they weren't healed, either. Doc thought they were a couple of days old, probably, maybe a day—torso, upper arms, legs, and ass. No place that showed when he was dressed. Doc thought he was beaten with some kind of paddle. But there were no defensive wounds, nothing on his hands, say. No broken fingers."

I felt fury rising in me. Beaten? "You fucking lied to me."

"I didn't lie to you. The bruises were not from that night. There were no fatal wounds. His lungs were full of water. He drowned. Period."

"But what about the bruises? Why didn't you investigate?"

"Investigate what? We don't know where he got them. We don't know when he got them. They weren't fatal, not nearly. They didn't happen that night—we're sure of that. For all we know, it was a jealous husband who taught him a lesson. Is that a possibility?"

It was, admittedly, a possibility. It also wasn't the only possibility, as we both knew. Suddenly, one of the screams from the basement of EL-DE Haus filled my head. But why would the Gestapo give a shit about Otto? I was about to speak again when Muller put a finger over his lips and shushed me. It was like he was drunker again and suddenly overcome by a drowning wave of paranoia. But there was one more burst of clarity:

"The bruises are not in the coroner's report. He will deny their existence. I will deny their existence. The body's been in the ground for nine months. I am sorry for your loss, I really am, but this is over. You need to remember where you are, which is in Germany, and you need to remember what year it is, which is 1937. Nothing you can do will bring him back. So you need to get on that fancy fucking train tonight and stop thinking about this. It was suicide. Case closed."

"So why did you tell me? Why bring up the bruises?"

Muller did not answer. He just got up and left.

30

The porter told me that every compartment on the train was taken. When I took the Orient Express in February, it was all business people and rich fossils with nothing better to do, and there was plenty of elbow room. In August, they were joined by vacationers of all flavors—heading out, returning home, new money, old money, the lot. Which meant that the bar car was crowded, even approaching 2 a.m. I sat at a table with a Turkish couple returning from their honeymoon in France, and a Bulgarian count, or prince, or something, who was 80 if he was a day and pretty much asleep in his seat. The honeymooners and I shared some rudimentary French for a few minutes, but we gradually slid into a comfortable alcoholic silence, the two of them also fading, the count faded, me wired and staring out at the darkness.

Beaten? Otto was all I could think about now. Only when I uncrossed and then recrossed my legs did I feel the microfilm in my shoe and remember, that, oh yeah, if the Gestapo were going to torture one of the Kovacs boys now, it would be me, not my uncle.

There is no way in hell that the Otto I knew would find

himself sideways with the Gestapo in Cologne. He had clients, and the clients did business with the military, and in that sense, the authorities were probably aware of him in the same way that they were aware of me. But there was no way Otto would do anything to put himself at risk. I'd often thought that he would crucify me if he knew about my courier work for the Czechs—and the truth was, if he were alive, I probably would never have agreed to do it in the first place. That I spent my adult life craving his approval, even his silent approval, went without saying.

I had to admit that the jealous husband theory was more than plausible. Otto was an impossible hound. He had a personal code with women that consisted of two immutable rules: Don't get too deeply involved, and don't get caught. That was pretty much it. I was convinced that the reason he never married Hannah was that he knew he could never change and that she knew it, too. I was also convinced that he would always keep a handful of clients, because, well, he would always crave the adventure of leaving the city limits—the chase even more than the sex. A raging husband turning the paddle he used on his children onto Otto, while his wife pleaded with him to stop, really was a pretty easy scene to picture.

But still, for all of this to happen within about a two-week period—the seemingly ominous news from the doctor, the beating, and the plunge from the bridge into the Rhine—was maybe one big event too many in such a short period of time. My gut told me that two of the three had to be related. I had become convinced that the medical news led to Otto's death. But what if it was the beating? If that were the case, the suicide was now likely a murder, unless the beating had somehow scared him into killing himself. But if that was the case, well, there was no jealous husband in Cologne who could possibly force Otto to kill himself. If the husband really was a lunatic, Otto would just give me that client—old Josef Kreisler—and stop traveling to Cologne.

So it was either the suicide I had already bought into, or something much more sinister than a jealous husband. And the more I thought about it, the more I owed it to Otto to try to find out. And if it led to the Gestapo somehow? As I sucked down probably my tenth drink of the day, there was an odd clarity: If I was willing to risk Dachau for some bullshit military secrets that really weren't all that secret, why wouldn't I be willing to risk it to find out the actual cause of death of one of the three people in the world I really loved? Because this was the list: Henry, Leon, Otto, fin. Not Johanna, not really, not yet. But if not for one of the three, who?

The police were going to be of no help—that was obvious. Their investigation was a sham. The paper trail was doctored and incomplete. But the fear that shone through Muller's drunken mask told me what he suspected. How he had gone mute when I asked him that last question in Herschel's: "So why did you tell me? Why did you bring up the bruises?" Silence was the lush at his most eloquent.

It was all I could think about as I ordered a final cognac from the bartender and walked it back to my compartment, the microfilm subtly nagging every time my right foot landed.

FEBRUARY 1938

31

My welcome home lunch with Johanna turned into a forgettable schnitzel followed by a long, lovely afternoon spent entirely within the confines of the bed that she had begun to refer to as "our rickety oasis." That it hadn't broken yet was a testament to good old-fashioned Austrian craftsmanship, or luck.

After I walked her home, I stopped in at Café Louvre to see if Leon was there, and maybe to catch up on the news. As I approached, I saw Old McGee—I think he was from the *Chicago Tribune*—running across the street from the telegraph office into the café. Now, Old McGee was probably 60 and must have weighed 250 pounds. As a matter of course, he did not run. He did not do anything quickly, for that matter, except shove schinkenbrot sandwiches—ham, rye, butter, gherkins, the whole mess—down his gullet for his gabelfrühstück. All of which meant that there was news, it seemed.

Inside, in the corner of the room where the foreign correspondents always congregated around the United Press man's stammtisch, there was a pandemonium in full roar. There were probably a dozen of them—London, Prague, Budapest, Paris,

New York, Philadelphia, Chicago, Baltimore, Washington; I'd been introduced to most of them at one time or another by Leon —and there was this insistent shouting among them, nobody seeming to listen but everybody hearing everything.

When there was big news, they all worked together on the stories. Leon explained how it was different for the locals, who all sold their newspapers on the streets and lived and died by their exclusives. The foreign correspondents really did not compete in the same way for breaking news. Yes, if one of them had a big exclusive interview with a government official, everybody bought the guy a drink the next day to congratulate him (and then shit on him and the story as soon as he left the café). But for day-to-day breaking news, they worked as one, pooling their information. It just made sense to them, especially given that most of them, while based in Vienna, were responsible for news throughout the region. If there was a political assassination in Bucharest, they had to write. If a bank failed in Budapest, they had to write. And if they happened to have taken their wife to the mountains for the weekend when said assassination or bank failure occurred, there would be someone to cover for them. Their bosses would have been aghast at the coziness of the arrangement, but their bosses were thousands of miles away.

I was seated at a small table on the edge of the swirl—most customers wanted to be nowhere near the noise, so there were plenty of choices. I asked the waiter what the news was. He screwed up his face and said, "Schuschnigg is in Berchtesgaden to meet with Herr Hitler. Menu?"

I ordered a drink and eavesdropped, which wasn't hard. The news of the trip was a complete shock, and the secrecy itself had become the story for many of the correspondents. They loved secrecy. It excited them in ways that women no longer did.

From what they knew, Schuschnigg had taken the overnight

train. Only a couple of embassies had been told—England, France, maybe a couple more.

The *Baltimore Sun* read loudly from one morning paper, I couldn't see which. "'There will be a Cabinet Council meeting today to deal with important matters.' Important matters, my ass. They knew he wasn't going to be here. Why the smoke screen?"

It was the question they were all asking, in a dozen different ways. Nobody knew anything until about 4 p.m., when the final edition of several afternoon papers hit the streets with the news of the meeting, nothing more. The government press office confirmed the bare bones soon after. Then the Austrian reporters were called in for a meeting with the commissioner for propaganda, Colonel Walter Adam—whose full name had been changed by the *Philadelphia Record* for the purposes of that evening's discussions to "that fucking snake, Walter Adam." The *St. Louis Post-Dispatch* went with "that lying sack of shit." I had never heard that one before, but I quite liked it.

The foreign correspondents got a summary of that briefing: It was a long-planned meeting at Hitler's invitation, and Italy and Hungary were aware of it, and it was meant as a way of strengthening the existing ties between the two countries, and the ultimate communiqué that was issued would emphasize the need for continued Austrian independence.

The news that Old McGee brought in his winded sprint from the telegraph office was the official government communiqué:

"The Austrian Chancellor, accompanied by Secretary of State for Foreign Affairs Schmidt, today visited Herr Hitler at Obersalzberg on his invitation. Herr von Ribbentrop and Herr von Papen were present. This unofficial interview resulted from a mutual desire to discuss all questions concerning Austro-German relations."

To which the *Times of London* replied, "McGee, you didn't need to run for that."

But what did it all mean? I knew what I thought—that Schuschnigg was bending over for the Corporal—and most of the correspondents seemed to be thinking the same thing. The problem was that nobody knew anything, so it was hard to know how to shade the story. Because of the time difference, the Americans had more time to wait for developments—or at least for the early editions of the morning papers for any hints. Some of the correspondents thought Hitler was in a weak position after he shook up the army and fired Blomberg and Fritsch, and so wasn't in a position to bully Schuschnigg about anything, but that was precisely backward to me. In my experience, cornered assholes just became bigger assholes. Hitler had no reason to make nice.

So this was all being debated when Leon walked in. He had a copy of the *Telegraf*, not his newspaper, in his hand. He was the only Vienna reporter in the café, the rest working their own sources.

He handed the paper to the *New York Times*. "It's been confiscated by the government, but I got one."

A torrent of "holy shits" rained down as they all crowded around. Government censorship was a way of life in Vienna—Schuschnigg was a dictator, too, but without the little mustache and with a tiny bit of sympathy for the Jews—but this was big.

"Why confiscate it? What do they have?"

Leon flattened the paper on a table and then pointed to about the eighth paragraph of the story, in which the reporter quotes Adam as saying the reason for the meeting was a fear that Italy and England were about to start getting cozy with each other.

The *Times of London* said, "Well, did he say it? Were you at the briefing?"

Leon said, "Yeah, I was there. And, yeah, he said it. But it was off the record—and nobody here quotes me or my paper on that, got it?"

They all nodded. Leon made eye contact with each of them individually before continuing.

"Adam said other stuff off the record, too. It's in the jump," he said, turning the page and pointing to the spot where the story continued. "He said Schuschnigg wanted to tell Hitler that he was being as lenient as he could with the Nazis here, but the bombings and the wrecking of Jewish businesses were becoming too big a problem to ignore."

The *Baltimore Sun* jumped in. "So what do your guys think? What do you think?"

Leon stopped for a second, gathering himself. "I'm not sure. But if I had to guess, Schuschnigg left with his pants around his ankles. When I hear 'Hitler's invitation,' that means 'Hitler's summons' to me. I don't know what that might mean, but can you honestly see him standing up to Hitler about anything?"

Around and around it went. Several of the correspondents left to attend the annual Press Ball, where the heurige was free, and there perhaps would be some new details to emerge. Kids the correspondents used as runners from the telegraph office brought bits of news, and copies of the first editions of the morning papers. They talked, and read, and sifted through the facts that they had and the suspicions beneath the facts, and then left in ones and twos to go across the street to type up their stories in the little cubicles set up for them in the press room. There, they would wait for any news from the ball attendees, and then send what they had by telegraph. I sat and drank with Leon, talking about this and that, watching as the correspondents acknowledged him with a pat on the shoulder or a nod of thanks as they left to write. He was basking. He was so in his element.

32

Heading home, I decided to stop for one more at Max's, the definition of a dive, maybe 20 feet wide and 50 feet deep, most of the space taken up by the bar and 10 stools, with a little bit of room to walk behind the stools and a hole-in-the-floor toilet in the back. The only customer snored quietly at the last stool. Heinz, the bartender, was washing glasses and seemed genuinely happy to see a live body.

"Herr Doktor Alex," he said, mocking me with the honorific. Doctor of what? Pimpography?

Heinz got me a drink and then pointed to the newspaper on the bar and the headline about the meeting with Hitler. "Schuschnigg—what do you think?"

"Other than that he's a lying sack of shit?" I really did enjoy that phrase.

Heinz laughed but then got serious. "You travel. You talk to people. What do you think is going to happen?"

I was about four drinks deep, and this conversation was suddenly approaching a tricky area. If you knew you were talking to a closet Nazi, you tried to be as noncommittal as your conscience would allow. Same with staunch supporters of the government. With monarchists, you mostly told the truth but always found a way to mention the good old days. And if you knew you were talking to a closet Socialist or a Jew, you mother-fucked Hitler with alacrity, albeit in sotto voce. The whole thing was complicated, and getting more tangled all the time, but getting through a conversation without somebody standing up and storming out had become a practiced skill and a sign of good breeding, kind of like knowing which fork to use for the salad.

I didn't think Heinz was Jewish, but I took a shot. What the hell—if he ended up hating me, there was another dive bar on the next block.

"We're screwed. You know it. I know it. Schuschnigg knows it. Hitler knows it. The only question is the timing."

Heinz's face fell. "You really think so?"

"I really do. The Germans are coming, if for no other reason than they need our money to pay for all of the fucking tanks they're building. Maybe Schuschnigg can make a deal where he hands over the gold in exchange for the Wehrmacht staying on the other side of the border, but really, how could that even work?"

"It would be like cutting off our balls at the whorehouse door. At that point, I mean, what's the point?"

I let that one kind of hang in the air, as vivid as it was nonsensical. Heinz went back to his sink at the other end of the bar. There wasn't a lot more to say. I always enjoyed my conversations with Heinz, because they were always about sports or women, and I was always already kind of drunk and having one more before heading home, and I barely even remembered them the next day. This one, though, I would remember. That was true even after a familiar face came through the door and sat down beside me.

"Ah, fuck," I said.

"And good evening to you, too," he said, slightly slurring. He was as drunk as I was.

"Were you following me?"

"Nah. I just figured I'd take a shot. You're a pretty predictable character, you know? So give me the microfilm, and I'll leave you alone."

"You think I have it on me?"

"Well, do you?"

I looked down at my feet. Same shoes. "Well, now that you mention it."

Tradecraft and secrecy take a back seat to expediency when there is alcohol involved, so I just took off the shoe and peeled up the leather strip. I looked over at Heinz, and he was washing glasses with his back to us. The light snorer at the end was still snoring.

I handed over the small envelope, which disappeared into my contact's pocket. He got up to leave, but I stopped him. "Sit. Have a drink. I have something to ask you. Like, I don't even know your name. What should I fucking call you?"

"How about 'Sir'?"

"How about fuck you?"

He laughed, whatever his name was. "I just saw a movie, *A Day at the Races*. Very funny. Call me Groucho Marx."

"So, Groucho . . ." With that, I began to lay out the story of Uncle Otto. I tried not to leave anything out, from the first phone call from the Cologne police to the chance meeting with Detective Muller in Herschel's. I tried to be as analytical as I could, given my biases and my emotional involvement. When I finished, we were quiet for a minute or two while Groucho processed everything I had said.

Finally, he spoke. "So you're thinking Gestapo, right?"

"The suicide just doesn't make enough sense. I mean, it

makes a little bit of sense, but not enough. Muller obviously thinks it's the Gestapo or he wouldn't have brought it up and whispered the whole thing as if one false word could get him strung up. That's how you read it, right?"

"Yeah. I wasn't there, but the way you tell it, it makes sense. Except for one thing—why Uncle Otto? Why would the Gestapo want to kill a semi-retired guy who sells . . . what's that shit called that you sell?"

"Magnesite."

"Right, magnesite. Hell, you guys are pretty much members of the Nazi's team—"

"Wait a minute—"

"No, you fucking wait a minute. You sell them the shit that keeps the blast furnaces humming in their steel mills. They need you. I'm surprised they don't stop the train every time at Passau and board a hooker for your exclusive use on the rest of your journey. I mean, why do you think we picked you? You have as much cover and as much protection as just about any businessman who travels to Germany these days."

I knew this, of course. It was bad enough when I allowed my mind to wander in that direction, but I couldn't stand hearing it out loud. I wondered if everyone thought that, deep down—Leon, Henry, Johanna? The truth was, I didn't want to know. The courier work was, in a way, my silent atonement. And I was just drunk enough that I felt like shoving it back in Groucho's face. But I didn't. The whole thing had become such a chore. Just living had become exhausting.

I said, "Look, if that's all true, then Otto had the same protections that I have—even more, because he was older and more respected by the clients, and he still had a couple of the biggest clients. It just doesn't make sense."

"Unless it was a jealous husband. I mean . . ."

"Look, let me tell you about Otto. He might have been a little reckless when it came to women, but I've really thought hard about this, and there's just no way he would have gotten himself killed over a piece of ass."

"So, what then?"

I asked what I had been wanting to ask all along: "So was he working for you guys? Or the Austrians? And could the Gestapo have found out?"

Groucho stopped, slugged down his drink, shrugged on his coat.

"There's no way—and I would know. I know who our guys are, and I know who Austria's guys are, and he wasn't one of them."

"What, do you all have a little spy club where you compare notes, all with the same outfits and a secret handshake—Groucho, Chico, Harpo? Fuck you."

"I'm telling you, he wasn't working for us. I never even heard of him until we started looking at you as a possibility and checked your background. That's the truth."

With that, he turned and walked out of the bar. Maybe it was the paranoia of drink, but somehow I didn't feel as if he was telling me the whole story. Then again, it wasn't the first time I had felt that way.

33

The train ride out to the western edge of the city, to the Pfarrwiese, took about a half-hour, give or take. With each stop, the cars became more crowded, the singing louder, the clapping more insistent. SK Rapid was the working-class team from Vienna, and the Pfarrwiese was their home ground. Seeing as how the serious drinking had not yet commenced, things were relatively orderly on the train. Given that Rapid was running away with the league that year, it was all good.

The Pfarrwiese was in Hütteldorf, the section of the city where Henry grew up and where his father established himself in the mobster trade. I was meeting Henry at the stadium, where his family held season tickets. It was February in Vienna, gray and miserable, the sky spitting just a bit of icy rain, not enough to keep you inside but an amount that would ensure an afternoon's misery. Thank God Henry's seats were on the side with the small roof overhead.

Hütteldorf was what you might imagine a working-class neighborhood to look like: crowded and clean and proud, where the kids played football in the street, in front of mothers sweeping the sidewalks, in front of six-story apartment houses, one after another after another. Late in the afternoon, they were joined by the men, many returning from the big oil and gas works. But there were a dozen major factories in the area, even after the Hütteldorfer brewery closed. It put a pinch on the local economy—and made the availability of spectators' post-game refreshments a little more complicated, seeing as how its beer garden abutted the stadium grounds—but as Henry said, "Hütteldorf takes care of Hütteldorf," and there were fewer of the obviously unemployed out there than you saw closer to the center of the city.

I met Henry at the ticket booth and headed for the covered stand. He stopped me. "First half with the people," he said, pointing toward the open side, the side with no seats and no roof.

"Really?" I said, holding out my hand to catch the falling ice.

"First half. Then you can rest your pampered ass."

The standing area at Pfarrwiese was notorious throughout Austrian football and had been for my whole time in Vienna. People were packed into the sloping terraces beyond all reason—singing, chanting, cursing, drinking to fabulous excess, and relieving themselves in place when necessary. But they weren't savages. As the guy in front of us demonstrated about two minutes after the opening whistle, a person could roll up a newspaper and piss into the funnel that they had created, sparing his neighbors any splashing before daintily dropping the sodden mess at his feet.

Henry watched and laughed. "You know, I was confirmed when I was 12, and my father taught me how to shoot a revolver when I was 14, but I didn't really feel like a man until I was 16 and he let me stand on this side of the ground. Right about here."

In about the 20th minute, this big, lumbering forward began

to lumber forward for Rapid. At six foot two, he was half a head taller than his next tallest teammate, easy to follow as he made his way from the center line, weathering one tackle and niftily shifting and avoiding another—niftily for his size, anyway—and launching a right-footed blast from the edge of the box and into the top-left corner. It was Franz Binder, the leading scorer in the league, and it was 1–0, Rapid.

As they chanted his nickname, "Bim-bo, Bim-bo . . ." Henry leaned in and said, "I think he has 11 goals in nine games. You'd need a poleax to stop him."

We grabbed a beer and switched sides at halftime, sitting under cover in Henry's prime seats. He seemed nostalgic the whole day, and then he told me why: He had just sold the bar.

He saw the shock on my face and held up a hand. "It's done. I got the money on Friday. I agreed to keep running things for a while, but it's over. The last of the Fessler empire is gone."

He stopped, laughed at himself. "Empire. I mean, that's the way we always thought of it—the old man, all of us. He had the numbers business here, and a little protection, and the little dive bar, and things were fine. But when he decided to take the business inside the Ringstrasse, it was a huge decision. I was only three or four when they did it, but my mom used to talk about the stress of it all. Some people in Hütteldorf thought he was putting on airs, 'too good for us now.' But my dad saw it as a business opportunity after this whole family that had a piece of everything inside the Ring died in a big fire in '03. He also saw it as the natural progression for his ambitions and his family. But he never forgot this place. He always hired from the neighborhood."

My turn to laugh. "Except the girls."

It was a more significant operation inside the Ring—the bar with the back rooms, the gambling well beyond a simple numbers game, the protection more widespread, extending up Mariahilferstrasse, a couple of miles past my house.

"So it's all gone?"

Henry nodded. "You know we sold off everything except Fessler's, and my dad took that money with him to Zürich, besides what he'd already squirreled away over the years—and it was a big fucking squirrel. He's fine. He couldn't spend it all if he wanted to. And he gave me Fessler's, to do with what I wanted. Well, I have."

I was still surprised. Henry was good at the bar business, and I thought he liked it. I knew he didn't want the rest of what his father did or the reputation it left him with, and his father knew that, too. Henry thought the gambling hurt weak people; it always bothered him, especially when he had to help with collections. He once told me he never beat anybody unconscious and considered that to be some kind of moral victory. But he hated it, and he hated the protection worse. He never admitted it, but he was relieved when his father and his Nazi fears left town in 1936.

But why sell the bar? And why now? Some of this had to be because of Liesl. We had all grown to like her a lot, partly because of who she was and what she believed—she referred to Hitler as "Herr Book Burner"—but mostly because of the bond she had built with Henry. They were so obviously in love that there was no chance Henry was packing up and leaving Austria if she wasn't going with him.

Just as he was about to answer, the clapping began. For the last 15 minutes of every game, Rapid fans joined in a rhythmic, almost hypnotic, clapping ritual. It began years ago, in a game where the team came from behind after the clapping started, and it became a tradition—and people looked at you suspiciously if you didn't at least half-heartedly participate.

So we clapped, and Henry talked. "Look, the old man was

right, Hitler's coming. That shit in the paper today, I don't care what Schuschnigg says—Hitler's coming. I sold for a decent price; my father would say it was a shitty price, but it was okay, more than okay, and it was in cash, and the cash is already in a bank in Bratislava. My whole account here, I emptied almost all of that, too. I'm set up for my next move. I wouldn't mind if it was here, but I'm just not sure it can be in Vienna anymore."

We watched the rest of the game, pretty much in silence, except for the clapping. Rapid won, 2–0.

34

For some reason, Groucho wanted to meet at Café Demel. I hated Demel. It was actually a little bit of a strain between Johanna and me, because she loved Demel. But it was just so fussy. All of the confections seemed as if they were there to be admired, like in a jeweler's display case, rather than eaten. Sitting there, slopping a cup of coffee and reading the paper amid the fur and the felt, I imagined myself being viewed as an animal that had wandered in off of the street.

Groucho came in, dressed as if he were coming from a meeting with the president of the bank. I looked him up and down with mock admiration. "Does this mean you have a real job beyond making my life fucking miserable?"

"Of course I have a real job. How could I not? Prague is paying me exactly what they're paying you."

"So you're a true believer? I took you for a mercenary."

"Fuck you. I'm risking a lot more than you ever will."

I fingered the material on the lapel of his suit. "I can see that."

We ordered breakfast and mostly talked about what was in the papers. It had taken a couple of days, but the government finally was admitting that Schuschnigg had taken it up the ass at Berchtesgaden. Well, they weren't exactly admitting it, but the facts were plain enough. Schuschnigg had agreed to put three Nazis in his cabinet. He also agreed to grant amnesty to all of the Nazis who had been jailed over the years—including the guys who killed Dollfuss. It was hard to decide which was worse. But Groucho had a definite opinion.

"Look at the cabinet. Look at that worm Seyss-Inquart. See the job he got? Minister of the Interior. He's in charge of the police. Half of them are Nazis anyway and now their new boss is one."

I started to interrupt, and he stopped me.

"No, listen. Know your history. When they first put Hitler in the government and made him chancellor—when Hindenburg was still alive, and they thought they could control him—he only asked for a couple of spots in the cabinet. One of them was Minister of the Interior, and another was Minister of the Interior of Prussia. He let the others in the coalition have the prestige jobs—finance, foreign affairs, all of them. Hitler didn't care. He was in control of the two biggest police forces in the country, and that was enough."

It was more than enough. We were so screwed, and everyone with eyes could see it. The only question was the timing. Groucho didn't have a good guess.

I asked him, "Weeks or months?"

"So you're discounting that it might be days?"

"Seriously?"

"Seriously, I have no idea. My guess would be months, but not a year. And they're just going to fucking waltz in unless Schuschnigg suddenly grows a pair. But I kind of think, deep in his heart, that he believes Austrians really are Germans, and he just couldn't ask them to shoot at their Germanic brothers."

We ate in silence for a few minutes. Then it dawned on me.

"Why did you want to meet me? Did you find out something about my uncle?"

"No, and I asked my contact, and he said the same thing. He'd never heard of Otto until we started scouting you. I don't know what to tell you. But that's not why I wanted to talk to you. You're going to Cologne on the 24th. We want you to change your train to the 23rd."

"That's the Wednesday train. No, I hate that trip. It stops in Frankfurt for, like, three hours. And then I'll have an extra day in Cologne with nothing to do. No. Why?"

"It stops in Frankfurt for two hours and 45 minutes. It's enough time for you to walk three blocks from the station and have lunch at Dimble's, on Mörfelderstrasse. When you're done eating, use the bathroom. Check under the lid of the toilet tank. There might be an envelope taped there. If there is, bring it home with you after the trip."

"If?"

"Yeah, if. We're not sure. But if it's there, bring it home. If it isn't there, enjoy the lunch."

35

The opening of Johanna's exhibition was set for Friday night. She was so busy in the days leading up to it, and so nervous, that we barely saw each other. I packed her a lunch and brought it to her desk on Thursday, trying to do the supportive-boyfriend thing, but I never saw her and never heard from her after. A problem with the program had her pretty much living at the printer's until it was straightened out.

Ernst. Nussbaum. Beckmann. Jew. Jew. Jew. The story promoting the event in the Wednesday *Die Neue Freie Presse* had been both cursory and buried in the paper. It contained none of the expected comments from either anyone at the museum or any of the artists. It was as if they couldn't ignore it, because it was the Rudolf Museum, after all, but they would be damned if they were going to promote it. Seeing as how most of the editors of the paper were Jewish, this seemed odd. Then again, survival mode is a peculiar state of being.

Henry had already noticed that ever since word of Schuschnigg's trip to Berchtesgaden, traffic in Fessler's had been down. He said that other restaurant guys had told him they had noticed the same thing. It was as if a switch had been flipped somehow, as if hope had suddenly morphed into grim reality. People were saving money all of a sudden, getting ready, preparing for a storm.

I was walking to the office, thinking about all of this, when there was a tap on the window of the café I was passing. It was Johanna's father, Karl, motioning me inside. Perfect.

The Baron von Westermann's morning café was Schwarzenberg, on Kärntner Ring. Its location and its history told you a lot about the man. It was never a place for intellectuals or authors, but for commerce. Financiers had always been the customers, not Freud. It was also one step removed from the real action, from the heaviest of the heavy hitters, who frequented the Imperial Café across the street. You could see the comings and goings, but you weren't really in the middle of the action.

Which, as it turned out, described the baron perfectly.

His stammtisch was by one of the front windows, giving him a perfect view of the Imperial. The sign at the front talked about a band on Friday nights, but I was pretty sure the baron had never been there at night, or even after noon. The remnants of what was undoubtedly his regular frühstück—coffee, roll and butter, soft-boiled egg—were being taken away by the waiter when I arrived, after I almost stepped on a little peanut of a dog who was sipping from a small silver bowl at the feet of a desiccated countess, lightly jeweled at 10 a.m., reading a newspaper.

"You almost stepped on Rudy," the baron said, by way of greeting. "That might have gotten a yap out of him. I'm not sure I've heard him make a sound this month."

The place was not silent if you counted the occasional tinkling of silver on china or the rustle of a turning newspaper page to be noise. There were eight tables occupied, six by single newspaper readers, one—in the far corner, away from the rest—by an ancient man taking a quiet nap, and one by Karl and me.

"You see those two?" he asked. He pointed out the window at

the door of the Imperial, where two men stood, buttoning their overcoats and waiting for a taxi, or a car, or something. "The older one is Himmler. The younger one is Heydrich. Do you know the names?"

Himmler, I knew. Heydrich, I did not. Karl proceeded to fill me in, adding details about Himmler I did not know—including that he had been a pig farmer when he fell in love with the Führer—and filling in a portrait of Heydrich as a genuinely frightening combination of both Aryan and Nazi perfection.

I read the newspapers pretty carefully—I read three every day, and I took a big stack on every train trip—and I traveled enough to hear plenty, but the good baron was offering a lot of details that I had neither read nor heard before. Still, that wasn't why he rapped on the window, to impress me with his inside knowledge of Austrian politics.

He pointed to the newspaper story. "This Jewish exhibit. It will ruin her career."

The thought had crossed my mind. "She is very proud of it. And as you know better than I, she is very strong-willed."

"She is acting like a petulant child. She refuses to see the consequences. Maybe she would listen to you."

"I think you overestimate my influence. Besides," I said, pointing to the same newspaper story, "it's too late. It's happening whether you like it or not."

The baron sipped his coffee. The expression on his face suggested it was cold. "She won't see the complications."

I looked, questioningly. He put down the cup and leaned closer.

"You've read the papers. You see what's happening. The way I figure it, Schuschnigg has one chance left. He has one card left to play—the restoration card."

Also known as the Return of the Vons. Like everything in Vienna, it was complicated. Everybody was using everyone else. Most of the Jews disliked Dollfuss and Schuschnigg but supported them out of fear of what might take their place. People like the baron, who wanted a return of the Habsburg Monarchy, were in kind of the same boat. They didn't like Schuschnigg, either, but they supported him because it was the only way to keep Austria together—and Austria had to be kept together if there was ever to be a restoration. If Hitler swallowed the country whole, he would belch pleasingly, and the monarchists would be done. There would be nothing to restore.

I always understood that. But this was a new twist for me.

The baron said, "Hitler is now knocking on the door. The people are split—you see the Nazis in the streets, getting bolder every day. I mean, is there a phone box inside the Ring that they haven't blown up yet? Schuschnigg's best chance here is to call for a Habsburg restoration—it can even be a constitutional monarchy if it has to be. But that's his chance, and we're actively making sure that he realizes it."

"Are you involved?"

"Behind the scenes, yes. He listens, and he's listening more in the last few days. It's very delicate, and I don't need this museum complication, not right now."

He stopped, locking on my eyes. "Fucking Jews," he said. "Fucking Jews."

That conversation was all I could think about as I walked up the museum steps on Friday night. The main gallery was set up for a reception, with waiters toting champagne, and canapés lined up and at the ready, and the works of Ernst, Nussbaum, and Beckmann arrayed around the great hall. My eyes caught Johanna immediately. She was stunning in a formal silver gown, her hair up, her smile perfect and perpetual. She was very easy to spot, for all of the aforementioned reasons but mostly because the place was almost empty.

"It's going to be a disaster," she said, leaning in as I kissed her.

"Come on, it's still early," I said, because it was the only thing I could think of saying.

But she was right. Leon and Henry and Liesl were there. A handful of the museum's patrons were there, but only a handful. Four hundred invitations had been sent. There was enough champagne and finger food for 250. But there weren't 30 people in the great hall. Disaster did not begin to cover it.

Time dragged—seven became eight, and eight became eight thirty, and 30 people became 15. Then 17, when the Baron and Baroness von Westermann arrived. Given our conversation at the café, I was shocked to see the old man (less so, his wife).

Johanna greeted them with a hug, and then walked them around the exhibition, and introduced them to a few of the patrons whom they didn't know, mostly because all of the patrons they did know were at home in their mansions, having tossed out the invitations the day they arrived. The smile on her face seemed just a tiny bit less forced. And while mother and daughter continued on, the baron suddenly showed up at my side with two glasses of champagne.

He handed me one. "The paintings, I actually kind of like them. She has no sense, but she does have a good eye."

I didn't know what my face was showing, but he caught something. He said, "You're surprised I'm here?"

"Well, after everything you said . . ."

"If you didn't think I would come, then you don't know my family very well."

36

Ever since I met him, my mind had wandered back to that day with Edgar Grundman in the quarry in Mauthausen. It didn't take a Freud or an Adler to guess that I was looking for a father figure in my life after Otto died. It got to the point where I wanted to talk to Grundman again but not only that—I wanted to see him, be with him, for reassurance or comfort or something. When I called, we talked about a time, and he seemed to think that Sunday would work best. He said, "Come to my house, and we'll listen to Hitler's speech. Sunday at noon—Nazi church."

The house was on the road toward the quarry—neat, tidy, with a couple of spare bedrooms. The radio sat prominently in one corner of the living room, warmed and glowing, playing German martial music. With sandwiches and beers, we got through the pleasantries in good order—the quarry was sold, and Grundman had occupied himself for the last couple of weeks with a home project: repointing the stonework of the house. He seemed content.

The music stopped at noon, and a voice thundered through the box. I didn't recognize it and shrugged. "Göring," Grundman said. Göring began reading off a list of the names of deputies of the Reichstag who had died in the previous year. Then he said, "The word is now given to the Führer."

After the applause died, and a long, uncomfortable pause, Hitler began. He said that this wasn't just a speech to commemorate five years in office, as most had anticipated, but an opportunity to correct some ongoing misperceptions about the military and about "certain aspects of our foreign relations."

Those words were barely out of his mouth when Grundman said, "We're screwed. As if we didn't already know."

We talked and listened. When he said Field Marshal Blomberg had stepped aside because of ill health, Grundman whispered, "Bullshit."

But Hitler was just getting started. He railed against a whole series of slights and misreporting he saw in the foreign press, this report, that report, a long litany ending with a report "that 14 generals have fled to Prague with Ludendorff's corpse; and that I have completely lost my voice, and the resourceful Dr. Goebbels is presently on the lookout for a man capable of imitating my voice to allow me to speak from gramophone records from now on. I take it that tomorrow this journalistic zealot of truth will either contest that I am really here today or claim that I had only made gestures, while behind me the Reich Minister of Propaganda ran the gramophone."

The laughter from the deputies was long and loud, exaggerated guffawing, fat-necked sycophants on parade. I started to say something, but Grundman shushed me.

"—Since this international smear campaign of the press must naturally be interpreted not as a reconciling element, but as one presenting a threat to international peace, I have resolved to undertake the reinforcements of the German Wehrmacht, which will lend us the certainty that this wild threat of war against Germany will not one day be transformed into a bloody reality. These measures have been in progress since February 4 of this year and will be continued with speed and determination."

"Fuck me," Grundman said. "Fuck us."

"It's not like he ever needed a pretense, but press reports? I mean, really?"

"He's drawing the roadmap. You wonder if anybody in Vienna is even listening."

Then Hitler got to the meat of the meal:

"Two of the states at our borders alone encompass a mass of over ten million Germans. Until 1866, they were still united with the German race as a whole in a political federation. Until 1918, they fought shoulder to shoulder with the soldiers of the German Empire in the Great War. Against their own free will, they were prevented from uniting with the Reich by virtue of the peace treaties. This is painful enough in and of itself. Yet let there be no doubt in our minds about one thing. The separation from the Reich under public law must not lead to a situation in which the races are deprived of rights; in other words, the general rights of völkisch self-determination—which, incidentally, were solemnly guaranteed to us in Wilson's Fourteen Points as a prerequisite for the Armistice—cannot simply be ignored because this is a case concerning Germans! In the long run, it is unbearable for a world power to know that there are volksgenossen at its side being constantly subjected to the most severe suffering because of their sympathy or affiliation with their race, its fate, and its worldview . . .

"Yet he who wields force in attempting to prevent a balance from being achieved in Europe in that the tensions are lessened will at some point inevitably call violence into play between the peoples. . . . Just as England looks after its interests in every corner of the earth, modern Germany, too, shall know how to look after and protect its albeit much more limited interests.

And these interests of the German Reich include protecting those German volksgenossen who are not, of their own power, in a position to secure for themselves on our borders the right to general human, political, and weltanschaulich freedom!"

I said, "That's the real roadmap—persecution of Germans in Austria and Czechoslovakia."

Grundman sat back in his chair, throwing up his hands. "Yeah, like jailing a Nazi who gets caught firebombing a Jewish restaurant is persecution."

Hitler started saying a bunch of stuff about his recent rape of Schuschnigg, but it didn't really add much to what we already suspected, and what he had just made clear. He said, "The idea and intention were to bring about a lessening of the tensions in our relations by granting to that part of the German-Austrian Volk which is National Socialist in terms of its views and Weltanschauung those rights within the limits of the law which are the same as those to which other citizens are entitled."

And then he said, "At this time, I would like to express before the German Volk my sincere gratitude to the Austrian Chancellor for the great consideration and warmhearted readiness with which he accepted my invitation and endeavored, with me, to find a solution doing equal justice to the interests of both countries and the interests of the German race as a whole, that German race whose sons we all are, no matter where the cradle of our homeland stood. I believe that we have thereby also made a contribution to European peace."

Now Grundman snorted. "I hope Schuschnigg is pleased with the Führer's gratitude. I mean, how does he sleep at night?"

"Maybe he's just playing for time. Maybe he's got a plan."

"He's definitely playing for time. But a plan? He doesn't have shit."

"Maybe he's hoping for Mussolini?"

"I don't think Il Duce is in the Austrian protection business anymore. I think that's over. I know he saved us in '34 when Dollfuss got killed, but four years is a long time. Somebody would have reported something by now if he's still on our side. But there's been nothing. I read everything I can get my hands on, and there hasn't been a hint."

Hitler droned on for a few more minutes, ending with, "Long live the National Socialist Movement, long live the National Socialist Army, long live our German Reich!" As the applause built again, Grundman snapped off the radio and said, "I'm not sure we have a month."

I asked him if he was still planning on resisting, and he laid out some of the plans he had made. Needing to unburden myself, in reply, I told him everything: about being a courier, and my suspicions about Uncle Otto's death, and my determination to find out more. I was looking for some kind of validation from him, I know. But after I finished telling him, his silence was unnerving.

"What?" I said. It was almost a panicked cry.

"I was just thinking about your mother and father. He would be cautious. I think she would be proud."

I felt like crying. "So you think I should keep pursuing how Otto died?"

"That's the part that worries me. The courier business is done for the right reasons, as a soldier in a just war. The rest is personal and personal scares me. Some of these kids I'm organizing, all they talk about is getting revenge against certain people: 'I'll strangle that so-and-so with his big red flag.' But that's not what this is. And getting revenge against the Gestapo? I'm as much of an idealist as you'll ever meet, but even I think that's fucking crazy."

"It's not revenge I'm looking for. I'm looking for information, that's all."

"Come on, that's bullshit. Make the assumption it was the

Gestapo. There's your information. What are you going to do about it?"

I thought for a second. It was the question I was avoiding as best I could. I was barely audible when I said, "I don't know."

Grundman grabbed me by the shoulders. "That's why I'm scared."

37

Frankfurt was a complete waste of time. I never liked the city—don't know why. Too many bankers, probably. But I got off the train, as instructed, ate lunch at Dimble's, went to the bathroom, checked under the lid of the toilet tank, and there was no envelope. Just the usual rust stains. And the food was crap. Three hours of my life I would never get back.

Because of the change in schedule, I was in Cologne by dinnertime, with nothing to do except pretend to be a detective. My first stop—really, the only stop I had planned—was at the Wasserhof, Otto's hotel of choice.

We both were slaves to our road routines. I always stayed at the Dom Hotel because it was nice and because they could accommodate me with the typewriter and supplies I needed. Otto always stayed at the Wasserhof, even though it had deteriorated over the years to the point where a nice person would call the appointments "tired." A less polite person, like me, would go straight to "shithole." But whenever I asked Otto why he still stayed there, he told the story about being snowed in one year—like in 1921 or something—and how they kept the kitchen and the bar open for him and three other guests when nobody else was in the hotel, and how he felt he still owed them his loyalty "even though the old girl's undergarments are getting a bit frayed." That was Otto.

I got there and headed straight to the bar; that made the most sense. It was a complete snooze. There was nobody in there except the bartender, who very much fit the surroundings —meaning that, in all likelihood, he'd probably been working a shift the night of the Armistice. When I sat down at the bar, I think I startled him. But he recovered nicely and returned quickly with a credible Manhattan.

He put down the drink. I reached into my breast pocket and removed the photo of Otto that Hannah had given me. I asked if he knew him.

The old gent didn't hesitate. "Ah, Mr. Kovacs. That's him, it is. It's a shame what happened. I have to tell you, the night manager and I drank a toast to him the next night, after we heard."

"What do you know about it?"

"Just what we read in the paper, that his body washed up along the river, and that it was presumed to be a suicide. It was a little, short article, a day or two after the police searched his room. We weren't surprised when we read it because the detective had told the night manager the same thing."

He stopped for a second, my inquisitiveness finally registering. "But who are you?"

I had rehearsed my story, which did not include the words "jealous husband" or "Gestapo." I told him I was Otto's nephew, and that our family was so shocked by the suicide, and that even though it was more than a year later, we still had so many questions, especially Otto's longtime girlfriend. So as a favor to her, and because I was here on business anyway, I figured I would take a little time and try to figure out whatever I could. This was the only place I knew to come.

The old man nodded. "That makes sense. But I don't know what I could tell you. I served him two or three drinks a night, three or four days a year. It does go back decades, that's true, but that was it. I didn't know anything about him—nothing about you, or a girlfriend, or anything really."

He stopped, smiled. "Sometimes he would have a lady with him."

"Ever the same lady twice?"

"Never." And the old man smiled again.

"What about the last night you saw him? I know it's been a while, but do you remember anything?"

"I do because I told the detective when he asked. Mr. Kovacs was in from about nine to eleven, which was pretty typical. Soon after he got here, another gentleman joined him. They sat over there," he said, pointing to a table by the window.

"They seemed to know each other well, but I don't know if your uncle was expecting him when he arrived—he had some notes he was looking through. They had three or four drinks, and they were laughing a lot—I couldn't really hear much because it was pretty busy, believe it or not."

I looked around. I was still the only customer.

"There really isn't much else to say. About eleven, they paid up and walked out into the lobby together. That's all I know. And nobody saw them leave the hotel or go up to your uncle's room or anything—I remember that, too, from when the detective was questioning all of the employees. The night manager was behind on his paperwork and was in his office behind the front desk. The police were here maybe three days later."

I asked him what the other guy looked like. He said he was about my uncle's age, nothing special, just a man in a suit. That's all he had. So I learned something, but I learned nothing. I didn't know who I was kidding, thinking I could come up with an answer so many months after Otto died. Real detectives would tell you that the trail grows very cold after only 48 hours. Fourteen months later, what chance did a fake detective have?

The answer: no chance. Before I left, I bought the bartender a shot, and he drank with me. He raised his glass and said, "To Herr Kovacs."

38

A terrible trip morphed into an absolute waste of time when the phone in my hotel room woke me at 7:30. It was the secretary for Michael Bader, owner of the family steel mill, my appointment for the day. He was Uncle Otto's client, maybe the company's oldest client in Germany. We didn't get along badly, but we didn't get along great, either. Anyway, the secretary was calling to tell me that Bader's wife had suffered a heart attack the previous night and was hospitalized. She asked if the appointment could be rescheduled in about 10 days. I checked my calendar and agreed.

I managed to reschedule my train for that night, but still had a day to kill. My first thought was to grab a beer and head for the river until I looked out the window and saw the rain. Also, the idea of sitting along the river with a cold one had lost a bit of its traditional appeal, given that a quick glance to the right would always leave me staring at Uncle Otto's bridge. So, it was breakfast in the hotel dining room, accompanied by a newspaper that featured a front-page story about the persecution of German Nazis by the good citizens of Salzburg, and how this couldn't be allowed to stand. There had been a different story the day before, and there undoubtedly would be another one the day after, all pretty much the same article, just substituting the name of the town and the number of Nazis who were supposed to have been roughed up. It was all bullshit, but it was relentless, and given the low growl I got from the waiter as he read the story over my shoulder, it also might just have been effective.

The rain stopped, so I decided to wander around. In Cologne, wanderers seemed almost automatically drawn to the cathedral. Something told me to go inside and sit in a pew. It was a massive place, not particularly beautiful but just so solid and imposing, comforting in its permanence. I hadn't been to Mass since Otto's funeral, and I couldn't remember the time before that, but I sat through the second half of this one, standing and kneeling at all of the right times, reciting the prayers by rote, the whole business burned somewhere into my consciousness. And when it was over, I just sat there and thought about I don't know what. I'm not sure how long I had been there when a priest in his black cassock slid into the pew next to me.

"Alex," he said. I looked up and didn't recognize him, except that I did. It was one of those situations where you see someone outside of their usual context and can't quite place them, although you know that you know them.

He smiled at my apparent confusion. "Peiper," he said. "Major Peiper."

Then it was my turn to smile. "So which are you, a Luftwaffe major or a priest? Because if you're really a priest, I personally would be thrilled, although I think I should tell you that your superiors probably frown on your walks down the back corridor."

"This is a fact: There is no specific mention of back corridors in scripture—so learn your Bible. But I'm in the Luftwaffe. I borrowed this from a friend who happens to be posted in the rectory here. A friend who happens to agree with what I'm doing and occasionally helps me out."

That he knew my travel plans and had been following me was as evident as it was unsettling. That I was a pawn in this entire business had become plain in recent months, but the number of people whose fingerprints were on me, trying to push me around a board I didn't understand—the major, the Gestapo, the Czechs—seemed to be multiplying. And there was no way for me to just turn over the board and run away.

Peiper started to say something, but I stopped him.

"My Uncle Otto," I said. "Do you know about him?"

Peiper looked at me quizzically. I told him the whole story. The last time I had seen Peiper, in August, I was still under the impression that it was suicide. I hadn't yet met Detective Muller in the bar, didn't know about the bruising on Otto's body. The Gestapo had not been a possibility that I had even considered.

So I told him everything, from the beginning. Peiper never interrupted, just took it all in before answering.

"First thing, I'm sorry about your uncle. But I didn't know him. I had never heard of him until you started talking five minutes ago. I'm sure you're wondering if he was an agent, but I'm pretty confident that he wasn't. I think I'd know. We're a pretty small circle. You know, I would definitely know if we were working with him. I would also know if he was working for the Gestapo against us because that would mean we killed him. And we didn't."

I had never even considered that Otto could have been working for the Germans as a spy. But if the Czechs thought I could be helpful because of my extensive traveling and my contacts, I guess the Germans could have felt the same way. Then again, what would the Nazis need Otto for? They had ministers in the Austrian cabinet, for fuck's sake. They controlled half of the Vienna police department, at least.

No, that wasn't it—and that was beside the fact that Otto hated the Nazis.

"Are you sure you would know?"

"Look, there are only six of us in this area. I promise you, I would know. Your uncle just wasn't working for us."

An old woman came into the pew behind us. It was a vast, empty church and she was right up our ass. Peiper leaned closer and whispered. "Stay here for five minutes and then meet me on the other side, in the last confessional on the right."

39

After five minutes, I approached the confessional, but the red light was on above the booth. Somebody else was in there, which didn't seem possible. I surveyed the area, and it was, indeed, the last confessional on the right. So I waited in a nearby pew. A minute or two later, an ancient woman wearing a rain bonnet tied tightly beneath her chin emerged. She walked with a cane.

I took her place in the booth and kneeled. The partition slid open, but the priest was in the shadows behind a screen, so I wasn't 100 percent sure it was Peiper. I began the rite from memory, just in case. But it must have sounded like a question as I said it.

"Bless me, father, for I have sinned—"

"Alex?"

"Thank God. You didn't really hear that old lady's confession, did you?"

"I did. There was nothing I could do—she followed me right in."

I was laughing, something I had never done in a confessional. "Anything juicy?"

"Haven't you ever heard of the seal of the confessional?"

"Yeah, but that's for real priests."

"All right. Let's just say she had some impure thoughts, the old girl did. I gave her three Hail Marys for her penance, but what I really wanted to do was congratulate her. God, she sounded like she was 80."

"She walked like she was 90."

We eventually got down to the reason why Peiper was following me into the cathedral in the first place. He said there was nothing physical to bring home this time. He just wanted me to listen and give a verbal report to my contact in Vienna.

"Just listen," he said. "About six months ago, Hitler and his generals had a meeting where he told them his plans—general plans, no timetables or anything like that. There wasn't supposed to be a record, but one of the junior officers, a guy named Hossbach, took some notes that we've seen. The basic summary is that he's about to move east—Austria, Czechoslovakia, Poland, you get the picture—for raw materials needed to continue the military buildup. The decision is made. We already kind of knew that, but now we really know it. It's not if, it's when.

"Okay, so there's that piece. The second piece is that a group of the big names—Blomberg and Fritsch from the military, Neurath from the foreign office—all thought the idea was crazy. They thought the army wasn't ready and that any move—against the Czechs especially—would bring the French into a war against Germany, and that the French army could kick their ass blindfolded. I should say our ass. And that's why all three of them have been replaced. Again, it's what people suspected, but this is the confirmation. It was all quite fishy—right after they expressed their skepticism, there was suddenly a rumor about Blomberg's wife and some nude pictures, and another rumor about Fritsch and a young boy in a public restroom, and they were both gone. Pretty convenient, it seems to me. When in doubt, sex it up."

"But you don't know when?"

"No. There's nothing from Hossbach about when, and I haven't seen any planning documents. Nobody here has. You have to think Austria is first, but there aren't any plans. Well, there's this thing called 'Case Otto,' but it's really just a training exercise that somebody drew up a couple of years ago in case somebody tried a Habsburg restoration. But it's nothing, a piece of shit. So there aren't any concrete plans that we know of. But really, how long would it take to draw up a battle plan to take over a country that is going to have brass bands playing to serenade us when we enter?"

"But what about the French?"

"Nah, nobody thinks they care about Austria. You know there are a lot of people in Europe who think Austria should have been a part of Germany to start with."

"A lot of people in Austria think that, too."

"Brass bands, I'm telling you."

"And you're telling me that there's nobody in Germany who can stop it?"

"That's what I'm telling you. You should go now."

"No Hail Marys?"

"I'll say a couple for you. And for Austria."

40

There wasn't a lot to do, or think about. On the one hand, Peiper didn't tell me anything I didn't already know; in fact, he kind of told me the same story as last time. I mean, everybody knew, deep down. Hitler was coming, and there was no stopping him. Once he got Austria, Czechoslovakia was next. It was just that plain, that certain, that final.

I was walking vaguely back toward the hotel, and some lunch, when the big-ass black Mercedes 260D, the spare tire sitting there on the running board, pulled up beside me and two black leather trench coats got out and sandwiched me, front and back, each then grabbing an arm. From the front passenger seat, the window rolled down, and a Gestapo officer I had not seen before said, "Herr Kovacs, your presence is needed at EL-DE Haus. I hope this is not too much of an inconvenience."

I had rehearsed for this moment, more than once, always praying it would never come but practicing just in case. And what I had decided on was to act naturally. That is to say, scared beyond belief. That was always the plan, and it didn't take a lot of acting. But as I settled into the back seat, between my minders, I did ad lib one question.

"Am I to see Captain Vogl?"

The officer in the passenger seat turned and smiled. "Eventually," he said.

The ride wasn't five minutes. We pulled up right in front. There were no screams that day from the array of knee-high windows along the sidewalk. On a cold February day, there were none of the fetid smells that were there in August. When they let me walk into the building without holding me by each arm, I allowed myself a few seconds of hope. But it ended quickly. We were not headed straight, up the staircase to the offices. We headed right, toward the big iron door, the door whose hinges screamed when they opened it, and the cellar behind it. The officer continued up the stairs; the trench coats and I headed down.

It was quiet. The doors of the first two cells were open, and they were empty. I was placed in the third cell. It was empty, too.

"Your clothes, sir," said the bigger of the trench coats. And so it was—topcoat and hat, suit and shoes and socks. They left me in my undershirt and shorts. My arms were folded, and I was shivering when they clanged the iron door behind them.

I kept telling myself not to panic. I also kept telling myself the fact that I had not seen or heard Peiper in another cell was a good thing. All I had done was go to church, and I didn't think things had gotten to the point where they would question a priest about what somebody had said in confession. As long as Peiper had been careful, I hadn't done anything. Then again, how many people admitted to doing things they hadn't done just to try to bargain their way out of whatever torture could be coming.

I wasn't sure how long I had been in there—maybe an hour, maybe a little more—when nature called. There was a bucket in the corner of the cell for that purpose. As I peed into it, the iron door opened. The Gestapo officer from the car and one of his henchmen stood and watched as I finished.

I suddenly forgot about my just-act-scared rehearsal. "Enjoying the view?" I asked as I pulled myself together.

The officer locked eyes with me.

"Take the underwear," he said, and walked out, leaving his aide to collect my shorts and shirt. I was naked now, alone and naked when the door slammed again.

I sat down on the wooden bunk. I had been sitting there before, but this time I rubbed my hand across it, to make sure I didn't catch a splinter in my ass—as if that was the biggest of my worries. For some reason, I wasn't all that scared about having a finger or toe lopped off with a pair of bolt cutters. But when I played this out in my nightmares, all I could think about was that same recurring dream, with wires leading from a battery's electrodes being attached to my balls—or, if they were feeling like kind torturers, maybe it would be my nipples. Those were the things that terrified me.

But I kept playing it out in my head, wondering if there was anything I could admit if I had to. It kept coming back to this: If I knew for a fact that they had Peiper in a nearby cell, and that he had admitted something specific to them, I could confirm it with a clear conscience. I mean, at that point, Peiper would be a corpse in waiting. There would be nothing I could do for him, and there was no reason not to try to save myself—and admitting a little something would probably play better than denying something they knew for a fact to be true.

But if not? Then I just had to deny everything. I mean, there was no physical evidence—not on this trip, anyway. And the more I thought about it, the more I could convince myself that they weren't going to kill me, even if they had something. It was tricky for them; they did need the magnesite, after all. I did have some level of protection because of that, and the Gestapo knew it. At least Vogl knew it. So maybe they would just threaten me and tell me that I would be under 24-hour surveillance any time I came back to Germany. Or perhaps they would tell me I couldn't come back to Germany at all. Or maybe I would be going to Dachau. But to kill me would risk international news coverage and repercussions, especially if Leon managed to make a stink about it at home; "The Two Kovacs Murders in Cologne" was my working headline. It was a small risk, granted, but it would be there. No, they didn't want that. That's what I kept telling myself.

Then I heard a scream—just one, but it was piercing. And as I sat there on that bunk, bare-assed and shivering, all I could do was try to convince myself that the scream didn't sound like the way Major Peiper would scream if someone showed him a wire attached to an electrode from a car battery.

41

I didn't know how long I'd been waiting—another hour, maybe more—when the iron door of the cell was opened again, the turning of the key accompanied by a loud, angry-sounding conversation, muffled by the iron barrier and then clearly heard as the door cracked open. The last bit of the rant:

"—EVER LEARN TO FOLLOW INSTRUCTIONS? HOW DID YOU EVER GET PROMOTED?"

Vogl was doing the screaming. The junior officer who had collected me off of the street was the one being screamed at. I was the only naked person in the room, reflexively covering my manhood as I stood, but it was the young officer who appeared to be holding his balls in his hands.

Vogl looked at me for a second, then exploded again.

"NAKED?" And then he paused a beat, leaned into his underling, nose to nose, and in a lower voice, lower but even more frightening, said very slowly, "Get . . . his . . . fucking . . . clothes."

The eunuch scurried off, and Vogl and I were alone. I couldn't have said how long the silence lasted. After a time, he walked out into the hallway, as if to offer me an apologetic gesture, to give me some privacy.

For the next minute or two, I ran the phrase "learn to follow instructions" over and over through my head. What could that have meant? Learn to follow instructions. For one thing, it meant that there were, in fact, instructions attached to my name. But what kind of instructions? Keep an eye on me discreetly? Or don't be discreet about it and make sure I knew I was being followed? Or do something a little more overt, like question me briefly, just to make it entirely clear that the Gestapo had suspicions?

Whatever it meant, naked in a cold cell appeared to have crossed the line. Unless, that is, this was all some elaborate bit of playacting, a good-cop/bad-cop routine like in the movies. Anything was possible. But the one thing was, Vogl really did seem enraged. If this was an act, it was a damn good one.

Soon, Vogl walked in with my clothes, folded and in a neat pile, shoes and hat on top. He placed them gently next to me on the bunk and returned to the doorway. "Please," he said, motioning to the pile.

I did my best not to display any emotion in reply. I turned my back on him, began getting dressed, and attempted to think of the proper response. I buttoned up slowly, tucked in fastidiously, tied my necktie with care. I went as slowly as I could and tried to think of what to say. There was a point where he coughed behind me. I thought he might be clearing his throat to say something, but no. There was just the silence, both of us clearly calculating.

I could be meek and essentially thank him for clearing up the misunderstanding. I could be curt and just nod and leave. I could be furious at this violation of my rights and promise to lodge a complaint with the Czech consulate. Or I could be silent and wait for him to say something. That's what I ultimately chose, silence.

In my stocking feet but otherwise dressed, I turned to face Vogl. As it turned out, he began speaking almost immediately.

"You must accept my apology. My man was overzealous. You have heard me reprimand him verbally, but he will be reprimanded formally as well. He will apologize, also, when we are leaving the building. I hope you can accept it with the sincerity it is offered."

I just looked at him, no nod, no acknowledgment of what he had said. He continued.

"I. am not excusing him, but you need to understand his motivations, all of our motivations. We are working here in the service of something great, something greater than all of us. It is an awesome responsibility."

He stopped again, seemingly seeking some sort of acknowledgment from me, some flicker of recognition. I did my best to remain expressionless. He continued.

"You have seen the Romerturm?" he asked. And I did nod here. The Romerturm was the remains of a stone wall and tower, built in the first century AD, when Cologne was part of the Roman Empire. It was only a couple of blocks away from where we were standing, although, when I'd seen it a few years earlier, I had no idea what EL-DE Haus was, or what it would become.

"I walk by it almost every day," Vogl said. "I can close my eyes and see it, every brick. This was the northernmost outpost on continental Europe of the Roman Empire—right over there," he said, extending his right arm and pointing. "We can almost touch it from here, the very edge. But why did it stop? And why did it end?

"You have read the history, I'm sure. You know why. It was rot from within that ended the Roman Empire. It was laziness, it was decadence, it was complacency—and it all came from within. You've heard about the barbarians, but that is rubbish. That wall was strong enough. The real problems were inside the wall, not outside."

He was speaking in a cadence now, a rhythm. He seemed like one of those preachers from the American south shown on a recent newsreel. Either that or like Hitler himself.

"This is our job, the Gestapo's job, my job—to protect against that rot while the Führer's vision is being realized, so that the realization can endure. Our job, my job, is to identify the small problems before they become significant problems, to root out the decadent and the subversive and make sure they can never become widespread enough or strong enough to challenge the vision. Because the vision must endure.

"I took an oath. It is a promise, and I take it seriously. So does that little shithead who pulled you in off the street. You must understand that I had no idea you were being detained and brought in here, and that it should not have happened. Again, I do apologize. But you also must understand that it was overzealousness in the name of a greater good—the most important good, in fact. Think about that old wall and you will recognize it. I know you will."

I did my best, again, to remain expressionless, to not give him the satisfaction. We locked eyes for a few seconds, just staring, and he blinked first, half-turning away, saying, "Finish getting dressed and I will drive you back to your hotel."

"I'll walk."

He seemed hurt. It seemed real. Then again, he might have been the Emil Jannings of the Gestapo. I just didn't know.

"As you wish. I'm sure you can find your way out." With that, he was gone. I turned to put on my shoes, resting my right foot on the edge of the bunk, tying it, then my left foot. Leaning over, my eye caught a few more wall carvings that I had not seen before. One was just a calendar marking off the days—eight days, it seemed, followed by God knows what for the poor sap in question. Near that was a single word, *Papa*.

Then I saw the third etching, and I stopped tying my shoe. I might have stopped breathing.

There, off by itself, was an O with three lines drawn neatly below it.

42

1) Could I kill him?

2) Did I have the guts?

3) Could I possibly get away with it?

4) Could I find out why he had Otto killed?

Those were the four questions I asked myself, over and over and over, as the train devoured the miles. It always came back to No. 2, of course. The rest were details.

We had all pulled the trigger on our rifles in the army—Leon, Henry, me, all of us. Presumably, we had hit somebody at some point. But that's not with this was. That was survival. This was an act of calculation.

Henry said he could never do it. His father had killed as a young man, establishing his credibility in a brutal line of work. He told Henry a couple of the stories, but only when he was drunk and only when he was an old man. He never used those stories to shame Henry in his formative time, to prod his son into doing something he otherwise couldn't do. Henry was not a killer, and nothing short of self-defense or war could turn him into one. He could barely rough up a gambler who was behind in his payments.

But what about me?

1) Could I kill him?

2) Did I have the guts?

3) Could I possibly get away with it?

4) Could I find out why he had Otto killed?

That I was even considering the possibility was an indication of where my head was. Seeing Otto's signature on the wall of the cell answered every question. It was not suicide. It was not a jealous husband. Otto had been in EL-DE Haus, the bruises on his torso were torture at the hands of Vogl's goons, and a day or so later, they were the ones who threw him off of the bridge and into the Rhine. One letter with three little lines drawn neatly beneath it told the whole story.

Except for one thing: the why. Was Otto a spy? Was that really possible? The fury I felt was tempered by that unanswered question. This was not to kid anyone, of course. People who knew me knew that Alex Kovacs didn't do fury, not even when confronted with the killer of the person he loved above all others. But my friends would be wrong in this case. The rage was not outward, true enough, but it was there, and it was real. And it manifested itself in an almost manic determination to consider actually killing a captain of the Gestapo and to do it on German soil, an act that was incredible on its face, falling somewhere on the spectrum between idiotic and suicidal. Yet I couldn't let it go.

Round and round it went, then, past Frankfurt and Würzburg and wherever. No sleep on this trip, just Hennessy followed by breakfast.

And the questions.

1) Could I kill him?

2) Did I have the guts?

3) Could I possibly get away with it?

4) Could I find out why he had Otto killed?

The truth was, as the train pulled into the Westbahnhof and I grabbed a cab from the rank on Felberstrasse, I didn't know the answers to any of those four questions. But I had ten days to figure them out, especially No. 2.

MARCH 1938

43

Johanna was furious. I liked it when she treated me like crap for fun, but this was serious, even if it was about a Fasching ball. Specifically, the most glittering and exclusive and expensive of all of Vienna's annual balls, which the von Westermanns treated like church on Easter but which I was declining to attend because of a previous commitment at the secretaries' and office workers' ball.

She was screeching. "I mean, it isn't even a choice. How can you turn down a ball in the Hofburg, right in the royal apartments, to go to one in the . . . wherever the hell it is?"

"It's in the Morgenthaler Hall."

"Oh, fine. And what was the last event they hosted? A swap meet?"

In truth, it was a sale of surplus housewares from a small chain of three stores that had gone out of business. But there was no stopping this rant.

"The royal apartments! Catering by Café Central! Desserts by Sacher! And what are the secretaries serving?"

"I'm sure we'll eat scraps of wurst off the floor, and drink homemade schnapps out of chipped porcelain jugs. Come on, Johanna. You know why I have to do this."

The truth was, I really wanted to do it—but I also had to do it. Otto, Hannah, and I had gone to the ball together every year. It was one of the dozens of balls in Vienna every winter, before Lent, organized mostly around professions. Everybody got dressed in formal wear and toasted the shitty weather. You would expect doctors and lawyers to have their own balls, and they did. But so did store clerks, government workers, even washerwomen. Leon said the newspaper ball was always a hilarious drunken mess. They were all the same—debutantes marched in at the beginning, a mass quadrille danced at midnight, a lot of waltzing happened in between—but they were all different, too, because the people were different. They were scheduled months ahead of time, but there were never enough days to avoid at least some conflicts. How was I to know that the secretaries' ball would be on the same night as the rich assholes' ball? Or that I would be invited to the rich assholes' ball?

The argument degenerated, but only a little. I was able to leave before Johanna said something really hurtful. She was already mad that I'd had to make the extra trip to Cologne, and this just tipped her over. Or maybe it was the lingering embarrassment she felt about the museum opening. She would sometimes swing, from the modern woman with an education and a career and opinions to the daughter of the Baron and Baroness von Westermann. I couldn't quite figure her out, even after a year. And I still didn't think I could tell her about my other life.

I couldn't tell Hannah, either. As far as she was concerned, Otto had jumped off of that bridge after receiving a bad diagnosis and that was that. She had come to live with it, to accept it. There was still a hint of sadness in her, but I was pretty sure most people couldn't see it. She had even considered accepting an invitation to the ball from the office manager at a law firm on the first floor of our building. Well, she said she considered it, but I didn't think she did.

As it turned out, Morgenthaler Hall looked great. The band was pretty good. The drink was plentiful. We danced and laughed and shared memories of Otto. It was what we both wanted.

"Here, let's sit," I said. It was about 11:30. We weren't at our table, but in two chairs near the edge of the dance floor. I grabbed two drinks from the bar, and we sat quietly, watching the waltzers waltz by.

Finally, I just blurted out what I had been practicing all day.

"You know it's time to go, right?"

"Go home? It's still early. We haven't even had the quadrille."

"Not go from here. Go from Vienna. Go from Austria."

The city had grown so emotional since Schuschnigg's trip to Berchtesgaden—the Christians sadly expectant, the Jews quietly frantic. They couldn't cancel the balls, but people just weren't going out at night anymore, weren't doing anything spontaneous or frivolous. The Nazis in the streets were getting more noticeable; they still couldn't wear the swastika, but you saw more and more of the white knee socks and the breeches, which had been their subversive trademark. They were just strutting. It was happening, and everybody felt it. Leon said they weren't putting it in the paper, but that their police checks the week before had turned up five Jewish suicides. One guy cut his throat with a razor while standing at a bar.

It was time for Jews like Hannah to get out if they could. It was past time.

Her response when I brought it up was the same as always. It had become a reflex at this point. "I can't. My whole life is here."

"You can and you must, because here isn't here anymore—or it isn't going to be, and soon."

I reached into my breast pocket. I handed her the bank book

from Zürich that Otto had left in the safe-deposit box. She opened it, saw her name next to Otto's on the "bearer" line, and began to weep.

I explained about the letter from Otto, and how he had asked me to wait until it was time for her to leave before giving her the bank book. "He told me to convince you. It was the last thing he asked me in that letter."

She held up the bank book. "But I already got the money from his apartment. I thought that was what he left me. Wait—"

"Shush. The apartment money was from me—and don't worry, he left me plenty, much more than I ever expected. Consider it your company pension. But you need to go to your sister's in London."

"But, how—"

I reached into my pocket again and showed her two train tickets from Vienna to Zürich, one for each of us.

"You have three days. You need to call your sister, and you need to go to your bank and get your money wired to this account in Zürich."

I could get her into Switzerland, traveling with me on business. They were starting to get nervous about Jews arriving and never leaving, but this would work fine. Getting a visa from Zürich to London would be harder, but doable, given her sister's sponsorship, and especially given the numbers in that bank book.

"But my furniture? All of my things? I can't."

"You can and you will. You know it's time. You read the papers—Hitler could be here by lunchtime tomorrow, and then it will be too late. You have to go. And I swear to God, I'll drag you if I have to."

She laughed. "Yeah, I'd like to see you try."

The laugh told me I had won. She grabbed my hand, and we waltzed.

44

On Monday night, Leon wanted to drink at Rudy's, of all places. It was a working-class bar on Kandlgasse, in Schottenfeld. I was surprised, because Leon once famously said, famously and drunkenly late one night, in a line that would be repeated by Henry and me every time we heard Benny Goodman's "Stompin' at the Savoy," because that was the song that was playing as Leon sang:

Wah-wah, the girls of Schottenfeld,
Wah-wah, they smell like shittenfeld.

But this was not about women. This was a night of what he called "winking," a combination of working and drinking. This was a derivation of our annual mid-December day of Christmas shopping and drinking, which he had dubbed "shrinking." Anyway, he said he needed to talk to a guy for a story, and wanted company while he waited for him to show up at his local. So, Rudy's.

As we drank and waited, we did our best to avoid talking about Schuschnigg, and what might happen next. But after exhausting a recitation of my fight with Johanna, and Henry's fixation with Liesl, there really wasn't anything else to talk about except the story Leon was working on—which, as it turned out, was about Schuschnigg.

"Look, I can't tell you," he said. "Not yet. If the guy comes in, I'll talk to him. Then maybe. But it's just too thin. Let's give it a little while more."

"But who is he?"

Leon paused. "Look, I'll just tell you this: He's the foreman at Hans Albrecht and Sons, the printing company. And I'm pretty sure Schuschnigg is arranging some kind of rush printing job. But that's all I know."

This was big, it seemed. Or maybe it was nothing. Leon just had that look about him, even though he also had that exhausted look about him. "Do you get the sense anybody in Café Louvre is on to it?"

"No, but you never know. I've stopped in to check the last few nights—give them a few scraps, an early read on what's going to be in the paper, maybe a little gossip, then I just listen. The gossip helps them a lot, makes their bosses think they're on the inside of things, spices up their stories—the guy from Chicago calls it 'the raisins in the pudding.' So they let me listen. The guy from Manchester has all the sources, but I don't get the sense they have anything. The truth is, they all look like shit. Nobody's sleeping. They're all afraid to. They know this is going to be the biggest story of their careers and they're nervous as hell. Because they know, but they don't know. They're like all of us."

I had never been a source for Leon, never told him anything I had learned on my courier trips, and he never asked. But it just seemed different now, time running faster somehow, all of us hurtling toward a horrible outcome. So I told him what I had found out in the confessional, about the Hitler meeting last fall, and Hossbach's notes, and Blomberg and Fritsch and Neurath, and how the major and his people were convinced that it was all happening soon.

Leon was suddenly alive. "In a confessional? Can I use this?"

"Not the confessional part. Not my name, obviously. But the information as background? Yes."

"A lot of this has been hinted at, but if I could tie it together and call you 'a source with connections to the German military,' would that be okay?"

I thought about it for a second and agreed. When I gave the information to my Czech contact, he pretty much yawned. I mean, what was the difference at this point? The bigger question was if I would tell Leon the rest of what happened that day in Cologne. When I did, well, it was because I had to tell someone.

Leon listened and then whispered, "I knew he didn't kill himself," as if his vindication was all that mattered. But then he caught himself.

"So what are you going to do about it?"

I paused, then just dove in. "I'm thinking of killing Vogl, the Gestapo captain."

Leon's first reaction was to laugh. But then he saw my face. "You're fucking serious, aren't you?"

"It's all I can think about."

"You can't. I mean, be serious."

"You're telling me to be serious? You're telling me to be cautious? You?"

"I mean, I'm impulsive. I'm an idiot sometimes, I'll grant you that. But even I know that killing a Gestapo officer in Cologne is crazy."

"But why does it have to be crazy if you plan it right?" And then I sketched out the beginnings of the scheme I had been concocting.

Leon listened, conceded a point or two, probed at what he thought were holes in my plan. But when I thought I was starting to convince him, he stopped the conversation. "No, this is absurd. Come on, this is real fucking life. This isn't just taking a swing at a couple of Nazi kids in a classroom. That was literally child's play compared to this."

He was talking about something that happened in 1924. Leon and I had enrolled for a semester at Vienna University—Leon because he was on a kick to become a lawyer and change the world, and me because, well, because Leon was doing it. Uncle Otto shrugged and told me I could go ahead if I paid with my own money. As it turned out, we didn't even last until the end of the semester.

Back then—and 1938 wasn't all that different, thinking back on it—the most rabid Nazis were at the university, true believers unencumbered by real-life experience, assholes with energy. The emotions seemed to boil over every few months—the signs posted on the notice boards more and more anti-Semitic, the speakers brought onto campus more hateful, and then the beatings of Jewish students. They were like mini-pogroms, tacitly supported by the administration and the faculty. And here was the beauty of the thing for the Nazis: Vienna city police were not allowed to set foot on campus because of some ancient law. They stood on the sidewalk and watched while Jewish kids were being curb-stomped 50 feet away. Then the stompers literally rolled the beaten kids the last few feet down the hill, where the police picked them up and dropped them into ambulances.

One day, I was late for an introductory philosophy class that Leon and I were taking together, and as I walked up the stairs to the second floor of the building, I heard a commotion in our classroom down the hall. I peered through the small window in the door and saw about 10 junior Hitlers surrounding Leon, calling him names, shoving him, then worse—because Leon was giving it right back to them. They were kicking the shit out of him while the professor and the rest of the class watched, all arrayed beneath a crucifix hanging on the wall. And I watched, too, outside the door, frozen, counting the attackers rather than rushing in, seven, eight, nine . . .

I didn't know what to do, or how long I was out there, but I saw a fire alarm and ran down the hall and pulled it. The loud ringing paused everything in the classroom for a second, and I just rushed into the vacuum. One of the Nazis kicked me in the balls, and another one shoved me headfirst into a desk, opening a small cut above my left eye. But with that, the bells were still ringing and the moment seemed to have passed. Their fun for the day over, the Nazis trooped out of the classroom, followed by the professor and the rest. I was left with a cut that didn't even need stitches. Leon was left with hamburger for a face and headaches that didn't go away for a week. I got him up and dragged him home.

We never went back to university. Leon veered to journalism, where you didn't need a degree, and I went back to selling magnesite. But when Leon told the story of that day, then and in years after, I was always painted as what he thought I was: loyal, brave, a great friend. Only I knew how long I had stood outside that classroom and watched as my friend was beaten nearly senseless, too afraid to move.

I thought of so many things in the days when I was planning what to do in Cologne. I thought of that day in 1924 a lot.

45

Johanna and I had not spoken since the Fasching argument, but we had made a date to drive out to her family's estate—that is, for me to drive her out in the big-ass Daimler that sat untouched for months in their garage. I showed up at the appointed time, not knowing what to expect. As it turned out, she greeted me with a long, dirty kiss and acted as if the argument had never happened.

I had expected the car to be like everything the Westermanns owned: top-notch and shiny on the surface but less so underneath, farting explosively out of the tailpipe at regular intervals. But the machine was a beauty, in looks and in action. Apparently, it was because they used it so infrequently and because one of the housemen maintained the engine as a kind of hobby.

The ride was about two hours, from city to suburb to farmland interrupted only occasionally by hamlets. Johanna started giving me driving directions at the end, and then we came upon an enormous iron gate that was closed.

"Honk the horn," she said.

I gave a polite tap. She leaned over, muttered one word

—"amateur"—and hit the horn with a long, insistent blast like a lorry driver stuck behind a double-parked taxi in a narrow street. Within seconds, a man in some sort of half-assed uniform, with no hat or gloves but epaulets on his unbuttoned coat, appeared on the other side, walking casually. When he saw it was Johanna, the walk became a sprint and he did his best to do up the buttons. He got all but one.

"I'm sorry, Miss Johanna, but we weren't expecting you." He fiddled with the lock on the gate but was obviously shaken.

"Just open the damn thing," Johanna said.

When he did, finally, she directed me forward with a wave.

"That was pretty shitty, not telling them you were coming," I said.

"Keeps them on their toes," she said.

We drove through woods for maybe a quarter-mile, and then the view opened up. The house—naturally, sited on a small hill —was there, in all of its massive granite magnificence. I had seen bigger—you know, like the Hofburg and Schönbrunn— and it's true that this was a cottage by comparison, but it was still twice as big as most resort hotels in Salzburg. I stopped the car and admired it from a distance.

"A dozen bedrooms?" I asked.

"Fifteen."

"And how many have you christened?"

"None, yet," she said.

There must have been a phone near the gate because, in the minute or so since, the troops had apparently been alerted. A butler in a tuxedo, a gardener in overalls, and a young housemaid in a hot little young housemaid getup were lined up outside the front door and waiting for us as we drove up. The butler opened the car door and said, "Miss Johanna, I'm sorry we did not—"

"I know, Merkins," she said. "Lunch for the two of us in an hour. Thank you."

Johanna took my arm and led me around the outside of the house. After we had traveled what they deemed to be a safe distance, the butler and the rest hurried off. As we got around to the back of the house, we climbed a few steps up to a massive patio that overlooked the back side of the hill, a sweeping lawn, a small stream with a tidy stone bridge, and then more forest. In the far corner, near the bridge, another gardener hacked at some tall grass with a scythe.

I pointed toward him. "So how many people do you employ to maintain this place?"

"I think it's eight now—Merkins, a cook, two maids, two gardeners, a houseman, and our pretend security man at the gate. But it used to be twice that when I was a girl."

"And how much time does your family spend here?"

"The month of August, maybe three or four other weekends in the spring—oh, and the week of the harvest celebration."

"Harvest? Is there a farm hidden out there somewhere?"

"It's a tradition," Johanna said. She actually sniffed when she said it.

I was getting the full von Westermann experience. It was the aspect of Johanna's personality that I liked the least. In fact, I hated it. It always amazed me how easily she swung from this cut-rate nobility bullshit to sitting naked on the floor of my apartment, cross-legged, drinking beer out of the bottle.

"You know, we're probably selling," she said, snapping me out of my naked/cross-legged reverie.

"Is that why—"

"Yeah, I wanted to see it again."

"So, when, do you think?"

"Soon," she said. "My father has an offer. He's considering it."

The legion of minor Austrian nobility was left with little

choice but to sell off their possessions, bit by bit. The question of houses was always the biggest one. Most people in the von Westermanns' position made the decision to sell the city house in Vienna and retire to the family home in the country, where their roots were and where they could live out their lives amid crumbling piles of granite, letting go of one servant after another and hoping to die of cirrhosis before it was time to fire the last gardener. But the von Westermanns were doing it the other way, and Johanna saw the questions on my face.

"They're city people now," she said. "Their parents, and a lot of their friends, always thought that they lived in the country and only visited the city. But my father and mother were always the opposite. Vienna is their first home—that's how they feel."

"But—"

"But there's a problem. Who the hell would have the money to buy this place? And who would want it even if they had the money?"

It was the Austrian dilemma of the 1930s. Who had the money to buy anything? There wasn't a whole lot of new industry in the country, so there wasn't that high-flier class of new-money shitheads to take over from the nobility. Besides, the small group of those people who were buying, well, they were purchasing petite palaces in the city like the von Westermanns. They had no use for this place, which represented a time long gone.

"So, if your father has an offer, what's to think about? Is it that low?"

"It's pretty low," she said. "But that's only part of it. The offer is from a man who is being very honest. His plan is to divide the estate and sell the pieces. The house will surely be knocked down. Because of the stream, there is a potential industrial use. Who knows? And," she said, pointing out beyond the woods, "the Museul estate is about a mile that way, and the Lindemann estate is really just past the last trees that way, and they would be furious. They would consider it a betrayal."

"But what's the alternative?"

"To sell the city house and come out here and die," Johanna said. "That's what his people are supposed to do. But he's just not willing to do it.

"But, you know, even then, it's just buying time. Father has been plain. He says, 'The money will keep us going for the rest of my life but not yours.' I'll have to sell the house when mother dies. It's why he's always encouraged me to get a proper university degree so that I could work."

I always thought she loved her work. Now she was spitting the word.

"Goddamn museum, that's going to be my life."

The notion that I was maybe going to be her life apparently had not dawned on her. When I realized that, my mood suddenly matched hers.

"Is it that bad a life?" I said. I really was hurt, but she didn't get the hint.

"I am a modern woman," she said. "But why can't I be a modern woman with a title?"

As it turned out, we never ate the lunch that the staff had hustled to prepare. It goes without saying that we didn't christen any of the bedrooms.

46

The trip to Switzerland with Hannah went off as planned. There were no problems at the border, her money had been transferred to the Zürich bank account, and the visa to England was, in the words of the man at the consulate, "in process, likely within a week." As we walked down the Bahnhofstrasse toward the station, past all of the grand merchants, we were silent. By the time we reached the big train shed, we were both weeping—not for each other, but for Otto. And as I boarded the train an hour before departure, had my ticket back to Vienna punched, tipped the attendant who had set me up in the compartment and brought me a drink, I allowed myself a small moment of satisfaction. Otto's last wish was for me to take care of Hannah, and now she was set.

One sip. Two. Then I got up, carrying my coat and the smaller of my two suitcases, and walked back two cars, away from the attendant's station and away from the conductor who had punched my ticket. Neither of them saw me as I got off the train. With any luck, the attendant would see the suitcase I left behind and assume I'd had a run of good fortune with a single woman whose compartment was in another car on the train.

Between that and the punched ticket, there would be ample evidence, if needed, that I had made the trip back to Vienna, just as the itinerary had said.

I walked a block from the station to pick up the car I had hired for what I described to the owner as an overnight visit to St. Gallen, paying for two days in advance plus a third day as a deposit. The identification I used for the transaction was all fake, obtained quickly and at great expense after visiting the man in the office down the hall from mine, the office that assisted Jews seeking a way out of Vienna. The conversation didn't total more than about a hundred words. I explained what I needed. He told me the cost. I paid. He stood me up against a neutral backdrop and took my picture. "Come back tomorrow night at about six." That was it.

Now I was driving to Cologne. It was an eight-hour trip, give or take, over uniformly good roads. I crossed the border into Germany soon after Basel, with nothing more than a stamp in the passport book and a wave on the Swiss side and only a quick chat and another stamp on the German side. Then it was really a nice ride—through Freiburg and Karlsruhe, Mannheim, Mainz, and Koblenz. I stopped for the night in Bonn, about 20 miles south of Cologne. This was where my meeting with Herr Bader would take place, nearer to his home than the steel mill. He said it would be an excuse for him to skip a day at the office and spend most of it with his wife, still convalescing from her heart attack. It would give me a free evening, as Bader was in no mood for nocturnal entertainment. And it would give me a chance to remain out of Vogl's range of vision, given that I checked into the hotel with my new passport. My real name would not show up on the nightly Gestapo report of new hotel guests.

Bader and I met at lunch, did our business in about 15 minutes as we drank our coffee and picked at our strudel, and spent the rest of the time reminiscing about Otto. Bader clearly missed him. They had worked together for 35 years. His steel mill was our first German client, and the two businesses and the two men had matured together. Bader wasn't a Nazi, but he was careful. We just didn't talk about it, probably because he didn't know me very well. I wonder what he had confided in Otto.

I had about three hours to kill after lunch before I would drive into Cologne. I had rolled the plan over in my head a hundred times during the drive from Zürich, to the point where I was seeking any kind of distraction. As I wandered upon the Beethoven Museum, located in the house where he had grown up, it seemed as good a distraction as any.

The woman sitting behind the desk at the front door seemed thrilled to have a visitor. I was pretty sure I was the only person in the place as I wandered from room to room over a couple of floors and a couple of houses that had been joined. It was mostly kitsch and crap but, whatever, it passed the time. And as I was leaning down to look at some sheet music in a glass display case —for what purpose, I didn't know, seeing as how I couldn't read music—I suddenly felt the presence of another visitor in the small room. It was Major Peiper, in civilian clothes.

I looked at him, shocked but maybe not so shocked. "If you're looking to get laid in here, I think you're going to be disappointed."

"I'm just looking for inspiration."

"From Beethoven? Really?"

"A complete hound. A fucking legend, apparently. Although they don't play that up in any of the exhibits. It's more of a local knowledge kind of thing."

Peiper pointed, and we walked to another room, farther away from the front desk. This was the ear trumpet room, with a couple of examples of the devices Beethoven used to try to improve his hearing. Whispering seemed somehow appropriate.

"I'd ask how you found me, but it doesn't really matter."

"We just followed the old man. You told us you were going to be meeting him, and it seemed easier to do it that way."

"So what's the big secret?"

Peiper told me. He said that there was a pretty solid rumor that Schuschnigg was going to call for a plebiscite in the next couple of days, an up or down vote by the Austrian people on the question of continued Austrian independence from Germany. At which point, the night in the bar in Schottenfeld suddenly began to make sense. I told Peiper about the hush-hush government printing job that Leon had sniffed out.

Peiper's face fell. "Ballot papers. Shit. I was hoping maybe it was just a rumor. That printing business adds a layer of credibility to it. Shit."

"Why shit? Schuschnigg will win. He might win really big."

Peiper looked at me like I was a stupid school kid. "Don't you get it? Hitler will go crazy when he hears—and for that very reason. His whole narrative is that the Austrians want to be part of the Reich. Well, not the whole narrative—he can still hang on to the bullshit about Nazis being persecuted. But the big justification is that we're all one big Germanic happy family. He can't have a vote that says otherwise."

"So you think—"

"I don't think—I know. Or at least I know in my gut. The German army is coming in, ready or not—and we're not ready. We don't have a plan except for some fucking training exercise called 'Case Otto.' I swear to God, we'll get stopped in our tracks by a loud fart. But the Czechs, your people, are both gutless and delusional, which is a fatal combination. And Mussolini, he could turn us around with a glare—but I think Hitler has that taken care of. So we're going to waltz in. Just watch. That vote is never going to happen."

"So what do you want me to do?"

"Tell your people—but it's not going to matter. They're already curled up in the fetal position, Beneš first among them. He's hopeless. They're all hopeless—they still think the French are somehow going to save them. Smart people with no street smarts, all of them. So go home and tell them. And maybe say a prayer that this is all just a fucking fever dream of mine."

47

Wednesday night. This was my only chance. I was counting on Vogl being a man of fastidious habits. I was praying that his workday had not intervened. Because this really was it: I wouldn't be back for six months, and by then, whatever nerve I had mustered would have dissipated.

My hired car was parked across the street and down a couple of hundred feet from Bischoffshausen, the café where Vogl told me he played chess and drank on Wednesday nights, his only drinking of the week. He'd told me about it the night I first met him, in the Dom Hotel lobby: into Bischoffshausen at 7:30, home by 10, right around the corner from the hotel. I was in the car and waiting at seven, scanning the street, praying that Vogl would park in the small street behind the hotel and walk from there down the alley next to Bischoffshausen. I had looked at it before and it must have been where he was talking about when he said, "It's a 30-second walk from the back of the hotel." It was an essential part of the plan, that alley. And right at 7:30, it was from that alley that Vogl emerged, turning right and opening the café door.

So, it was happening. Part of me couldn't believe it, but the rest of me couldn't consider backing out. It was a good plan. I kept repeating that to myself like a mantra. It wasn't just blind vengeance, even though it was. It wasn't crazy just because it seemed impossible to kill a Gestapo captain in the middle of Germany. Because it wasn't impossible. It was a good plan.

I patted the knife in my pocket. It was a beauty, a flick knife from Solingen in Germany. The handle that concealed the blade until it was summoned with the push of a button was sheathed in brown leather, worn down over the years in places but even more handsome as a result. It was Otto's knife. I never saw him carry it—I think he used it as a letter opener—but it always sat on the desk in his apartment. And if it was the movie cliché of all time to kill Otto's killer with that knife—and it was—well, fuck it.

If the plan wasn't foolproof, it was entirely sane. I would be waiting at the far end of the alley at 10, near to where it joined the little street behind the hotel, which wasn't much more than an alley itself. Vogl and I would meet, me smoking a cigarette before going into my usual hotel. Vogl would not be alarmed by my presence, and maybe a little tipsy. He would reach out to shake my hand. I would reply with the flick knife, straight into his throat. That was the area I would attack, bare skin not covered by his coat, first his neck and then his head. He would be stunned. It would not take a minute. The only risk was somebody ducking into the alley to take a piss.

I thought about planting an envelope with some money on the body, to suggest it might have been a private Gestapo shakedown that had gone wrong. I thought about unbuttoning his pants and yanking them down to his ankles, as if it had been some kind of illicit encounter. But in the end, I decided against any embroidery. Don't waste time. Just kill him and walk back up the alley, nice and comfortable, across the street, down to the car and away. The Dutch border was only about 50 miles to the west, just past Aachen. With any luck at all, I would be out of Germany before they found the body. The odds of somebody stumbling on it weren't that great. His wife probably wouldn't call work looking for him for at least an hour. The Gestapo night crew would take at least a few more minutes after that before rousing themselves to go out and check. It would be some time after that before any kind of organized search for the killer would begin. And there would be every reason to believe it had been a local grievance, because Vogl dealt with local people. That's where they would start investigating, not at the Dutch border. This was going to work.

I sipped schnapps from a flask as I sat in the car. The street was dark and there was nobody out. Between 7:30 and 9:30, only two cars drove past. I closed my eyes at one point and woke with a start, but a look at my watch told me I hadn't been asleep a minute. In that short time, though, I felt this flicker of photographs streaming through my subconscious, of Otto and Hannah and Henry and Leon and even Johanna—I was surprised at that—and of me in two particular places: hiding in that barn during the war, and peeking through the window of that classroom door.

At about 9:45, I got out of the car, crossed the street and walked toward Bischoffshausen. As I reached the alley, I ducked, walked halfway down, and took a piss against the wall. If anyone had happened upon the scene, they would think nothing of it.

Buttoning up, I headed toward the end of the alley, where it met the little street behind the hotel. There Vogl's car was, the big black Daimler. I stood at the end of the alley and began to smoke. It was a habit I had given up 15 years earlier, and it actually dawned on me that Vogl might have noticed I had never smoked in his presence before, not even after dinner that first night I met him. But I could live with that contradiction—it wouldn't register with him right away, and he wasn't going to have much time to think about inconsistencies or anything else.

Standing there, smoking, checking my watch every 30 seconds, the adrenaline rose and the hand that held the cigarette shook. I really was doing this. I thought of Otto for a second, and how he would crucify me if he knew what I had planned. Otto did not do vengeance. And Otto did not take personal risks. But if I could tell him, I would say that, yes, I was doing this because of him—but I was also doing it for myself.

After waiting a few minutes, I decided that standing on the street behind the hotel and not in the alley itself made the most sense. Just a step or two around the corner, leaning casually against the brick wall, finishing a last smoke before heading back into the hotel—again, if anyone came upon me, they wouldn't think twice.

I leaned then, left shoulder against the brick wall, facing the alley about two feet ahead, smoking. The night was quiet. Then I heard someone, first footsteps in the alley, then a soft whistling. I couldn't make out the tune. I looked at my watch quickly. It was 9:55. This had to be Vogl.

I tried to look casual. I decided I would walk into the intersection between the alley and the street and then turn on my heel, as if pacing as I finished my cigarette. The whistling had stopped but the footsteps grew louder. I fingered the flick knife in my pocket. I did not look down the alley—easy now, relaxed, casual, not to appear as if I were expecting to see anyone, no less Vogl. I threw the cigarette to the ground and stubbed it out, prepared to turn and head back for the hotel's rear door, fully expecting to be stopped by a shout of, "Alex, is that you?"

What stopped me instead was a blow from behind, and then a handkerchief held over my nose and mouth, and then sleep.

48

The cell was lit by an overhead fixture. The walls were plaster painted white, amplifying the light. The bunk was just a mattress on the floor, the straw spilling out of the sides. I fully expected to see bugs crawling on the bed, and on me, but when I finally opened my eyes, I couldn't see anything, not with any degree of focus. I was in a kind of fog, much worse than the worst hangover.

Where was I? I could tell I wasn't in the cellar at EL-DE Haus —this cell was different, everything about it, size, shape, and including that there was no writing on the wall—but, beyond that, I had no idea. The last thing I remembered was being in the alley, hearing the whistling, waiting for Vogl. I coudln't remember seeing him. Whatever was done to me, he didn't do it —at least not physically. But he probably ordered it.

But then, why wasn't I in EL-DE Haus? If Vogl had somehow sniffed out my plan—and I really didn't think that was possible —why wasn't I in Gestapo headquarters in Cologne? Maybe someone had seen me sitting in the car and became suspicious, but they would have called the police, and I would have been cuffed and arrested, not knocked down and then, I thought, drugged. When I was hit, it was on the shoulder, not the head—at least my shoulder was what still hurt. And I remembered a kind of chemical smell on the handkerchief that was clamped onto my face. The fogginess was likely a hangover from whatever had been on that handkerchief.

I didn't know where I was. I didn't know how long I had been in the cell—day or days, night or nights, no clue. I had a vague sense that I'd woken up at one point, lying down in the back of a car, but it might have been a dream. I wasn't sure. I wasn't sure of anything—except, that is, that I was fucked.

Leon had warned me. Grundman had warned me. Groucho had warned me. But here I was, too smart for my own good, loading on the self-pity. Then the key turned in the lock of the cell door. A guard I did not recognize came in carrying a tin tray with a cup of black coffee and two slices of brown bread.

"Good, you're awake. Eat up, use the facilities," he said, pointing to the bucket in the corner. "Try to make yourself look presentable. The tribunal is in 15 minutes."

Then he was gone, the door clanging shut. Tribunal? That sounded like a military court, but what did any of this have to do with the military? The truth was, what did they possibly have me on? Nobody in Germany knew the details of my plan, or that there even was a plan. All I had done was loiter in an alley, smoking a cigarette, behind a hotel where I was well known, where I had been a guest twice a year for the last 15 years. If they caught Major Peiper, and he talked, then I had a problem. But even then, even if that had happened, how had they found me so quickly? Peiper didn't know where I was going. And I had driven around Cologne for over an hour before parking across the street from Bischoffshausen. There was no way anybody was following me.

None of it made sense. But it didn't matter because, after about 10 minutes, the guard was back and I was cuffed, hands behind my back. We left the cell, crossed an interior courtyard of some kind and headed into a different part of the building. It was night, but I still didn't know what day it was.

The room we entered was kind of a mock courtroom, with a table on the right, a table on the left, and a third table on a raised platform in front of them and between them. In the back, there were about a dozen chairs in two rows. I was directed to sit in one of these chairs, with the guard standing beside me. There was no one else in the room, except for a couple of other guards.

I turned and looked at my guard, with a questioning shrug. He looked right through me.

In a minute or two, the door opened and Vogl walked in, accompanied by another man in a Gestapo uniform. They sat together at the table on the left. Vogl didn't look at me. He didn't even look in my direction.

A minute later, two more men walked in, also in uniform but not Gestapo. It took me a second, but then I recognized one of them: General Fritz Ritter from the Abwehr, Uncle Otto's old running buddy, the guy who I had met at dinner in Nuremberg. We made eye contact, but only for a second. Friend or foe? I thought friend, but I couldn't tell for sure. It was a swift glance, and his face betrayed nothing.

What the hell was this? What had I gotten myself into? I had no idea. I couldn't even imagine. But then came the order, "All rise." And so we did, as the man who would sit at the table on the raised platform entered the room and climbed onto his perch. I didn't know him, but I knew him. Everybody in Germany knew him, everybody who had ever seen a newsreel in a movie in the last five years, everybody who had heard his slavish, almost cartoonish speeches in praise of Big Adolf.

"All right, let's get to it," he said, oddly fidgeting. The judge, or whatever you wanted to call him, was Rudolf Hess, the Deputy Führer.

49

It is hard to overestimate what those newsreels meant—and we saw plenty of them in Austria, given that the government needed to play nice with Germany to get Austrian films distributed in the Reich. They took our crap films, we took their crap newsreels. That was the deal.

So we saw all of Hitler's top henchmen on a pretty regular basis. Mostly, you were left with snapshot impressions, one-liners to describe them. Goebbels was a little weasel. Himmler was an evil worm. Göring was just a fat fuck. But Hess was different, a bit squirrelly, kind of a nut. The other guys seemed like operators. Hess seemed slavish by comparison, the truest of true believers, without an original thought of his own. Whether it was true or not was beside the point. That was the impression.

And now, sitting in the same room with him, I couldn't shake that notion. He was up on that platform, clearly annoyed to be there, foot tapping, both hands on the table in front of him, fidgeting with a coin. He had no paperwork before him. He was accompanied by one aide, dressed in civilian clothes, who sat in a chair back by the door and immediately began reading the *Völkischer Beobachter*, the Nazis' favorite rag. The headline screamed, "The Shame of Vienna." I could only guess what atrocity they had concocted.

"Gentlemen, the Führer has chosen me to mediate this dispute between your two services. But I have important business later this evening in Berchtesgaden. You have one hour. General Ritter, begin. You have five minutes to make an opening statement, then Captain Vogl will follow. Then we will hear, I assume, from the witness."

Looking around the room, seeing no one else besides the guards, it seemed that the witness was me.

Ritter stood and made this charge: that Vogl was guilty of treason against the Third Reich. "He has, over the course of many months, traded information with an agent of a foreign government in exchange for money. His motive was not ideological. It was simple greed, and we have the incontrovertible proof. He believes in nothing. He is loyal to nothing. He betrayed the Führer and the Fatherland for filthy lucre, nothing more."

Vogl shook his head as Ritter spoke. He looked tired, almost beaten. I had no idea what the look on my face was, but it likely approximated astonishment. Because if Vogl was a traitor, then Göring was a swimsuit model. There was just no way, unless he was an actor of unparalleled skill. But beyond that, how were they planning to use me to prove it? Because there wasn't anything. If they asked me under oath what kind of Nazi I thought Vogl was, I would honestly answer that I thought he was the creepiest true believer I had ever met. But beyond that, why had Ritter chosen me to be a pawn in this? I was usually pretty good at reading people, and I'd thought he was a decent guy who genuinely liked my uncle. But he had just identified me as a spy.

Ritter sat, and Vogl stood. His voice was hoarse. He really did seem beaten. "The deceit of the Abwehr and of General Ritter is clever but reprehensible. He has fabricated a case against me for a simple reason: He is the traitor, and he knew I was getting too close to his despicable secret."

That was it. Vogl sat again. Hess seemed stunned that Vogl's presentation was so short—he used about 30 seconds of his allotted five minutes. It took Hess a few seconds to say anything as everyone waited. Finally, "General Ritter, what is your proof?"

"I would like to interview the witness, Herr Deputy Führer."

"And what is his name?"

"Alex Kovacs."

"The witness will stand."

So I stood. So it was me. There was a dangerous game being played here, but I knew neither the rules nor my part. I didn't know if I should tell the truth or lie or what. I didn't know if it even mattered, seeing as how I was likely fucked either way. I mean, I was the only one wearing handcuffs. And then came the first question from Ritter: "Herr Kovacs, have we ever met before?"

I wanted to believe that Ritter was on my side somehow, but I couldn't figure out the play. I thought the thing to do was tell the truth whenever possible, just for consistency's sake. I also figured he wouldn't have asked the question unless he wanted people to know the answer—or he thought they already knew the answer and just wanted to get it out of the way. Anyway, I decided on the truth, for now.

"Yes, we have met."

"And what were the circumstances?"

"I was dining with a client in Nuremberg. You knew him from your service in the Great War. You sat down at our table and reminisced."

I decided to leave out the part about Ritter knowing Uncle Otto. I figured Ritter would lead me there if that was where he wanted me to go. He didn't.

"What is your business, Herr Kovacs?"

I offered a short spiel about selling magnesite. Hess appeared to be preoccupied with the coin that he was now spinning on the table.

"Are you a spy for the Czech government, Herr Kovacs?"

"Absolutely not. I'm just a magnesite salesman."

Ritter returned to his table to retrieve a piece of paper from which he read. "Herr Kovacs, did you have lunch at Dimble's restaurant in Frankfurt on February 23rd of this year?"

Shit. What was this?

"Yes. While my train to Cologne was making an extended stop, I had lunch at Dimble's. It's close to the station."

"Did you visit the toilet in that restaurant?"

"Probably. I don't remember."

"Did you retrieve an envelope taped to the underside of the toilet tank in that restroom?"

I denied it because it was the truth. But the question opened up two more for me. One: How did Ritter know I'd had lunch in Frankfurt? Two: How were Groucho and the Czech intelligence service involved in this? Because they'd sent me on that pointless errand to the restaurant in the first place. Had they been setting me up?

It was getting hard to focus in the fog. Then Ritter turned from me to Vogl, pointing and saying, "And isn't it true, Captain Vogl, that you had a gabelfrühstück at Dimble's restaurant in Frankfurt several hours before Herr Kovacs did on February 23rd?"

Again, as if the life had been beaten out of him in the cellar at EL-DE Haus, Vogl replied in a monotone, "Yes, I ate in the restaurant."

"Were you in Frankfurt on official business?"

Pause. "No."

"Why were you there?"

Longer pause. "I was meeting a friend."

"A woman? Is her name Elsa Haas? Was this an illicit relationship? You are married, Captain Vogl, correct?"

Vogl did not answer, instead looking down at his hands, folded on the table in front of him.

Ritter went on, ignoring the silence. "And the envelope, sir? You taped it under the lid of the toilet tank, correct?"

Barely a whisper. "There was no envelope."

"You are honor-bound to tell the truth, sir."

"There was no envelope."

Ritter returned his attention to a folder on the table. He opened it and removed what looked to be a bank book along with a separate sheet of paper. He approached Hess and handed them over. "Herr Deputy Führer, I offer this as further proof of Captain Vogl's treason. The bank book, from the Brust & Co. Bank in Zürich, was taken from Captain Vogl's coat pocket on Wednesday night when he and Herr Kovacs were taken into custody in the alley behind the Dom Hotel in Cologne. As you can see, several deposits totaling ten thousand Swiss francs have been made over the last 18 months. As you can also see, the name on the bearer line of the account book is that of Captain Vogl."

Vogl replied in a voice so low that I wondered if Hess could hear him. "I have never seen this before."

"The document accompanying the bank book, Herr Deputy Führer, is a report of a fingerprint analysis of the bank book performed by Abwehr technicians, an analysis attended by a Gestapo observer. Both the Abwehr and Gestapo representatives have signed the letter. There were two identifiable sets of fingerprints on the book and two that were not. The identifiable prints belong to Captain Vogl and Herr Kovacs."

Ritter turned to me. "Do you have any dealings with the Brust & Co. Bank?"

I had no idea what was going on. I could barely focus. I

defaulted to the truth, even though I was pretty sure there was no way they could know about my private dealings with a private bank. I mean, that was the whole point of a Swiss bank. "I have an account at Brust & Co.," I said, leaving out Hannah.

"And did you make the deposits in Captain Vogl's account?"

"No."

"Did you arrange for those deposits?"

"No."

"Did you give him the bank book?"

"No."

"Then how did your fingerprints get on it?"

I had no answer. Ritter sat down. It appeared that he was finished.

50

The silence lingered for several seconds before Hess finally looked down and said, "Captain Vogl?"

A ghost in a black uniform, appearing as dead as the death's head emblem he wore so proudly, Vogl stood and began speaking. He talked about a suspicion that an unnamed Abwehr officer had traveled into Czechoslovakia in the summer of 1936 with a briefcase full of secret papers about Gestapo troop strength in various sectors of Germany and their field radio codes—information that the Gestapo later found out was in Czech hands from a double agent of their own. Researching travel records of Abwehr officers in the eastern sector indicated three possibilities. Two were eliminated with a reasonable level of confidence, leaving Ritter by process of elimination.

"That is when we began following General Ritter on an intermittent basis. The truth was, he eluded us for hours at a time, occasionally days at a time, and this elusiveness, in and of itself, continued to fuel our suspicions."

As he spoke and got into the narrative, Vogl seemed to regain a bit of his strength. He opened a file folder on the table and picked up a sheet of paper to which he referred as he continued:

"In the fall of 1936, while surveilling General Ritter in Cologne, our agents observed him meeting in the bar of the Wasserhof Hotel with Otto Kovacs, the uncle of our star witness today. Otto Kovacs also was an executive in the family mining company. I personally supervised the subsequent questioning of Otto Kovacs, but he denied being a spy for either Czechoslovakia or Austria, his countries of birth and residence, respectively. Otto Kovacs subsequently committed suicide, but it appears that his nephew has taken his place. We observed General Ritter meeting with Alex Kovacs in the restaurant in Nuremberg, a meeting that Mr. Kovacs acknowledged in his testimony."

The portrait Vogl was painting, and the mention of Otto, brought back every conflicted feeling I had experienced since his death. I now knew who he drank with the last night of his life. But could he have been a spy after all? Or was this just two old friends getting together to tell old stories? As those questions swirled, my hatred for Vogl was reinforced. He had tortured Otto. He just admitted it.

Vogl looked up at Hess. "Again, Herr Deputy Führer, agents of the Gestapo assigned to the task of surveilling General Ritter lost track of him on several occasions. On at least two of those occasions, Alex Kovacs was within fifty miles of our last sighting of the general at the same time, traveling as he did for his magnesite mine. We believed we were getting close to catching the general in the act."

Vogl lifted another paper from the file folder. "Besides the circumstantial case we had assembled, our double agent in Prague told us that there was concern in the Czech intelligence service, and I quote, 'that our most productive information source is sensing he is in jeopardy.' That was about two weeks ago, Herr Deputy Führer. That is when this smear against my name was obviously concocted."

He stopped, then smiled. "With permission, Herr Deputy Führer, I would like to question Herr Kovacs."

Hess waved his assent. Vogl turned toward me.

"Just one question, Herr Kovacs. What were you doing in the alley behind the Dom Hotel on Wednesday night? Were you not there at the direction of General Ritter, as a part of this plot to frame me?"

"I was not."

Vogl picked at still another piece of paper. "Then why, sir, did you enter the country with a false passport on Tuesday, in a car you had hired in Zürich, a car that was parked a block away from the alley? Why did you stay in Bonn on Tuesday night at the Stark Hotel, using that false passport? Why the secrecy, if this was just a normal business trip?"

I thought for a second. But the problem was, I didn't know if I could trust anybody. I could say that I was in the alley to give Vogl the bank book, but that would be an admission that I was a spy. I could say that I was there at Ritter's direction, to frame Vogl, but I would be in the same spot.

So, the truth. "I was in the alley to kill you, Captain Vogl, to avenge the death of my uncle."

At this, Hess dropped his coin. It rolled off the platform, and everyone seemed to watch it until it settled on the floor. Hess seemed interested for the first time. "I thought Captain Vogl said your uncle committed suicide."

"I believe that was a lie."

Vogl was silent. Hess was now fully engaged. "How did you plan to kill him?"

"With a knife."

"Is the knife in evidence? Let me see the knife."

Ritter lifted a briefcase from the floor, removed a large envelope, reached in, grabbed the knife, and handed it to Hess. He fondled the leather, weighing it in his hand, feeling the balance.

Then he flicked open the blade. He positioned it just so under an overhead light and squinted to read the manufacturer's engraving. "Solingen, I knew it. Excellent quality. Excellent."

At which point, Hess pocketed the knife. He was taking it for himself. "Captain Vogl, from the look on your face, I will assume you did not know of Herr Kovacs's plans. And you, General?"

Ritter stood and spoke confidently. "We believe Herr Kovacs is lying. He is a spy for Czechoslovakia; we are confident of that. His entry into the country with a false passport just added to our confidence. We were following both him and Captain Vogl, and we believe we interrupted a clandestine meeting between two espionage professionals who were working to sabotage the Führer's vision and the Third Reich's future."

With that, Vogl sat. Both sides appeared to be done. The room was silent, awaiting some signal from Hess. But all he did was clear his throat to get the attention of the aide who had been reading the newspaper, then motion toward the wayward coin on the floor. The aide walked over, picked it up, and handed it up to Hess on his little platform. Hess began to spin it again on the table.

As before, there was only one certainty: that I was fucked. Both sides had called me a spy, sacrificing me as a pawn in a bigger game. How either of them knew for sure was beside the point. It was the only consistency that existed in the two stories: Alex Kovacs, spy. However Hess decided, I was still going to be leaving the room in handcuffs. If I was lucky, they would just deport me. But I wasn't feeling lucky, not even a little bit.

I didn't know how long we waited—five minutes, 10 minutes. The only sounds I heard were my own breathing and Hess's damn coin. Then Hess suddenly looked at his watch and, as if startled at what he saw, began to speak.

"The guards will come to the front of the room." Three of them did just that, one carrying leg chains.

"Captain Vogl, you will be taken into custody and delivered to the Abwehr for further interrogation. General Ritter, you are free to go."

That was it. Hess offered no explanation for his decision. Vogl had seemed resigned to the verdict all along and stood calmly as the leg irons were attached. Ritter gave no reaction, gathering his papers and then standing at attention as Hess descended from his perch.

Perhaps no one else noticed, but it certainly caught my attention that Hess had said nothing about me. But then, as his aide helped him on with his overcoat, he caught my eye.

"Oh, yes. Herr Kovacs will be transported to Dachau in the morning."

Then he was gone, followed by Ritter, and then by Vogl, clanking along, one guard at each elbow, one behind. As he trudged by, he stopped for a second at my side and leaned in and smiled.

And then Vogl whispered to me, "The walls are strong enough. The real problems are inside, not outside."

51

Dachau wasn't a secret place—they'd done newspaper stories on it when it opened, and we saw at least one newsreel on it. I couldn't remember the term they used—something like "re-education facility," I wasn't sure—but the pictures showed people who were doing a lot of physical labor, then listening to lectures and eating happy meals together. They wanted to make it out like it was a rustic summer camp just outside of Munich—the kind of rustic summer camp where you sent enemies of the state, mind you—with no downsides except for maybe a sore back from all of that good, honest heavy lifting, or water that was too cold in the showers. I didn't believe it, not really, but as I lay there on the straw mattress, back in the same cell, I began conning myself into believing parts of it. You know, hey, it looked like there was meat in the stew they served on that newsreel.

I didn't think I fell asleep, but maybe I had because I was so startled when I heard the key turn in the lock and the door of the cell open. It wasn't the customary guard. It was Ritter, alone.

He tossed me an overcoat and a hat. "Put them on, quick."

When I did, I saw that I was suddenly an officer in the German army. I couldn't tell the rank.

"Quick, quick, just walk right behind me and don't say anything." And so we walked, out of the cell, down a hallway, across the courtyard, through an archway, into another courtyard, and then into a waiting car. We did not see a guard.

"I'll get in the back. You drive. At the guard shack, just point to me in the back. He won't say anything. Then make a right turn, drive a block, and pull over."

It went exactly as he said it would, at which point he got into the driver's seat and handed me a civilian overcoat to change into.

I got into the passenger seat and tossed the hat into the back seat. "Seeing as how I'm a civilian again, I have a question to ask you. With all due respect, sir, what the fuck is going on?"

Ritter smiled. "Can you just shut up and listen for a little while longer? We have a little less than an hour to drive."

"Drive where?"

"Just listen, okay?"

With that, Ritter began to tell the story. I had just spent the night in Traunheim, in a prison where, during the Great War, they had rounded up civilians who had a background in France or England. We were driving to the Austrian border, near Salzburg. I was going home, my role now finished.

And that role? "Vogl was right—I am a spy for the Czech government, and he was on to me. We needed to use you to get him. It was the only way we could think to do it. But look, I wouldn't have agreed if I hadn't been confident we could protect you."

"Confident? In that lunatic playing with the pfenning? Are you kidding me?"

Ritter ignored me and continued. The operation had been a couple of weeks in the planning. The blank bank book had to be obtained from Zürich. "That might have been the hardest part—you wouldn't believe how much money we had to pay one of their clerks to get it."

Ritter said the fingerprints were easy enough; they can be lifted with tape and transferred from a drinking glass, say, to another surface. The selection of Dimble's in Frankfurt for my lunch was easier: Vogl took his mistress there for a second breakfast every time he visited. That was really the key—that Vogl did have a flaw they could exploit. Without it, Ritter said, he wasn't sure they could have pulled it off. "Even with the bank book, convincing people that a completely straight arrow like Vogl was a spy would have been doable, but a stretch. But add in the mistress, and the arrow is suddenly a little bit bent. Just enough."

"But why didn't you just kill him? Or why didn't you let me kill him? You must have known what I was thinking. Groucho must have told you."

"Who's Groucho?"

I held two fingers over my upper lip. "My Czech contact."

"I haven't had the pleasure. And, yeah, he told his bosses about your plan. But it wouldn't work. I mean, first off, we couldn't count on you following through, and I was running out of time. We couldn't afford it if you chickened out. But more than that, killing Vogl wouldn't solve the problem—it would just put it off. If he's dead, his replacement just picks up his old cases. But if he's disgraced, and found guilty of fabricating evidence against me to preserve his dirty secrets, the case is closed. Nobody's going near me now."

It was the middle of the night. For the first half-hour or so, there was pretty much no traffic on the road. But as we got closer to the border, we began to see more of a military presence: not soldiers so much as trucks and other materiel, parked along the shoulders here and there on both sides of the road.

"What are they going to say back in Traunheim when they find my cell empty in a couple of hours?"

"It's been taken care of. Germans are great record-keepers but, well, let's just say that people get lost in Dachau all the time. Don't worry about that. Do you have any other questions?"

There was just one. It was the question that had started this whole thing. It was the line that intersected with all of the other lines.

"Otto?"

Ritter nodded. For a second, he looked as if he was going to cry. "I got him killed, and I have to live with that. It wasn't intentional, and there wasn't anything I could have done about it, but I got him killed. I got him killed by running into him in the bar at the Wasserhof that night.

"It was a total accident. We hadn't seen each other in probably close to 10 years, but there he was. Suddenly, we were retelling our old stories—we had a couple of others, besides Munich—and getting drunk and just laughing our asses off. But I was traveling early the next morning, and I couldn't make it too late a night, so we said our goodbyes and promised not to wait 10 years before doing it again, and that was it. When I found out he killed himself, I couldn't believe it. But I had no idea that Vogl had begun to suspect me at that point, no idea I was being followed. That didn't come until months later."

"So he wasn't a spy?"

"Otto? No way. At least not with me. It was just a terrible misfortune. I found out much later that they questioned him the same night we met. I'm convinced they threw him off that bridge. And it's my fault."

If Ritter was looking for me to let him off the hook somehow, to offer some kind of absolution, he was disappointed. I just sat there and stared out the window. Soon we were stopped, stacked behind a column of trucks carrying troops. I pointed. "What's going on?"

"Oh, shit. You don't know, do you? About the plebiscite?"

I told him what I had heard.

"Well, your source was good. Schuschnigg announced it Wednesday night in a speech in Innsbruck. You were probably in the alley when he did it. The vote is supposed to be Sunday, but Hitler won't let it happen. We're invading. That's why Hess was in such a hurry—big planning meeting tonight in Berchtesgaden. It's Thursday night now going into Friday morning, and we're coming over the border on Saturday morning."

Ritter looked at his watch. "Maybe 30 hours from now, give or take. We've already closed the border. No trains are getting through."

The military column finally began to move, and Ritter made a left turn onto a smaller road. We were in the middle of dark farmland within a minute, with few visible landmarks, but Ritter seemed confident as he maneuvered right after one farmhouse, then left after the next, and then right again soon after that, past more farms set in small valleys among the mountains.

After another right turn into the woods, there was nothing for a while, just us on a single-track road, and then we passed another farm. "Okay, we're in Austria now, through a little back door. Almost there."

Farms quickly gave way to small houses, and then Ritter pulled over. "The Salzburg station is two blocks down the road and to the left. There's a night train to Vienna in twenty minutes. Here's some money. Make sure you're on it. But just so long as you understand . . ."

"Oh, I understand. I can't stay in Austria. That's pretty goddamn obvious at this point."

I opened the door, got out of the car, and started walking. I didn't say thank you. I didn't say fuck you. I didn't look back.

52

The train ride didn't take four hours. I tried to sleep a little and might have succeeded. I figured it was going to be my only chance to get a rest. Still, back in my apartment by 6 a.m., with a pile of newspapers—each more hysterical than the last, even the serious ones—I half fell asleep again. Then the banging on the door began. It was Henry.

I looked at the wall clock: 7:30. "A little early for a visit, isn't it?"

"Man, you look like shit."

"Right back at you, buddy."

"No, I mean, seriously. Are you okay?"

I hadn't seen myself in a mirror, so I decided to take Henry's word for it. Then I couldn't help myself and walked into the bathroom to see. He was right. But the thing about it was, I wasn't kidding about Henry. He looked as if he hadn't slept, and like he'd been wearing the same clothes for days.

He joined me for a peek at the mirror, then winced. "Look, it's a risk, but we both need to get cleaned up. You first, then me. Fifteen minutes."

"Risk? What's the risk?"

"I'll tell you when we're done."

The bath felt like a forbidden luxury, even if only for five minutes. The shave almost made me feel human again. Then I was out of the bathroom, and Henry took my place, having scavenged my wardrobe for clean clothes. Fifteen minutes turned into 25, but then we were out, walking down Mariahilfstrasse, away from the Ring. About three blocks down, we came upon a tired-looking café, the Linden.

Henry stopped. "You ever eaten here?"

"Are you kidding me? It stinks. You can smell it out here on the street."

"Perfect. Let's go in."

We ordered what turned out to be a more than serviceable breakfast—and the thing was, you got used to the smell. After the waiter brought the food, I finally said, "So what's going on?"

Henry pointed to a newspaper that a customer had left on an adjoining table. "You mean other than the obvious?"

"Yeah. What's the issue? What's the risk? Is it Fuchs?"

Henry's face indicated that he was shocked I knew about Captain Fuchs, or that I had guessed.

"I saw Max giving him an envelope. I figure that had something to do with it."

"That isn't the half of it. You probably figured that he goes to the back room at the club sometimes. Nothing unusual there—that's always been a part of the accommodation with the police, back to my father's day. Well, sometimes there's a young man in one of the rooms to meet him. Our friendly captain is, how do you say, of equal opportunity?"

"Oh, man." I could see where this was going.

"It's not my place to judge," Henry said, "and I don't. We don't advertise it, but it's a service we can provide. And as long as he needed me and I needed him, there really wasn't an issue."

"Except now Uncle Adolf is coming . . ."

"Exactly. So this is my problem now. Most of the cops are Nazis anyway, and you just know our boy wants to move up in the ranks once the Germans get here. So who can cause him trouble with his new bosses? Well, there's the guy who ran a small organized crime ring, the guy who paid off the local captain to protect just the kind of thing that the Nazis hate. And then there's the guy who can tell the Nazis that this ambitious little fascist is into the fellas. The problem is that both of those guys are me."

"Oh shit."

"Oh shit, indeed. But there's more. I haven't been in the bar in three days, and I haven't been home—a couple of my father's old boys have been giving me some cover. But my friend Captain Fuchs has been in there twice in the last two days, asking if they've seen either me or you. So what's with that? Why you? He only met you the one time, right?"

I could only guess that the Gestapo had put out a few feelers with their soon-to-be coworkers. It was the only thing that made sense—because Henry was right, I had only seen Fuchs the one time.

Whatever. It was time to tell Henry everything, and so I did. It took a while, from the very beginning to the scene in the alley and the mock trial and my being spirited across the border about eight hours earlier. Henry was either stunned or had suffered a stroke because his mouth was half-open for about the last two minutes of my story.

He snapped out of it when I stopped talking. "God . . . God, that means you can't stay, either."

He had known he couldn't stay, and I had known I couldn't stay, but the combination—and the very act of him saying it out loud—added a crushing finality to it. We both just looked at each other and shook our heads.

Henry began to wipe a tear, and I started talking to distract him. "Liesl?

He smiled. "We're leaving together. We're getting married, wherever. What about Johanna?"

I shrugged. "I don't know. We haven't talked about it."

"Does she know about all the cloak-and-dagger stuff?"

I shook my head. Henry was quiet again. "Leon knows—he's the only one. He figured it out from the start. Have you talked to him?"

"Not for a week, at least."

"But he knows he can't stay, right?"

"I don't know. But we both know the only way we'll get him to leave is by dragging him."

"Then we'll fucking drag him," I said.

Henry said he had access to a car and a plan for leaving that he had been working on and that it would accommodate all of us, plus Johanna if she wanted to go. I told him what I knew about the timing of the invasion, that the Germans would be in the country by this time tomorrow.

Henry stopped, seeming to calculate something in his head. "Okay, then it's got to be tonight. That's fine. I can get it together. But there are a couple of details I need to nail down, and I need to get Liesl ready and get her down to one small suitcase. That's all Johanna can take, if she's coming. You and I are going with the clothes on our backs."

"My clothes, you mean."

Henry opened the jacket, looking at the tailor's label on the inside pocket. "Same shit I wear. I thought you were better than that."

Henry reminded me that I couldn't go home, or to the office —Fuchs was probably checking both, growing increasingly frantic. He said we should meet at Café Louvre at seven. He asked me what I was going to do in the meantime, and I said I had to talk to Johanna, but first I had to find Leon.

"His apartment?"

"Nah."

"The Louvre?"

I pointed again to the newspaper on the adjoining table. "Yeah, I think that makes the most sense. If he isn't there, he'll be there soon."

53

Café Louvre was just this side of pandemonium. There were no regular customers that I could see, only reporters—almost every one that Leon had ever introduced me to, plus some others. Their wives were there, too, at least some of them, working as secretaries. One ran past me for the door, clutching a sheet of paper, likely headed for the telegraph office across the street. Another rushed past me the other way, returning with a sheet of paper of her own.

A waiter scooted past with a tray crammed with empty schnapps glasses. They weren't staffed for a big crowd, so I broke every rule of Viennese waiter–customer decorum and just caught his eye and pointed to an empty table on the periphery. He nodded. I ordered coffee with a shout, and he nodded again. It came in a few minutes, on a small metal tray, with two glasses of water, decorum partially restored, but only after he had delivered a bigger tray of full schnapps glasses to the journalists. It wasn't yet 11 a.m. Leon wasn't there.

They were in the midst of the biggest story of their lives—at least the biggest for most of them. You could sense both the excitement and the nerves. To blow this one somehow would be to blow their jobs, and they knew it.

Suddenly, I had a table-mate. Leon.

He leaned in. "See them over there? Scared shitless, every one."

"But wouldn't they be excited? I mean, a scoop on this one . . ."

"Scoop? They're not interested in scoops—they're just worried about being left behind. Look at them standing there—they're standing so close to each other, they're nearly hugging. It's kind of unspoken, but as long as they all write the same thing, everything will be fine with their bosses. So they're not out doing any reporting—they're just watching each other like hawks."

Just then, the man from the *Philadelphia Inquirer* walked into the café. A dozen reporters immediately surrounded him, grilling him, debriefing him. Philadelphia had been over by the Kärntnerstrasse, and he had seen some Nazis openly demonstrating. He also had a copy of the latest government handbill, urging a yes vote on the plebiscite. He said they were just throwing them out of the backs of trucks.

I pointed at the handbill. "Your printer friend?"

"Yeah. That would have been the story of my career if I'd been able to nail it down."

Just then, the *Chicago Daily News* brushed by, nodding at Leon. One of the reporters called out, "Stephansdom, one hour then back here, no more," and it was understood that he was going on a reporting excursion for some color from the streets, at which point he was expected back to share his work.

Leon scoffed. "Most of those old fucks are too scared to go out and do any reporting themselves." Then Watson from the *Manchester Guardian* walked in and calmly hung up his coat and hat. "But even more than the streets, they're scared of him most of all. He's been at this a long time and has diplomatic sources that even the guys at my paper don't have. And everybody knows it. If anybody is going to get a break on this one, it's him."

"But didn't you tell me he was generous with his information?"

"Yes. Ridiculously generous. Some of those lazy blockheads, I can't believe how patient he is with them. But would you share this story if you had it alone? If you were the only one who knew when the invasion was starting, would you share it with anyone?"

At which point, the obvious suddenly dawned on me. While the reporters crowded around the *Guardian* for a few crumbs, I told Leon everything that had happened in the last couple of days, beginning with Zürich and ending with my clandestine drive to the border, and what Ritter said to me about the invasion plans.

Suddenly, Leon was in full-on reporter mode, the questions coming quickly, one after the other—describe the military vehicles, approximately how far from the border were you, what time was it, what time again did he say the invasion was, when was the planning meeting at Berchtesgaden?

"Why aren't you writing any of this down?"

Leon nodded toward the pack of reporters. "Don't want them to think this is anything but a couple of friends having a cup of coffee."

"So we're not friends anymore? I'm hurt."

"We're best friends, but right now we're even more than that. I'm a reporter, and you're a 'diplomatic source' giving me the biggest story of my life."

Leon said they were running extras all day, special editions, every three hours. He looked at his watch. "I've got an hour to get this into the next one. I've got to get to a phone, and away from here."

I grabbed his arm and stopped him as he began to stand. I told him that Henry and Liesl and I were leaving and that he had to leave, too. I explained everything about us, and he nodded. I made my case, but he was defiant.

"Are you kidding me? I'm not leaving."

"Leon, be reasonable."

"No, you be reasonable. This is the biggest story I'm ever going to cover."

"It isn't worth dying over."

"I'm not going to die."

"They'll arrest you in an hour. Come on, think about it. Jews will be the first ones they come after when they get here, and Jewish newspaper reporters will be the first of the first. You think you'll be covering this big story, but they won't let you. The papers will never be allowed to print the truth. It isn't worth the risk."

I pointed over to the pack. "They'll probably throw all of them out in the first couple of days—but at least they'll get to leave."

"You worry too much."

"You're staying because of some fantasy. They'll never let you print the truth."

"But they're not here yet, and thanks to you, I have my biggest scoop ever. So let go of my arm."

Which I did, after getting him to promise to come back at seven. Leon walked out of the café slowly, so as not to attract attention. But once he was out the door, I watched him break into a run.

54

I rang the bell at Johanna's house, and Gibbs answered as he had a dozen times before, all formal dress and stern demeanor. After about my third visit, I started trying to get a laugh out of him with some kind of smart-ass remark, but it never worked. I never got a reply, never even a smile, just an escort to a chair in a little sitting room off of the entrance hall and a promise to fetch Johanna.

This time, I asked, "How's tricks, Gibbsy?"

This time, he answered, "Tricky, sir."

He walked me past the usual waiting place and into the family's main living room, a coldly formal space that happened to be warmed by the biggest fireplace I had ever seen, the opening six feet high and just as wide, the logs stacked to my waist. It was big enough to roast a Göring.

Johanna and her mother sat in matching wing chairs, 10 feet apart, staring at the fire, not talking. The old man wasn't with them. The radio glowed in the corner and played nondescript music. It was about a quarter till six, when the next scheduled news bulletins were customarily read.

Gibbs announced me and left. Johanna's mother did not

move a muscle in acknowledgment. Johanna looked over her left shoulder at me, but that was it. I was a day late on my scheduled return from Cologne, and I hadn't called or sent a telegram, all of which I was sure had frayed things between us even more. I leaned over for a kiss and received the royal cheek, warm from the fire. I sat down and embroidered a story about being late because the Germans had closed the border and the train connections were a mess, but for all of my efforts at lying, Johanna wasn't really listening. So then the three of us sat in the silence broken only by the forgettable music from the radio.

After an eternity, or five minutes, the baron arrived, shucking off his coat and handing it to Gibbs, who was struggling to keep up. The old man headed straight for the drinks cabinet, and poured himself a whiskey and his wife some port, or something similarly disgusting. The drinks were both in crystal tumblers, and they weren't small.

He plopped on the couch as we all looked at him expectantly. Finally, he said, "It's over. It's . . . it's just over."

His wife took a big slug. Johanna started to cry. The baron continued, "Look, he used us. That's just the truth of it. He's a goddamn snake, and he used us, and now he's thrown us away."

The baron stopped. I wasn't sure what he was talking about, so I punctured the silence with a question: "Schuschnigg?" He responded with a cold stare directed not so much at me as at Johanna, as if to ask her, "How could you last so long with this idiot?"

Finally, he said, "Yes, Schuschnigg. He told us for weeks that we were his trump card, that if it all went bad, an appeal to restore the monarchy would be his play. Well, it's all gone to shit, and he won't see us. He won't take a meeting. He won't take a phone call. He just used us."

The baroness took another gulp and then, so quietly, said: "And we used him, too. And it got us nowhere."

It had been going on for years—the monarchists supporting the government in general, and lately Schuschnigg in particular, because their only chance at a restoration of the monarchy was if Austria remained free. An Anschluss with Germany was the end of the monarchists' dreams. It was worse than any war. So they needed Austria intact, and Schuschnigg needed the monarchists, mostly because he couldn't count on support from the Nazis and the other nuts on the far right, or the socialists on the left.

So he strung them along, always telling them that a restoration was the long-term play even if it was impossible in the short term. And they strung him along, still feeling in their hearts that Schuschnigg was just their errand boy and that he recognized that an appeal to restore the Habsburgs was the ultimate hammer, the one that would unite the people against Hitler.

But now, this. The baron refilled his tumbler, then looked at his pocket watch. "I stopped at the café for a drink before I got here." The café was a little dark place on Bankgasse, about a block or so from the parliament, a gathering spot where the right people were able to stay informed. It didn't have a name over the door, and I didn't even know what it was really called.

"I don't know if the radio will announce it now, but Schuschnigg is probably resigning tonight," the baron said. "That's the talk, anyway. The plebiscite is going to be called off. It's over. They'll be here tomorrow."

They. No explanation necessary.

Johanna let out a noise that was half gasp, half cry. I grabbed her by the elbow. "Come on, we have to talk." She resisted, then relented. We crossed the hall to the sitting room where I usually waited for her.

"I have to leave."

"Of course you do. You just got here."

"I have to leave Austria, tonight."

Then I explained why, the whole truth—the spying, the plan to kill Vogl, the trial, the escape, all of it. When I finished, I was expecting some acknowledgment of my predicament, and maybe my courage. Instead, she just laughed—that fake fucking rich person's laugh, like out of a British drawing-room comedy.

"You never cared, did you?"

"What are you talking about? I risked my life."

"You never cared about us."

"I could never figure out us. Or you. Your father is a raving anti-Semite, you're not—except maybe a little. You're all about being a modern, independent woman, but you're also all about this house and whatever old money it still represents."

"And you're a coward who has never come close to getting married and never will. What are you afraid of? I'm committed to my family. I'm committed to this country. I could have been committed to you. What have you ever been committed to? Ever?"

I just stared at her. I was going to ask her if she wanted to come with us, but I didn't—partly because I didn't want her to come but mostly because Johanna turned and left me standing there with my mouth open, returning to her parents, and the big fireplace, and the radio announcer who might or might not have been spelling out the final details of their doom. But even if I did ask, she was never leaving. I think I always knew that. The three of them were going to sell off their lives, piece by piece, and throw parties for their new overlords, and kiss whatever Nazi asses were presented to them, and do whatever it took to survive. Gibbs was probably downstairs already, fashioning a Nazi armband for the old man out of whatever scraps of old cloth he could find.

55

Café Louvre at 7 p.m. was the same as it had been at 11 a.m., only more so. There still were no regular customers, not one, but even more reporters. They probably hadn't been drinking nonstop for eight hours—there were some half-empty coffee cups on the tables to go along with the completely empty schnapps glasses, and the remnants of a couple of picked-over schnitzels—but they had apparently been drinking plenty. Their clothes were just a bit more disheveled—neckties looser, shirttails untidier—and the volume of the place was much louder. It was as loud as I had ever heard it.

Two questions pierced the maelstrom:

"What time is he starting?"

"Where is the fucking radio?"

It turns out that the "he" was Schuschnigg and that the radio was being carried in through the door leading to the kitchen by two of the busboys. We had always thought that waiters spent their time making things just so for the customers when they went through those doors. Now we knew better.

The belief was that Schuschnigg was going to speak at around 7:30, but nobody was exactly sure. What he was going to say was also unknown, although everybody had a guess: that Mr. Plebescite was going to head for the hinterland. Every calculation he had made had been wrong. He thought he could deal with Hitler face-to-face at Berchtesgaden, that he somehow had some leverage over him, and instead ended up wetting his pants. Then he thought he could call the snap plebiscite and show the world that the country wanted independence, and instead ended up giving Hitler no choice but to take the army out for a morning constitutional. And now he was going to quit and run away. Idiot.

I had grabbed a copy of the latest edition of *Die Neue Freie Presse* and read it while I waited for Henry and Liesl. Leon's story was on the front page, at the top, under the gigantic headline, "Invasion Expected Saturday."

It was a long story that rounded up information from all over the city, including the notion that Schuschnigg had been ordered to resign by the Germans and that Seyss-Inquart would take his place. It included a box near the top listing a half-dozen reporters who contributed. But the byline was Leon's.

I looked up and saw Watson from the *Manchester Guardian* sitting next to me. He pointed to the byline. "Your friend, he does good work."

"Has anyone else confirmed it?"

"I have, but please keep that between us. And I have a few other details that no one else does, that I will be filing soon. But Leon deserves the credit. Every one of the rest of them will have to credit his paper if the story holds for a few more hours. American deadlines are just about here."

It was, as Leon had said, the biggest story of his life. I couldn't help but wonder, for all of their sweat and stress, if anyone outside of this room would even remember at this time tomorrow.

"What do you expect from Schuschnigg?"

He stopped for a second. "Well, he has surprised us a few times lately, so I'm not sure I would put money on it. But I think he's quitting. He's afraid to fight. I'll never quite understand him —he's this great Austrian patriot, but I think he's got a German soul. And that conflict, it's just led to so much confusion."

He got up just as Henry and Liesl arrived. She was calm. Henry was bouncing. "Where's Leon?"

I told him that he promised to be here at seven and that we had to wait until at least eight. Besides, Schuschnigg was going to be on the radio, and we should listen.

"Fifteen minutes, not a big deal," I said.

"You don't know that. I don't know that."

I looked at Liesl. "Has he been like this all day?"

She smiled. "This is calm. But he's right, we don't know."

"Fifteen minutes."

"Are you sure he's coming with us?"

I hesitated, then admitted that I didn't know. At which point, Henry's bouncing stopped. "If we have to kidnap him, we kidnap him. But you'll have to be the one who knocks him out."

I laughed. Liesl laughed. Henry did not. The awkwardness was saved by a chorus of shushing as the correspondents gathered around the radio, notepads and pencils in hand. We joined on the periphery. It was Schuschnigg.

"The German government today handed to President Miklas an ultimatum, with a time limit, ordering him to nominate as chancellor a person designated by the German government . . . otherwise, German troops will invade Austria."

Leon walked into the café, and we made eye contact. Grim did not begin to describe his face. He joined us.

". . . I declare before the world that the reports launched in Germany concerning disorders by the workers, the shedding of streams of blood and the creation of a situation beyond the control of the Austrian government are lies from A to Z. President Miklas has asked me to tell the people of Austria that we have yielded to force since we are not prepared even in this terrible hour to shed blood. We have decided to order the troops to offer no resistance."

So that was it. The Germans would waltz in, one-two-three, one-two-three. Austria wouldn't even pretend to resist. There was some other stuff, and the reporters were all scribbling with a particular fury. Then came the end:

". . . So I take leave of the Austrian people with a German word of farewell, uttered from the depth of my heart: God protect Austria!"

That was it, followed by the national anthem, over and over. The reporters spent a couple of minutes going over their notes, making sure they had identified the key quotations and that they had all heard them the same way—especially the ending. Then they flooded across the street to the telegraph office. The four of us, and the waiters clearing the tables, were the only people left in the place.

Liesl looked at me. "Johanna?"

I shook my head. That would have to do, because I just didn't have it in me to tell them what had happened. Then I looked at Leon.

"So?"

"I wasn't going to leave. I really wasn't."

"But you are now?"

"About a half-hour ago, I called the office. I was over near the Chancellery, and I didn't have anything much to add, but I was just checking in. I dialed direct to Althauser's office—he's the editor. You've heard me talk about him. Somebody else answered. I asked for Althauser. He said that he was no longer the editor and that he had been replaced by the guy on the phone. I didn't get his name. He asked me who I was and I hung up.

"Then I called directly to Keil's desk in the newsroom—he's another reporter. He picked up, and I asked him what was going on. He said Althauser had gone for dinner with his family—he'd been in the office all day, putting out all of the extras. When he came back to put out the morning edition, they arrested him. Said they were the police, and that they were taking over."

Henry looked confused. "They're not even here yet. How can they be here?"

Liesl grabbed his hand. "They've always been here."

Leon said, "Keil is Catholic, so he's okay. But he told me not to come back. He said they grabbed every Jew in the newsroom. He's calling Jewish reporters at their homes and telling them to stay away."

Leon was crying. "It's over. It's fucking over."

We all sat, exhausted. I wasn't sure I had ever seen Leon cry. After a minute, Henry looked at his watch. "Look, we have to go now. After what you just said, now more than ever. The car's right outside."

As we got in, an open truck pulled up in front of the telegraph office, and a dozen Brownshirts jumped out and ran for the front door. We kept our heads down. From what Henry had said, Liesl had the one bag in the trunk. The rest of us, friends for 20 years, had each other and the clothes on our backs and nothing else—except for Leon, who had scooped up from the table the copy of the extra from *Die Neue Freie Presse.*

56

The car had belonged to Henry's father. It was a massive black Daimler that we used to call the Love Tank when we were triple-dating in our twenties—Henry and whoever up front, Leon and I and our whoevers in back, three couples in all manner of embrace and with room left over besides. Honestly, a family of four could have lived comfortably inside, and besides that, it was heavy enough that it could have stopped an artillery shell. The glass was double thick, too. "As Pop said, 'I don't know if it would slow down a .38 from six feet, but maybe 20 feet—so why not?'"

When Henry's father sold off the loansharking part of the family business, he included the car in the deal. The guy who bought it, Putzi Brandstetter, was one of his father's oldest friends, and he sold him the territory for half of what it was probably worth. So when Henry asked Putzi to borrow the car, there was no hesitation; he said he'd have somebody pick it up in Bratislava next week: "He said, 'Just leave the keys at Café Milos.'" Putzi had even restocked the bar in the back.

The drive to Bratislava was about 50 miles, most of it right along the Danube. Not that this was a sightseeing trip, but you could see it off to the left sometimes, or at least the moon reflecting on the water. While we drove, Henry laid out the details of his plan. He didn't think the regular border checkpoint made a lot of sense, and I couldn't disagree. As he said, "Me and Alex could be on a list at this point, and Leon—every Jew—is always going to be on a list. But—oh shit—Leon, do you even have your passport?"

He didn't, which clinched it. That and the fact that, as we approached the border, a ribbon of red taillights greeted us. A long ribbon. Henry said, "We're more than a half-mile from the border. Maybe a mile. That could be 200 cars ahead of us. It'll take hours. This is why . . ."

He stopped and jerked a U-turn—which was really a three-point turn in the Tank—that sent us heading back toward Vienna. "The turnoff was up there, but I don't want anybody following us. We can get to it another way, from back here."

After about two minutes, Henry made a right turn at a forlorn-looking farmhouse, dark and maybe abandoned. No one followed us as he drove us into the black. The fields were still frozen, weeks from planting. That moon—less than full, more than half—bathed everything in a soft glow.

This was Henry's plan: Up ahead, after a couple of turns, we would pass another farm that belonged to the guy who had supplied the lamb to Fessler's for as long as Henry's father owned it. On the far side of his land was a little road—it was on all the maps—that led into Czechoslovakia. Before the war, when we were all one big happy Austria-Hungary, it didn't matter. After Versailles carved us up, though, this was suddenly a border crossing—this road that was about eight feet wide. So the Austrians and Czechs each dutifully built little guard shacks on either side of the imaginary line and then proceeded to forget about them. The farmer told Henry—and he'd checked with him again last week—that the Czechs staffed their side for about six months in 1919 before quitting, and that the Austrians had never even bothered. The shacks were barely standing, all of their glass broken. The roof of the hut on the Austrian side was gone completely—at least, that's what Henry said.

"The farmer told me that kids have been using it as a back road into Bratislava forever—it's cheap to drink there—and the farmers have been using it to avoid customs inspectors and do a little business on the side. It's like their own private pipeline."

So, for the second time in as many nights, I was going to be fleeing the Nazis by sneaking across a border on a darkened back road. The truth was, I was just being carried along at this point. The last decision I had made was to go into that alley in Cologne. Everything since then was just me clinging to a piece of driftwood in a rushing river.

As Henry snaked around the dark farm roads, Leon was getting worried. He was riding shotgun, with Liesl and me in the back. "Are you sure about this? Do you know where you are?"

"Calm down. That's our friendly farmer's house on the right —up there, with the flagpole and the Austrian flag. It's the next left."

The flag, red and white, hung limp as we passed. That's when it really hit me: He'd have to take it down tomorrow or deal with some officious Nazi in no time.

We made the left turn, and the road really was about eight feet wide. The tank came close to filling it. If somebody came in the other direction, one of us would be in a ditch. We drove for about two minutes, and the farmland gave way to forest, and then Henry warned us, "Hang on, there's a hairpin turn to the left, right before we get to the guard shacks."

When he turned, two spotlights suddenly flashed on, blinding us. Henry stopped. Quiet curses filled the car. There was no way to turn around. We were maybe 200 feet from the guard shack, and we were paralyzed.

Then, from a bullhorn, "Get out of the car, please, and approach the checkpoint."

We all looked at each other. To get out was to get sent back to Vienna. That wasn't an option, not now, not if they were suddenly guarding border crossings that had never been defended. They had seized the newspapers, and probably the telegraph and radio stations, and they had manned a border crossing on a cow path—all before the Germans even invaded. This was so over.

The silence in the car was almost scarier than that thought. Nobody knew what to do. Finally, I said, "Okay, here's what we do. Liesl, lay on the floor and don't get up. I'm going to open my door and get out. I'll just stand there for a second, shut my door, take a step. You two start to open your doors. Then I'll run for those woods."

I gestured to the left. It was maybe a hundred feet to the tree line.

"That will distract him. Then you just fucking floor it, straight ahead, right at him. First, he'll be looking at me, then you'll be going right at him—he'll just tumble out of the way. Just stay down as low as you can."

Henry and Leon were silent, and then they started to disagree, and then the bullhorn again: "Get out of the vehicle and approach the checkpoint. This is your last warning."

I opened the door, got out, yelled ahead, "Yes, sir, we're coming." I leaned back in through the window. "I'll take two steps forward and then run—that's when you gun it. Open your doors, just a little, and now I'm going to start to walk."

They opened their doors.

One step.

Second step.

I ran. The doors slammed, *bang-bang*, and the Love Tank accelerated with a roar. I heard the slams and the roar, and I heard my breath as I ran, and I heard some yelling—there must have been more than one man at the checkpoint—and I heard the gunshot. It was such a pure and clean sound, piercing the rest of the noise.

57

Café Milos was a Hungarian caricature plopped down in a Slovakian nightmare. Everything—carpet, tablecloths, napkins, curtains, wallpaper, everything—was red, or at least red-dominated. Everything on the menu tasted at least a little bit like goulash. But by the third night, Leon and Henry had taught Milos how to make a Manhattan, which was how they passed the time, drinking and trying to ignore Milos's accordion-playing daughter and wondering about Alex.

The plan had gone exactly as Alex had predicted. The guards dived out of the way, and the car wasn't even scratched. But where was he? There was no way they could go back and look for him, but Henry did call the farmer, who had heard the gunshot. He drove his truck down to the border and innocently asked the guards if there had been an incident, and the two of them looked at each other and said that they had shot at a suspicious person but scared him away.

Whether that was true or not dominated the conversation among the three for about the next 36 hours. They debated back and forth and decided that, if the guards killed Alex, they would have boasted to the farmer about bagging an enemy of the

German state. There was no reason to lie. The story they told made them seem kind of weak, to be honest. You wouldn't tell a lie that makes you look bad, so it must have been true.

So where was he?

The smart play would have been for Alex to go back to the farmhouse and hide—unless he decided that they would be searching for him, and hiding would just put the farmer in danger. So maybe he went through the woods and into Czechoslovakia that way—although who knew how hard it would be to make his way through a pathless forest in the dark. He could have easily gotten himself turned around. Hell, he could have wandered right back to the guard shack. And besides, if he did do that, and if he did make it through, why wasn't he here? Café Milos was only a couple of miles from the border, right on Michalska in the Old Town, and it was the only place they had talked about.

So where was he?

Saturday night, they drove right to Café Milos and waited, sleeping in the car after it closed. Sunday, they rented two rooms when they woke up and were back in the café by noon, listening to radio reports of the German arrival in Austria. Monday, the same thing, long silences between radio bulletins punctuated by a variation on the same conversation:

"Okay, so if he got through the woods by dawn . . ."

"If he hid out for the night, and then tried to get through . . ."

Over and over. By dinner on Monday night, Liesl said she couldn't take another night, especially when the lovely Zsofia and her accordion returned for her evening set. So Liesl headed back to the rooms—they were just across the square—and Henry and Leon kept drinking.

The radio was a nonstop Hitler travelogue—Braunau and then Linz on Saturday, right behind the army, to see the home folks. Then stops here and there on Sunday, then Vienna on

Monday, crowds cheering the whole way. There were a few other Austrians who came in and out of the café, mostly Jews, drinking and listening to the radio, shaking their heads and drinking.

At one point, Leon looked at Henry and said, "My God, it just hit me. We're refugees. We're fucking refugees. We don't have a home."

So they drank and sat. What else was there to do? Zsofia's repertoire, which wasn't that bad if you arrived without expectations, was mostly standards and folk songs—and just as all of the food kind of tasted like goulash, all of the songs kind of sounded like "Ochi Chernye." Which was fine.

But that night, she got a little daring, offering a sampling of American big band songs—which was, well, interesting. But you could tell what the song was after a couple of notes: first Tommy Dorsey, then Teddy Wilson, then the first few notes of Benny Goodman.

Which was when Henry and Leon heard someone behind them start to sing:

Wah-wah, the girls of Schottenfeld,
Wah-wah, they smell like . . .

GET A FREE STORY IN THE ALEX KOVACS THRILLER SERIES

My interest is not just in writing, but in building a community of readers. My plan is to be in contact occasionally with news on upcoming books, blog posts and other special offers.

If you sign up to the mailing list, I will send you a **FREE** copy of "Otto's End," a story in the Alex Kovacs thriller series that explains exactly what happened on his trip to Cologne in November of 1936.

It's easy.

IT'S FREE.

Sign up here: https://dl.bookfunnel.com/kpuyzx4un8

ENJOY THIS BOOK? YOU CAN REALLY HELP ME OUT.

The truth is that, as a new author, it is hard to get readers' attention. But if you have read this far, I have yours – and I could use a favor.

Reviews from people who liked this book go a long way toward convincing future readers of its worth. It won't take five minutes of your time, but it would mean a lot to me. Just click the link below to leave a review on the book's Amazon page. Long or short, it doesn't matter.

Just click here.

And THANKS!

I hope you enjoyed *Vienna at Nightfall.* What follows is the first four chapters of the sequel, *The Spies of Zurich.* It is available for purchase now at https://www.amazon.com/author/richardwake

Thanks for your interest!

The heart of Zurich -- the heart and maybe the soul, too -- were at the Paradeplatz, a vast expanse just off of the Bahnhofstrasse where about 10 tram lines converged. The lake and all of its beauty, and Switzerland really is a beautiful country, was off to the right. The temples of conspicuous consumption and commerce made this country go more than any place I had ever been, dotted the street to the left as it led ultimately to the train station and the transportation links to still more commerce. But what held it all together was in the Paradeplatz, because that was where the banks were.

It was two banks, two substantial buildings, stone fortresses, staring at each other across the expanse. Kreditanstalt was on the north side, and Bankverein was on the west side. Those two ran everything. The truth was, they ran the country. There was plenty of money to be made by the minnows, the small private banks tucked into the side streets between the Paradeplatz and the Grossmunster -- different churches, yes -- thanks to the Swiss secrecy laws. But the whales on the Paradeplatz made the biggest decisions, funded the biggest developments, and controlled their smaller competitors by throwing them morsels of side work, or not.

That was the dynamic on a beautiful September day in 1939. It was still more than a month away from the sun's autumnal retreat, and three months away from the cold and miserable gray that descended upon the city every winter. It was bright and blue and much too nice to be inside, but the massive fourth-floor reception room in the Kreditanstalt building was filled that day with that great oxymoron, the smiling banker. One of the bank's directors, Gerhard Femmerling, a miserable prick even by Swiss bank director standards, was retiring, and we had all been summoned with engraved invitations to wish him well at a noontime reception. Looking around at the assembled dozens, grins plastered in place, I did a quick head count, and it appeared that everyone had RSVP'd in the affirmative. It was just business, after all. You had to retain your place in the queue for when it was morsel time again.

I had two rules at these kinds of things. The first was to make sure to be seen by the person or people who needed to see me and to do it quickly. There was nothing worse than waiting your turn for an audience. So I took a direct line to old Femmerling as soon as I walked into the room, and barged in on the group surrounding him, and offered a random sampling of pleasant conversational nothings, and was done with the work of the day in five minutes. That allowed me to attend to my second rule, which was never to be out of direct contact with the bar.

This was a rarity, seeing as how Swiss bankers didn't drink at lunch, except for maybe a glass of wine -- one glass, and not drunk to the bottom. But it was a full bar this day, and the scotch was really from Scotland, and the bartender was pouring my second when I received a nudge in the ribs followed by, "Bonjour, Alex. I see that Zurich has not changed -- that there are almost no women in the banking business, and that they have never been seen in public without every button of their blouses buttoned all the way to their eyebrows."

Freddy Arpin had made the trip up from Geneva, where his family owned Banc Arpin, a little private joint whose principal customers, in Freddy's words, "were either French pseudo-Fascists or outright Fascists, hedging their bets." We had met at a conference in Basel and immediately hit it off, mostly because we were clearly oddballs in the banking business in that we didn't give a fuck. Or, as Freddy put it, "My father and brother are in the sharp pencil and green eyeshade business. I am in the cognac and silk stocking business." We got along fine.

"Long way to come for this, huh?"

"My father insisted," Freddy said. "It's OK, easy to kill the time on the train. There's plenty to read in the papers."

"Anything new?"

"No. Warsaw is still holding out, but --"

"Poor bastards," I said. "Any sign the French or the Brits are getting off their asses to help?"

"Nope."

"Useless fucks."

Some variation on this conversation was happening all over the room, no doubt. The Germans had invaded Poland two weeks earlier. The British and French had declared war on Germany a couple of days after that, but sat and watched as the Wehrmacht went about its business. The conversations -- and I had participated in my share as president of my own little bank, Bohemia Suisse -- were all about the sober calculation of the effects of war on European business in general and Swiss business in particular. I could do sober calculation if the social or business setting demanded it.

But this was a little more personal for me. My adopted home, Austria, had been seized by the Nazis in March of 1938. My real home, Czechoslovakia, had been gifted to them, bartered away a couple of months after that by Chamberlain and Daladier. So, yes, useless fucks.

I asked Freddy, "Are you guys seeing an increase in deposits?"

"You might say that. We actually had a guy show up last week from Lyon in his car, and he had the driver get out and carry in a picnic hamper stuffed with French francs. We sold him Swiss francs --"

"At an obscene markup --"

"That is getting more obscene by the day. Or, as my brother says, 'Add a point for every drop of piss you see dribbling down their legs.' So his deposit is in Swiss francs. Then we had a guy drive the French francs back to Paris and bought gold coins -- at a markup, yes, but not yet obscene. Then he brought the gold back, and it's in our vault."

"All in the same picnic basket?"

"The very same."

Freddy was saying that his father was calculating that they wouldn't be able to accept French francs at all in a couple of weeks, the way things were going -- unless, that is, the bank wanted to get into the business of using them to buy French real estate.

"If the little corporal keeps going, we could probably get houses in Paris at knockdown prices," Freddy said. "But that's a really long game. Maybe buying artwork is the way to go."

He stopped as if he were hearing himself for the first time, then said, "You think we're shitheads, don't you?"

"I don't know who isn't a shithead anymore, me included."

I went to grab two more drinks and returned to find Freddy talking to the only woman in the room with her top button undone. Her name was Manon Friere, and she was a trade representative from the French consulate, and she was more than a pleasure to look at. In this room, her red lipstick was like a beacon in a gray flannel night. She apparently had been working out of the consulate in Geneva but now was stationed in Zurich.

I waved my arm toward the windows to point out the expanse of the Paradeplatz, lit by the sun. "So how do you like our fair city? Freddy hates it, but you probably already knew that."

"You mean Tightassville?" Freddy said.

"Freddy is a Parisian at heart, trapped in a Swiss hell," Manon said

"Hell?" I said. "All of it?"

She shrugged.

Hell it is, then.

"Are you a tiny banker, like Freddy?"

"No one is as tiny as Freddy."

"That's pretty much what I hear --"

"Your vengeance is unbecoming," Freddy said. He pointedly turned away from Manon and looked at me. "Here's the story. I was dating a friend of Manon's in the consulate. At the same time, I might have also made an attempt to date Manon. It was honestly a mistake."

"You're honestly a pig."

"And my penance is her indiscriminate use of the word 'tiny' in conversations such as these."

"If the name fits," she said.

"I think it's more like when I was in high school," I said. "We had this buddy who was about 6-foot-4, and we called him Shorty."

"Exactly. Alex Kovacs, you are a true friend," Freddy said.

"No problem, Tiny," I said.

She snorted. Freddy made a face. I was smitten but also in a hurry. I had a 1:30 appointment that I couldn't miss. So I said my goodbyes and walked out into the Paradeplatz. I'm not sure I had ever been there without stopping on the way home at Confiserie Sprungli, on the south side of the square, for a small bag of something sweet and rich and decadent -- although, as everyone knew, the truly rich and decadent things happened on the north side and the west side. Anyway, I stopped, collected my little stash, and began the 10-minute walk back to Bohemia Suisse.

As I turned onto Rennweg, I looked ahead and saw a small crowd had gathered outside of Gartner, a little restaurant that I had walked past about 500 times and never once thought to enter. As I got closer, the crowd grew, and I could see the frightened looks on the faces and hear the cries and the shouts for help. Then, in the distance, I heard a police siren.

I got to the edge of the crowd and shouldered my way through it. Finally to the front, I looked down and saw that I suddenly wasn't in a hurry anymore. Laying on the ground was my 1:30 appointment, his head framed by a puddle of blood. He had been shot through the left eye.

A few blocks away, on Fortunagasse, was Bohemia Suisse. The bank was tucked in amid a row of houses, each with a ground floor and four floors above. It could have been just another residence in the hilly line of homes, but for the small gold sign on the door that identified the bank and said, "By appointment only." I always thought that it seemed to be more of a warning than a statement of information.

I moved slowly away from the crowd surrounding the body. I walked for five minutes in the wrong direction and did my best to check behind me while looking in the reflection of shop windows. I turned and walked in a circle around the Fraumunster and actually said a little prayer to myself somewhere behind the church, although I wasn't sure, in retrospect, about the effectiveness of a prayer that included the phrase, "Please let this not be completely fucked." Only then, when I was sure no one was following me, did I start walking toward the bank.

Even I couldn't let myself in during business hours -- such was the show of security required for private banks in Switzerland. And it was a show. At night or on the weekend I just used my key, but at 1:30 in the afternoon I rang the bell and was greeted after about 30 seconds by Anders, the security guard. He was dressed in a blue blazer and gray slacks. He was dressed that way every day, the coat specially tailored to smooth the line of the pistol he carried beneath it. He was a retired captain in the Swiss army, which I always thought was a hoot. I had fought in Caporetto for the greater glory of Austria-Hungary, for the emperor and his whiskers, while Anders oiled his gun on weekends in some barracks beneath an Alp. I made a joke about it when I first met him. His reaction, not in words but in the more powerful language of the body, made it quite clear that there would be no need to make the joke a second time.

"Herr Kovacs," he said.

"Anders," I said.

This was pretty much the extent of our conversation most days. He returned to his desk in our small lobby. What he did all day was beyond me, seeing as how most days we had no appointments. I never even saw him read a newspaper. He would let himself in. He would let me in. And he would let in Marta Frank, the office manager. She handled everything when I wasn't around, which was often. She could authorize cash deposits and withdrawals. She could, in the presence of Anders, open the vault and assist customers with their safe deposit boxes; she knew the lock's combination while he held the required key. Only I could open it by myself.

Marta had heard the police sirens. She said, "What is going on out there?"

I told her that a man was dead outside of Gartner and that he had been shot. And just as she got done gasping about that, I told her the dead man was Michael Landers, our 1:30 appointment, at which point she pretty much collapsed into the chair beside my desk, clutching my diary to her bosom. The diary was always either open on her desk or open in her hands.

She pulled herself together and looked down at the diary. "Landers. You wrote this one in. Who is he? Did I ever meet him?"

She knew very well that she had never met him, and I knew that she knew. We had only about 50 clients, most of them ancient Czech expats, so it really wasn't tough to keep track.

"He's one of the nephews in the Kerner Trust."

"Rich fool setting his money on fire," Marta said. She had been disapproving of the setup from the first time I explained it to her.

"But it's his money, and he pays his fees, so as far as I'm concerned, Bohemia Suisse will always be happy to supply Herr Kerner with all of the kerosene and matches that he requires."

The Kerner Trust was the fiction that had been created during my first months at the bank. The original depositor was a 40-year-old who had, with the aid of some stage makeup, a hunch, a limp, and a cane, passed himself off as an 80-year-old when he made his one and only appearance at the bank. It was important that Marta and Anders saw he was a real person, living and breathing. There was no way, after all, to hide a mysterious account from them, and especially from her, seeing as how the client base was so small and she kept the books.

The deposit he made was sizable, 200,000 francs. The money could be withdrawn by any of four of his nephews, all of whom I was to meet personally later that evening at Herr Kerner's home. There were no restrictions on the withdrawals. I would bring the required account identification materials on the home visit and distribute them so that a withdrawal could be made if I wasn't around.

Marta actually snorted and said, "The whole thing is ridiculous. And what are you now, his butler? Going to his house?"

"Look, it's a lot of money, and it's a service business, right? And you're acting like he's the only eccentric on the client list. What about Herr Lutz?"

Rudi Lutz was one of our wealthiest depositors. He never made a withdrawal but, once a month, he came in and asked to see a full accounting anyway. Then he inspected the contents of his safe deposit box. This did not make him eccentric in my book, just untrusting. The eccentric part was that he showed up for every visit with a chauffeur whose job, besides driving the big black Daimler, was carrying in a small fish tank, and the several fish swimming inside, and placing it on my desk as we went through the accounts, and then on the table in the room where deposit boxes were examined in private.

"Ah, he's just an animal lover," Marta said, conceding the point with a smile.

"He's batshit is what he is," I said. "But we're happy to have his money, and we're happy now to have Herr Kerner's money."

That seemed to satisfy her. She usually said something snide when she took note of the withdrawals on the accounts that I had posted -- they tended to be at night or on weekends and handled by special appointments with me -- but that was it. "Shiftless" was her favorite word to describe the nephews. She did meet one of them once and handled his transaction, and told me later that "he had obviously been drinking at lunch." That also was by design, to assist in keeping her suspicion level low.

Marta was going to meet a second nephew that afternoon. Until, well.

She pulled herself together pretty quickly and asked, "Are you going to inform Herr Kerner?"

"No, I don't think so. It's not my news to tell. I'm sure the police will get to him soon enough."

Of course, Marta did not know how right she was. I was going to have to tell somebody else -- not Herr Kerner, but Herr Kerner's handler.

Because Herr Kerner was actually Fritz Blum, the man in charge of an espionage network working in Switzerland, Belgium and Holland on behalf of the French, the British, and my old bosses, the Czechs, whose spies had fled to London along with the leaders of the government after the Nazi takeover in 1938. My Czech bosses, who were actually running the operation, shared everything with their hosts. My job was merely to be in charge of this sleepy bank and to distribute funds for operations to the spy network on demand. The truth was, it was the easiest and best-paying job I had ever had.

Well, it was until that day. As Marta got up and went back to her desk, I was wondering how quickly I needed to contact London, and pretty much immediately was my conclusion. But the contact information was back in my house, the return address on a random postcard currently being used as a bookmark in a book I had never read, "Dante's Inferno." And while I contemplated precisely what circle of hell I was about to enter, Marta poked her head into my office.

"There's somebody to see you," she said.

"Is there an appointment I forgot about?"

"Nope. He says he's a police detective."

I stood, and buttoned my jacket, and batted a flake of dandruff off of my shoulder, and walked out to fetch him. What circle of hell indeed?

Anders and the cop were talking as I approached. They were laughing, in fact.

"You guys know each other?" I said.

They stopped laughing. Anders said, "Army training together."

Perfect. That Anders did not like me had been made pretty plain over the prior 16 months. I'm not sure I had seen him laugh -- or, if I had, I didn't remember. But here he was, laughing with the cop. The two of them had probably been drunk together more than once, because what else do you do during Swiss army training but march and drill and...drink? And what do you when you're drinking but tell each other endlessly, in some variation, "Fuck them -- we are so real soldiers."

I stuck out my hand and introduced myself. The cop's name was Peter Ruchti, and he was a detective. He said his goodbyes to Anders and suggested we head into my office. The look on Anders' face indicated that he knew all along that I was a pick-pocket or a pervert or something, and that I was about to be found out. In his heart, Anders was likely hoping for pervert.

Ruchti sat down, didn't want anything to drink. I tried small-talk, which is about the only professional skill I possessed. "So, were you in the army long?"

"Just two years -- I didn't make it a career like Anders. That was enough time for me to make the world safe for democracy and the bankers."

Great. Just great. "So what can I do for you?" I asked.

"Do you know a Michael Landers?"

In the minute or so I'd had to think, I had played this question out in my head. Would I admit it or not? There were upsides and downsides to both answers. Telling the truth is always best when dealing with the police, and there would be no harm in admitting that I knew the guy other than having to endure a series of follow-up questions. But then, the more I thought, there was a problem. There was no way Ruchti could find out that Landers was able to draw on an account at the bank because the Swiss banking secrecy laws were pretty much impenetrable. And there was no self-respecting Swiss banker who would ever identify one of his private clients. So if I told Ruchti that I knew Landers, I would have to invent some other context for knowing him, and that lie would be more complicated.

The alternative was to deny knowing him. Again, the banking secrecy laws protected me there. But it was a lie, and if Ruchti could ever put Landers and me in the same place at the same time, it could be a problem -- and we had met for a drink once, and he had made a previous withdrawal on a Saturday afternoon, and who knows who on the street might have seen us together.

So there were risks either way.

I went for the lie.

"No, I don't think I know him. Why?"

"He's dead. Murdered about three blocks from here. Shot through the head. You must have heard the sirens and the commotion."

"It is pretty quiet in here," I said, pointing to the leather padding on the walls behind him, and on the door. "That's official, standard-issue private bank wall paneling, gracious soundproofing. It really works pretty well -- but I did hear a little something. I thought it was maybe an ambulance siren."

"You mean maybe 10 ambulance sirens. I think the whole police force is on Rennweg. This would be a great time to rob a bank."

I shrugged. Maybe I was going to get out of this after all. "So you're just asking everybody in the neighborhood?"

"Street cops will get to that in the next few hours," Ruchti said. "I came to you because the deceased had your business card in his wallet. When I saw that and saw how close you were, I took you for myself. Besides, I'd had enough of the crime scene. Puddles of blood turn my stomach."

He removed the card from his breast pocket and flipped it on to my desk blotter. It was, indeed, my business card.

"You sure you don't know him?"

"Pretty sure."

"So how did he get your card?"

"Beats me."

As soon as I said it, I was pretty sure I was going to need more than "beats me" to end this conversation. Flippant doesn't work with these guys. So I started to tell Ruchti how I spent my time. When I wasn't in the office, I was going through the motions of drumming up business -- and being seen drumming was significantly more important than actually signing new accounts. So besides lunching with prospective clients, mostly wealthy friends of friends who lived to have their asses kissed and their lunches paid for, I attended banking conferences and trade shows and sat through boring speeches at arts festivals and municipal project unveilings and whatnot. The truth was, I gave out 50 business cards a month, easily. For all I knew, the next random dead guy they found would have my card, too.

If Ruchti was swayed at all by my explanation, he wasn't letting on. He had that cop face perfected, that vaguely-smelling-shit-on-your-shoe look. I didn't know if I had made any progress, but I was out of things to say and didn't want to start babbling. So I just shut up.

He stared back at me, three seconds, four seconds, five seconds. Silence like that can be better than thumbscrews sometimes, and it took everything I had to match him, wordless second for wordless second. Finally, Ruchti gave up.

"Okay, we'll be in touch," he said, standing and shaking my

hand and heading for the leather padded door. I scrambled to follow him, but he stopped me. "I can show myself out."

I sat at my desk and grabbed a stack of letters to sign and a pen, playing over that one phrase in my head: "we'll be in touch." About what? I said I didn't know the guy. There should be no need for any other questions, no reason to be in touch. Maybe he didn't mean anything by it. Maybe it was nothing.

I began signing the letters and, after each signature, took a quick peek. One letter. Two letters. Three letters. Four. And Ruchti and Anders were still talking as they stood near the bank's front door.

One of the privileges of friendship, when the friends you are talking about are the owners of a cafe, is your own personal stammtisch. Mine was a tiny booth in the back corner of Cafe Fessler, where I could see the whole place. The table was designed for two people, max, but the space was big enough that I could spread out a couple of file folders stuffed with paperwork, and there was a decent light overhead.

I had never been an office guy, and much preferred a more comfortable environment when I was wading through the black-and-white avalanche that came with my job, as it did with a lot of jobs. Order forms and delivery schedules back when I was a magnesite salesman in Vienna had morphed into legal compliance forms and weekly deposit reports in my bank job, but it was all just shitwork, there to remind you that your job was, indeed, a job. And in my experience, it tended to go down easier with a beer or two.

Cafe Fessler usually did an early dinner business, as it was a family kind of place and an old guy kind of place. I was 40 and single, and there was precisely zero chance of me finding a date in the cafe most nights, this one included. It was 8 p.m., and we were already down to what I liked to call the "fossil collection." They were all over 70, all men. Their conversations were dominated either by jokes that traveled another mile along the rutted road from risqué to raunchy with the consumption of each successive round of drinks, or by spirited-beyond-all-sense arguments about the FC Zurich vs. Grasshoppers football rivalry.

I was plowing through the latest compliance schedule and half-listening to an anguished debate about the substitution patterns employed by "that fucking Bohm," the FC Zurich manager, when Henry sat down.

"Shouldn't you be massaging your wife's feet or something?" I said.

"She's out at dinner with a couple of girls from work."

"What do you think librarians talk about at dinner?"

"I think they rage on about the Dewey decimal system."

"Or they talk about the male librarians," I said, and Henry shrugged. Henry was one of my dear friends from Vienna, and also one-half of the Fessler empire. He ran the cafe during the day while his wife, Liesl, was working as a librarian at the Central Library, the biggest in the country. Henry's father, Gregory, was the other Fessler, still automatically Mr. Fessler to me. He took over in the afternoon and closed up at night. They both lived above the shop in enormous apartments -- it really was a big building -- with Gregory on the second floor and Henry and Liesl on the fourth.

Henry stood up almost as soon as he sat down. "I'm just getting my drink," he said. I hadn't seen Henry legitimately drunk in a while, probably years. He was on a one-Manhattan-per-day plan, a regimen from which he rarely deviated.

"Besides," he said, with a quick flick of his head toward the circle of fossils that included his father. "You know how he gets."

How Gregory got was angry if he perceived that Henry was hanging around because he thought the old man was letting things slide. Henry ordered the provisions and the alcohol, supervised the deliveries, scheduled the staff, kept the books, and made sure to go upstairs when Liesl got home from work. Gregory was the central presence in the cafe from lunch till closing -- pinching babies, telling tales, very much the charming rogue. And if he tore up a few checks now and then, well, Henry would just have to understand.

Alone again, I got back to my pile. At the bottom was the note to write the letter to London, which I was saving for last. I felt into my breast pocket, and the postal card with the return address was there. I had stopped at home long enough to scoop it up before coming to Fessler's. This was going to be only the second contact I'd had with Czech intelligence in the 16 months I had been in Zurich. The first had been to alert me to the mechanics of setting up the spy account. Now, this, the matter of the dead client.

A knot of the old men was grabbing their coats. Henry was still by the bar, and he was talking to his father and shaking his head, and Gregory was smiling and shrugging and heading toward the kitchen. Henry walked over.

"None of those guys paid a franc," Henry said. "The old man's going to ruin us. Sometimes I think we just should have stayed in Bratislava."

"Yeah, maybe you could have bought Cafe Milos."

"And smelled like goulash forever."

"And I could have married the accordion player."

"And smelled like goulash forever," Henry said.

We had escaped to Bratislava in March of 1938 when Herr Hitler decided to add an addition onto his country and nailed Austria to the back of the house. We had to leave for different reasons. Henry had gotten in trouble with a Vienna police captain who was about to be given a free hand by the Gestapo, so he had to go, and Liesl was going with him. Our other great friend, Leon, had to go because he had two blots in his official Nazi copybook -- he was not only Jewish but a Jewish journalist besides. Then there was me. I had to go because I had been recruited by Czech intelligence to act as a courier during my sales trips to Germany, and had tangled with the Gestapo along the way. So all of us slipped into Bratislava on the night of the Anschluss and tried to figure out what was next.

The answers came pretty quickly. The Czech intelligence people owed me, and they knew it. This was handy because we needed some favors in return. Leon had no passport because, in the hurry to escape, he forgot to bring his. Henry wanted to be able to get full-time resident status in Switzerland, where his father had settled in 1936 -- Gregory had seen Hitler's moves coming even back then and wanted to beat the rush to the exits, a rush that never happened. Liesl wanted to go to Switzerland with Henry, whom she was to marry, and also wanted an introduction at the library.

So we made a deal. Leon received a Czech passport and a plane ticket to Paris, where he knew a guy who knew a guy who could get him a job on one of the newspapers. Henry and Liesl received their Swiss paperwork, two plane tickets to Zurich, and a letter of introduction at the library. I received a Swiss passport to go along with the Czech passport of my birth, along with a high-paying job as president of Bohemia Suisse. In exchange for all of this, I had to agree to keep working for Czech intelligence by becoming the banker for their network based in Zurich.

It was impossible to make the deal without everybody knowing the details, or at least most of them. With the three of them sworn to secrecy, we embarked on our new lives. They really were pretty good lives, too. As Henry walked away, I thought about how happy he was. He could be a moody guy, but Liesl had pushed most of that out of him. The truth was, he was even kind of happy when he was bitching about his father.

It really was a good time, if you could find a way to ignore the Hitler drumbeat that was never far below the surface.

I got through my stack and was left with the letter to write to London. I had been made to memorize exactly one thing by my Czech handler, and it was the title of the book I was to request if I needed an in-person meeting. So I wrote to the Smedley Bookshop on Charring Cross Road in London:

Sirs,

I am in search of a copy of "Northanger Abbey" to complete my Jane Austen collection. Please inform me at your earliest conve-

nience if you can obtain a copy, as well as the cost. My request is urgent, as I hope to present the collection as a gift on a special family occasion upcoming soon.

Thank you for your consideration.

The addition of the sentence containing the word "urgent" was meant to tell London just that. As I was sealing it and copying the address from the postal card, Gregory began making his way toward my booth.

The Spies of Zurich is available for purchase at https://www.amazon.com/author/richardwake

ABOUT THE AUTHOR

Richard Wake is the author of the Alex Kovacs thriller series. His website can be found at richardwake.com. You can connect with Richard on Facebook or you can send him an email at info@richardwake.com.